ROBERTS & M

THE GOLDEN PATH

A TOM WAGNER ADVENTURE

Thriller

Translator: Edwin Miles / Copyeditor: Philip Yaeger

Imprint: Independently published / Paperback ISBN 9798501801554, Hardcover ISBN 9798449091901

Cover Art by reinhardfenzl.com

Cover Art was created with photos from: depositphoto.com, Plane: icholakov01, smoke Plane: YAYImages, Fire Plane: Noppharat_th, Bullet: iLexx, Waterfall: dubassy, Wall: jipen, river: adamov_di, Temple small: lunamarina, Temple big: diegograndi, Bridge: pawopa3336, Mist: shmeljov, Big Smoke: v74, Big Fire: bisagraph . gmail.com, Sky: portokalis // Person: neo-stock.com

www.robertsmaclay.com

office@robertsmaclay.com

“The best revenge is not to be like your enemy.”

Marcus Aurelius

1

SOMEWHERE IN THE JUNGLES OF CENTRAL AMERICA, FEBRUARY 2018

Leaves and branches whipped painfully at her face. The formidable humidity drew perspiration from every pore of her body, and sweat flowed in small streams down her back. Panicked, panting, she ran on through the undergrowth. She had no time for caution, no time to check that she was not about to run headlong into a poisonous plant or dangerous beast. Something far more menacing was right behind her.

Dr. Sienna Wilson was running for her life. She leaped over rocks, vaulted tree trunks in her path, ducked beneath low-hanging branches. The rest of her team was dead. Or more precisely, they had murdered each other, simply because they had been ordered to do so. She herself had managed to escape her colleagues' fate only at the last moment. Luck had been on her side, and she had survived. Only now did she realize that they had crossed into sacred territory, had desecrated holy soil. Although the native inhabitants had been outwardly remarkably friendly toward them, something had seemed off. Alarm bells had been ringing in her gut from the start.

Days before, she had set off with a small team—herself, her boss Dr. Emanuel Orlov, three other researchers, and two soldiers that Orlov had hired to protect them. The Central American jungle was home not only to poisonous animals, insects and plants, but also to local cartels and freedom fighters who regularly kidnapped employees of the Western companies that were making inroads into their lands. The kidnappers then extorted millions out of the companies to finance their guerrilla wars. Scientists and tourists were also common targets, and some had never been seen again. And then, of course, there were the indigenous tribes.

Just a few weeks earlier, the press had reported on the case of two employees of the food company NutriAm. They had been working at a drinking water bottling plant and armed men had abducted them on their way to work. The company had been forced to pay two million dollars to free them and prevent a public execution on YouTube. Two million was pocket change for a company like NutriAm, but it was a fortune for freedom fighters waging a war against a corrupt regime. Orlov had read the reports, and insisted on bodyguards. They were cheaper than the insurance premiums.

The team had been tasked with finding exotic plants for the Genesis Program, a non-profit research center in the southwest of England. The ambitious botanical project comprised two enormous domes on 120 acres in Cornwall. Inside the larger dome, they simulated the climate of a tropical rainforest, while the smaller replicated a

Mediterranean climate. The artificial ecosystems housed more than five thousand different kinds of plants.

The Genesis Program was a popular tourist attraction, but the scientists employed there were more than just well-paid gardeners. They also carried out invaluable research. The two domes had answered the question of whether such closed ecosystems were viable at all, a crucial issue for long space missions, especially NASA's planned mission to Mars. But it also applied to the very real possibility that climate change and environmental degradation might soon make parts of our own planet uninhabitable, causing famine and leading to a shortage of drinking water. The Genesis Program could well provide much-needed solutions.

The team had battled through the jungle for several days without success before finally stumbling across something they could use. It was Dr. Wilson who'd found it. The plant she discovered—or rather rediscovered—had long been thought extinct. Others in her field had held this rare species of orchid to be no more than a fantasy. But there it was, in all its glory. Sienna and Orlov had gazed at its glorious blooms in disbelief. A seaman who had sailed from Spain to Central America with Hernán Cortés in the 16th century had described it in his diary, and in honor of his homeland had christened it *Orchidea espagnola*.

It was this same plant that might now cost Sienna her life. In rediscovering the orchid, they had wandered into a region that no white person had ever walked out of alive. And now Sienna knew why. Just minutes before, she had witnessed what the orchid could do. And she had succeeded in escaping its power.

She had no idea how long she ran without looking back. Fear and adrenalin drove her on.

"Sienna!" she suddenly heard someone call behind her. She knew the voice—it was Dr. Orlov. Like her, he was on the brink of exhaustion. But also like her, he had survived.

"Did you see it, Professor? Did you see what happened to our team?"

Orlov nodded and lifted his hand. In it was an orchid.

2

KULIBIN PARK HOTEL, NIZHNY NOVGOROD, RUSSIA

"Can we finally concentrate on the next job? It's important!"

Theresia de Mey was head of Blue Shield, the UNESCO-associated organization for the discovery and protection of cultural heritage. And right now, she was pissed. Three tired pairs of eyes looked back at her.

"Mother, we were sealed inside a cave just a few hours ago. We barely managed to escape with our lives. I want to find El Dorado just as much as you do, but can't we take a couple days off before we start again?" Hellen de Mey asked.

Tom Wagner looked over at Hellen. It was obvious to him how exhausted she was. He was used to the kind of adrenalin rollercoaster they'd just been through, but it seemed to be taking a toll on her. "Give Hellen and François a couple of days' R&R," he suggested. "Then we'll all be ready to focus on the job. Meanwhile, maybe you can tell us exactly what it's all about?"

"Wagner, if you made the effort to actually read the brief, you'd save us all a lot of work."

François Cloutard, behind Tom, chuckled. He'd been quiet since the meeting began but seemed to be having a fine time. Still, his wound was not making things easy for him, and he, perhaps even more than Hellen and Tom, had earned some time off. He'd been shot in the thigh just the day before, but had refused to stay in the hospital. The doctors had patched him up but he'd signed himself out again despite their protests. A man like François Cloutard was not about to let a mere flesh wound slow him down. "Madame, you know me and you know my past. I am an art thief, a smuggler, and a grave robber. I would like nothing more to go in search of El Dorado, but . . ."

He paused briefly and sipped the coffee that a waiter had served them there in their suite just a few moments earlier. He grimaced. "*Un moment*," he said. He reached into his jacket pocket and took out his hip flask, poured a solid dose of Louis XIII cognac into the coffee cup, then took another sip. His face brightened. Theresia de Mey sniffed impatiently and drummed her fingers on the table. "*Beaucoup mieux*," Cloutard said, "Madame, Hellen is exhausted. I am injured. You do not want to send us back to the front like this, do you? Even with new clues to the location of the greatest hoard of gold in human history, I am sure you would like us to be at our very best for the search."

Cloutard gave Theresia de Mey a wink, and a hint of a smile appeared on her face. For a moment she lowered her eyes. Then she abruptly stood up, sighed, and paced back and forth through the suite.

"Is everything all right, Mother?" Hellen could see that something was weighing on Theresia.

"Everything is all right, yes. It's just that we've already postponed this project too long. We have to get things moving."

"Then let me start alone," Tom suggested. "I can kick things off, and Hellen and François can rest up a little and join me in a few days."

"The problem is that we need Hellen at the start."

Hellen suddenly pricked up her ears. "What do you mean?"

"I'll have to go back a little if we want everyone—" here, she looked disdainfully at Tom "—to understand."

Tom tilted his head to one side. He could take a hint. It was about time he did something to counter Theresia's image of him as no more than some rent-a-goon.

"The Albertina museum in Vienna has an enormous collection," Theresia began, "most of it not even catalogued."

"You mean the Albertina folks have no idea what they've got stashed in the basement?" Tom said.

"You could put it that way," Hellen confirmed.

Cloutard was sitting up now, his interest aroused. Simultaneously, Tom and Hellen waggled their index fingers in front of Cloutard's nose. "Don't even think about it.

Nothing gets stolen from the Albertina, understood?" Tom brusquely made clear.

"*Bien, bien. J'ai compris,*" the Frenchman said, raising his hands defensively.

Theresia de Mey shook her head. She was starting to realize what a motley crew she'd fallen in with: Thomas Maria Wagner, a former officer in the Austrian counterterrorism unit Cobra, who had a problem with authority and a talent for creating chaos. François Cloutard, art thief and erstwhile head of a global organization of grave robbers and smugglers—she could never be certain whose side he was really on. And her own daughter, Hellen de Mey, archeologist and historian, with whom Theresia had had a frosty relationship ever since the death of her husband, Hellen's father. Altogether a far cry from a professional special ops team.

"All done with kindergarten, are we? Can we move on? Thank you!" she said icily.

"What have they found in the Albertina, Mother?" Hellen asked.

"We don't know exactly. What we *do* know is that documents have turned up in which the name 'Cortés' appears and which mention some sort of 'Golden Path'."

Hellen's and Cloutard's eyes widened. Tom pretended to be just as fascinated, but was already getting annoyed at Theresia again. "Cortés was the Spanish conquistador who slaughtered the Mayans and the Aztecs, right?" he said.

Hellen nodded. "Yes."

"Then how did the documents find their way to Vienna?"

"The Spanish line of the Habsburgs," Cloutard said drily. "To explain all the connections now would take quite a while."

"There's just one problem," Theresia said.

Tom grinned. This was where he came in. He was the problem solver.

"Officially, Blue Shield knows nothing about these papers. We were tipped off from the inside, but we can't simply walk into the Albertina and start analyzing the documents."

"Then let's steal them," said Cloutard, clapping his hands.

"I appreciate your enthusiasm, Monsieur Cloutard," Theresia said. "But perhaps we should take a more subtle approach."

"I've got an idea," said Tom. "I'll fly to Vienna and contact the chancellor. I've saved his skin several times, as you know, and he's eternally grateful to me for that. And then there was that whole Florentine diamond thing. He's got contacts who can help us."

"Knowing the bureaucracy in Vienna, that's going to take a few days," Hellen threw in. "So Tom goes ahead and sorts things out with the chancellor, and we stay here and treat ourselves to a little rest and relaxation, then we can join him later."

"Sounds like a plan," said Tom.

Cloutard nodded, too. He had gotten slowly to his feet,

supporting himself on his walking stick, and laid one hand on Theresia de Mey's shoulder.

"You can rely on us, Madame. We will get the job done, as always."

Theresia de Mey looked up and smiled. Hellen, however, was suddenly unnerved. She did not recognize the look on her mother's face at all. Warmth? Affection? Before she could follow the thought any further, Cloutard had already put it into words.

"Allow me to invite you to dinner this evening? I happen to know an excellent restaurant here in Nizhny Novgorod."

"Why doesn't that surprise us, François?" said Tom, who had spotted Hellen's chilly gaze.

"All right, Mr. Wagner," Theresia said. Tom flinched as she deliberately mispronounced his name. "You fly to Vienna tomorrow. Hellen and you, Monsieur Cloutard, will follow in a few days. But don't keep me waiting long. It is extraordinarily important for Blue Shield that we find El Dorado."

"I will put out my feelers, too," Cloutard suggested. "Maybe there are others who know about the documents in the Albertina. We may have competition to deal with."

"That would be marvelous, Monsieur," Theresia said with a sweetness in her voice that made Hellen roll her eyes.

"Why don't we talk about this in more detail over dinner, Madame?"

Theresia and Cloutard were both on their feet now and already heading for the door of the suite.

"Mother," Hellen began, although she was not entirely sure what she wanted to say.

"Yes?" Theresia de Mey stopped and looked back over her shoulder at her daughter.

Tom placed a soothing hand on Hellen's arm.

"Oh, nothing," said Hellen. "Have a nice evening."

A moment later, Tom and Hellen were alone.

"You're not thrilled about that at all, are you?" Tom asked —a rhetorical question, he knew.

"Not even a little bit," Hellen said with a snort.

"Let's go get a drink in the bar and you can tell me a bit more about El Dorado. I don't want to be completely clueless."

Hellen laid her head on Tom's shoulder and closed her eyes for a moment. He made her feel safe just by being there.

3

CAMP DAVID, COUNTRY RETREAT OF THE PRESIDENT, MARYLAND

The man pulled the woman hard against him with the last of his strength, holding her tightly, and they both moaned loudly. His mind was blank, focused entirely on never letting her go again. Seconds later, an eruption rocked the two drained, perspiring bodies, a shuddering explosion that almost drove them out of their senses.

Exhaustion overtook them completely. The sweat poured from their naked bodies and their hearts hammered wildly against their ribs. The woman slumped onto the man's body with a blissful smile and lay without moving, as slowly but surely their pulsating climax ebbed.

"Thank you, Mr. President," the woman whispered breathlessly into the panting man's ear.

"No, thank *you*, Ms. CEO," George William Samson, the president of the United States, replied exhaustedly.

She rolled off him to the side and they lay on their backs, gazing at the ceiling. "I didn't think I'd ever get used to this," she said, slowly starting to catch her breath.

“Get used to what?”

“Sex. Like this. With four Secret Service agents standing outside the door making sure no one tries to attack you while you’re fucking my brains out.” She paused and looked at him intently. “As only the leader of the free world can.”

President Samson didn’t really know what to say to that, but the chime of his mobile phone saved him from having to. He looked at the display.

“Armstrong,” he said, although she could have guessed as much.

“Your chief of staff knows your every move, doesn’t he? So he also knows what you’re up to right now.” The thought startled her. “Christ, that’s something else I’ve had to get used to. Can’t the man wait a few minutes?”

“Until we’re finished, you mean?” Samson looked back at Yasmine Matthews, CEO of NutriAm, and smiled.

“Exactly,” she said, grinning. “Until Mr. President is finished.”

They both laughed, and Samson read the message from his chief of staff.

“It’s about my re-election. We need a strategy, and the sooner the better,” the president said.

“But it’s still three years away.”

“That’s a very short time when you’re talking about a U.S. presidential election,” Samson explained as he disappeared beneath the blanket. She playfully pushed his head away from her belly.

"Mr. President, duty calls."

He sat up with feigned exasperation and looked at her, pouting like a little boy who's had his favorite toy taken away from him.

"I think I have an idea," she said, her voice suddenly cool and calculating.

"An idea for what? How I can tell my watchdog and chief of staff, Armstrong, that I'm not coming to the meeting?"

"No. How to make sure you get re-elected."

The president's expression changed instantly. "What do you mean?"

"Maybe I'm getting ahead of myself. A week ago, we had another confidential meeting of the country's leading food companies."

Samson raised his hands. "Sorry, I don't want to hear it. I don't want to know anything about price fixing or whatever other antitrust escapades you indulge in."

She laid her index finger on his lips, then kissed him.

"Don't worry, that's not what it's about. You won't be compromised. We're all on your side, and we've done no more than start brainstorming ways we can support you —in addition to our substantial donations, of course. We also think long-term."

She ran her hand playfully through his hair and kissed him passionately. Her mouth wandered down his throat and on to his chest. Pleasurably, slowly, she traced a path unerringly toward his lower regions.

"And what did this brainstorming come up with?" Samson groaned, although his head was somewhere else entirely.

"I didn't get to be CEO by gossiping about half-baked plans," she said, kissing his navel. "You'll have to be patient a little longer." Samson's phone beeped a second time. Yasmine, halfway down his body, looked at the annoying device dispiritedly. "With that, too," she said, and she sat up and got out of bed.

"Don't keep me in suspense too long," he said.

"I thought you liked it," Yasmine replied flippantly. "I'm just going to jump in the shower."

She went to the bathroom, and Samson followed her with his eyes. He was suddenly struck by a pang of conscience. His wife had passed away just a year before. Was it too soon to get caught up in another relationship? Was it all right to start an affair, to have a little fun, so soon after such a devastating loss? When was he supposed to tell his daughter, Bethany, about it? Should he tell her at all?

His brain was beginning to pick up speed again; the brief respite offered by his tryst with Yasmine was over.

If there was any chance the food industry could ensure his re-election, he had to take it. Of course, publicly, everything had to be above board. In the past, entire campaigns had been derailed because trivialities, like his affair with Yasmine, had been leaked. But that's what he had Armstrong for. He would make sure that everything stayed kosher.

With no warning at all, memories of his deceased wife, Sloane, returned. And of the promise he had made her. He and Sloane had first met as college students at a campaign rally for Al Gore. Back then, she was an ardent young warrior in the fight against the gun lobby. And like him, she had stood at the threshold of a huge political career—a career that, for his sake, she had put on hold.

Back then, they had made a crazy pact. If he ever became president, he would devote his entire second term, if he got one, to one thing: dismantling the gun lobby and tightening gun laws. Sloane's brother had been killed by a madman on a rampage with an assault weapon. Ever since, she'd campaigned tirelessly for gun control.

He had promised her that, and had reaffirmed his promise twice: at their wedding and at her deathbed. Samson knew that it would be a long, hard battle to make her wish come true and to complete her mission. But she had earned it. Of course, he had a second iron in the fire, too.

His phone rang. Chief of Staff Armstrong seemed no longer content just to send text messages. President Samson answered the call.

"I'm already on my way, Jordan." He looked out the window to see Marine One landing in the garden.

"Thank you, Mr. President. It's very important."

4

THREE DAYS EARLIER, GENESIS PROGRAM, CORNWALL, ENGLAND

Dr. Sienna Wilson leaned on the railing of the narrow bamboo bridge and gazed down pensively into the stream sparkling beneath. The oppressive humidity did not bother her at all. In fact, she loved this climate. For the first time in two years, she was standing in the middle of the biggest indoor rainforest in the world again. After her return from Central America, she hadn't set foot inside the rainforest dome once. The traumatic loss of her research team ran deep, and still gave her nightmares. But with the help of her therapist, she had come a long way.

After a few minutes, she returned to the entrance. This place was at its most beautiful in the early mornings—until the tourists started swarming in, at which point the idyll transformed into Disneyland.

She left the dome, boarded her Segway, and rolled through the lush green paradise of the surrounding park and up to the research center located above the larger dome. There was a shortcut she could take, but Sienna enjoyed this morning ride through the verdant wonderland. She looked up and saw one of her colleagues zooming past in midair.

"Morning, Sienna," the man called. He waved as he flew overhead, crossing the grounds on England's longest zip line. Every morning, he tested his equipment before the paying guests were snapped into their harnesses.

When Sienna entered the laboratory wing, she shivered. England wasn't the warmest of countries, of course, but there in the laboratories, the air conditioners were still working overtime. Moving directly from the tropical dome to the research center was quite a shock. She moved through the labyrinth of white passages until she reached her lab, slid her key card through the scanner, and stepped inside.

She knew immediately that something was wrong. It was too quiet. She pulled on her white lab coat and hurried to the rat cages. For a moment, Sienna's breath caught in her throat. It was a horrific sight. The five lab rats she had requested especially for this project lay lifeless on the floor of the cage, torn apart. Covered in blood. They looked as if they had bitten each other to death.

But what had happened? She glanced at the observation camera she had set up to watch the rats in her absence, then quickly turned to her laptop and called up the recordings. She scrolled back to the moment when she had mixed the plant extract into the rats' water and watched in horror as the rats began to attack one another shortly afterward. It was a gruesome spectacle. Repulsed, she closed the laptop. What had happened?

She had to get to the bottom of it. She immediately carried out an autopsy on one of the rats; within hours, she had her answer. And it was far from pleasant. Exhausted, she sat on one of the rolling stools and stared at the results of the computer analysis, her mind racing. Was this what Otto Hahn had felt when he discovered how to split the nucleus of an atom? Had he also known what his discovery would mean for the future of humanity, what terrible things people would do with it? When Sienna finally dragged herself out of her gloomy thoughts, she realized that she had been sitting at her computer, unmoving, for far too long.

What was she supposed to do? The properties of this plant extract could change the world forever. She had to sleep on it. One night, then she would decide what her next step would be.

The following morning, after her usual stroll through the dome, Sienna had made up her mind. She hurried to her laboratory to gather the papers she wanted to show to her boss, Dr. Orlov. But as she drew her key card through the scanner, she got a rude surprise: the card no longer functioned. "Access denied," she read on the display above the scanner each time she tried.

Finally, Sienna gave up and strode off furiously to her boss's office. She raised her hand to knock, but paused. She could hear Dr. Orlov's voice through the door. He was talking to someone on the phone. She listened.

" . . . it is beyond belief. The properties are simply unprecedented, and the applications are limitless. I'll send you the documents as soon as I've gathered everything. You can send my fee directly to my Caymans account."

Stunned, Sienna leaned against the wall behind the office door when Dr. Orlov emerged. Had that really just happened? As the door swung closed, Sienna stepped forward.

"What did it take to buy you?" she asked from behind the professor's back. Startled, her boss swung around. Pale as chalk, he looked Dr. Wilson in the eye. She glared back at him. "You're the head of this laboratory. Aren't the thousands of pounds you get paid every month enough? Do you have to peddle your employees' work to the highest bidder, too?" Taken aback, Orlov just stood there. Sienna slapped him hard across the face. "Do you even know what you've just sold? Don't you care at all what this substance is capable of in the wrong hands?"

Orlov was able to fend off the second slap. He grabbed Sienna's wrist and held it in an iron grip. "Dr. Wilson, you're fired." With his free hand, he took out his portable phone and dialed a number. "Send two men to my office, now," he said into the phone, then hung up.

Sienna tried to twist free of her boss's painful grasp, but in vain. She beat her other hand against his chest. "Let me go. You're going to regret this," she hissed.

Dr. Orlov grabbed her other wrist, pulled her closer and snarled into her ear: "No one will ever believe *you*, sweetheart. You had a nervous breakdown after you came into contact with toxic substances. And your little trauma two years ago, the visits to your therapist—they all support my story much more than yours. So do yourself a favor and hold your tongue. A few calls is all I need to end your career." He paused, unable to suppress a self-satisfied grin. "Understood?"

When the two security men turned the corner, he let her go. Sienna rubbed her wrists where Orlov had held her.

"Escort Dr. Wilson off the premises. She's just been fired. We'll arrange for her things to be sent to her."

"You'll be sorry," Sienna shouted after Dr. Orlov, who had already turned away and disappeared around the next corner. "Get your hands off me," she snapped at one of the security men as he tried to take hold of her arm. "I know my way out."

With her head held high, Sienna walked in front of the two security guards, who followed her dutifully to her car.

She had to think of something, had to tell someone what had happened. Someone would believe her. But it was going to be difficult without any proof.

Then she had an idea. She started her car and drove onto the A390, heading for London.

5

SECRET PRISON COMPLEX, NEW MEXICO

Ossana Ibori was disappointed. And furious—at herself. The last weeks had taken their toll on her. Physically and mentally, she was exhausted. And that was the source of her anger: she couldn't believe how soft she had become.

She'd been a proud woman once, but that pride had not been her birthright. She had grown up in extreme poverty in South Africa, one of eight children and only two girls, and from birth she was condemned to servitude and misery. She could no longer remember the deprivation and abuse she'd had to endure as a child and as a young woman, nor did she want to. She had known only one thing: no one in the world had ever been able to break her, no one had ever forced her to her knees, and no one would ever rule over her. Where that inner strength had come from back then, she did not know.

Not from God, certainly. As far as she was concerned, God did not exist. If He did, there wouldn't be so much cruelty in this world. But Ossana had been destined for bigger things. She had freed herself—from her family, from the laws of her tribe, from the obstacles put in her way. She had fought through it all alone, and had reached a point where she no longer believed that anything in life could be easy. Until the day she met the Leader and he adopted her. She was eternally grateful to him and would forever be in his debt.

But recent weeks had made her realize that the luxury yacht, the fast cars and the expensive clothes had done her no good. The five-star hotels, the first-class flights—all the comforts that she had enjoyed because of the Leader and her mission for AF had also turned her into a pathetic shadow of what she'd once been. As a child, if she had been as weak as she now felt, she would never have broken out of the hell of South Africa, never killed her biological father or escaped from her brutal tribal brothers.

She heard someone tap in the ten-digit code for her cell door. The lock beeped and the door sprang open. Three guards stepped into the cell. Two held automatic weapons trained on her while the other snapped shackles on her wrists and ankles without a word. After the interrogations of the previous week, she knew what was coming. And she suddenly realized why she was so angry at herself: she was afraid.

6

BAR IN KULIBIN PARK HOTEL, NIZHNY NOVGOROD

Hellen closed her eyes and listened to the music. She loved Cole Porter, and "I've Got You Under my Skin" was one of her all-time favorites. Goosebumps stole up the back of her neck as she opened her eyes and looked around.

The patrons had all left. Only the barman remained, leaning tiredly on the counter. And Tom was still there, of course, sitting at the piano. It was his mother who had taught him how to play the piano, Hellen knew. Back then, when she had heard him play for the first time, she'd been utterly bewildered: his sensitive, almost fragile playing style had nothing in common with the rough-and-ready, crude, occasionally cold and brutal man she knew. It was these contradictions that so fascinated her.

But it wasn't just the song. His presence was getting under her skin as well. So much had happened between them in recent months. When they had met again in Vienna after a long time apart, she hadn't thought for a moment that Tom would ever mean something in her life again. But then one thing after another had happened: in Malta, Barcelona, Alexandria, Washington, Ethiopia. And now here they were, deep in Russia, and she felt closer to him than she ever had before. Tom lingered on the last, wistful chords of the song, his foot on the sustain pedal. It felt like forever before the final notes died away, and as it did so Tom swiveled around and looked her in the eye.

"Excuse me, I not like disturb," said the barkeeper in broken English, his voice demolishing the moment, taking Hellen and even Tom by surprise. Both frowning, they turned to the man. "I have to do my cash. I leave you for few minutes, yes?"

The question was purely rhetorical—he was already moving from behind the bar and heading for the exit.

Tom smiled at Hellen.

"Now's our chance for a drink on the house. François's taught me a trick or two."

For a second, Hellen regretted that the moment had been so rudely interrupted, but then she smiled back. "Surprise me with your cocktail artistry," she said.

"A White Russian for m'lady?" Tom asked playfully. He'd already fetched the cream from the refrigerator and was checking out the mixing options. Hellen had left her table and was now sitting on a stool at the bar. She was watching Tom at work when the phone on the wall at the end of the bar began to ring.

Tom ignored it. He poured vodka and coffee liqueur into a tumbler over ice cubes, then inverted a spoon and slowly poured the thickened cream over it and into the glass. The telephone continued to ring. Tom jabbed a short straw into the glass, laid a cocktail napkin on the bar and set the drink in front of Hellen. She smiled at him. The telephone rang and rang.

"Before I conjure up a whiskey sour for myself, let's have a little peace and quiet," said Tom. He went to the phone, picked it up and dropped it back onto its hook. "Let there be silence," he said with a grin and began looking around for a good bottle of bourbon.

The telephone rang again.

Hellen tilted her head to one side and looked at Tom. "If this goes on much longer, my drink will get warm and you can forget your tip," she said with an impish smile.

Irritated, Tom strode to the phone and picked it up.

"Hello?"

"In front of you is the remote control for the TV on the wall," said a voice with a strong Russian accent. "Turn it on."

The caller had already hung up. Mystified, Tom looked at Hellen.

"Who was it?" she asked.

Tom reached for the remote. "He said to turn on the TV."

"How romantic," Hellen teased.

The flat-screen TV sprang to life. On CNN, a report about wildfires in Central America was just finishing, and the anchorman moved on to the WHO conference in London. The camera swung across the crowd and zoomed in on the director-general of the WHO. At the same moment, Tom and Hellen saw who was standing directly behind him.

7

CAMP DAVID, COUNTRY RETREAT OF THE PRESIDENT, MARYLAND

"I didn't say a word, sir!"

Chief of Staff Jordan Armstrong raised his hands defensively as President George William Samson took his seat in the beige leather chair bearing the presidential seal. They were aboard Marine One, the president's helicopter, and the two Secret Service men accompanying the president took their seats at the other end of the cabin.

"But you said it very loudly, Jordan," Samson said. He thought his chief of staff was eyeing him a little judgmentally.

The modified Sikorsky VH-3 took off and joined two identical helicopters, which flanked Marine One as they flew.

"It's been a year," Samson said. "I think the American people will learn sooner or later to get used to the idea that I've got a girlfriend."

"Not when it comes to your re-election, Mr. President. Your focus should be on nothing but the election and your objectives. A sex scandal is the last thing we need, and—with all due respect—least of all with a CEO who is under constant fire because of her corporation."

"I see. Well, what's so important that you felt you had to interrupt my brief return to normal life? And why couldn't it wait for the daily briefing?" Samson asked.

"The NSA picked up a phone call." Armstrong pushed a file marked "Top Secret" across the folding table set up between them.

"You don't say. That's one for the books," Samson said ironically. Smiling, he accepted the file from Armstrong and opened it to find a photograph of an attractive woman and a few loose documents: scientific papers and chemical analyses.

"We don't know much. In 2018, in a jungle in Central America, a young botanist, Sienna Wilson"—Armstrong leaned forward and tapped on the photograph—"rediscovered a plant that many thought had died out long ago. The research team behind the discovery perished in mysterious circumstances, all except for Wilson and her boss. They were the only survivors, and Wilson has spent the last two years researching the plant."

"And why exactly are we interested in a plant?" Samson asked, furrowing his brow.

"It shows enormous potential. We are very close to having a new biological weapon out there to deal with. You can imagine what that would mean in the wrong hands."

Armstrong paused to let his last words sink in. President Samson raised his eyebrows and leafed through the file.

"The NSA alerted us to the situation after they picked up a phone call from one of the leading scientists of the Genesis Program, Dr. Emanuel Orlov. Unfortunately, so far, they haven't been able to trace whoever was on the other end. They seem to have used some kind of extremely advanced encryption. So we don't know who Dr. Orlov was passing information to."

"So, you're telling me that Great Britain—our most important ally—is home to some scientists who, by pure chance, have stumbled onto a new kind of biological agent and that apparently they're about to sell it to the highest bidder? Have I understood you correctly?" Samson leaned forward and looked keenly at Armstrong.

"Yes, sir."

"I'll be sitting across from the British Prime Minister at the WHO summit. What do you suggest I say to her?"

Samson looked steadily at Armstrong, who took his time answering. As an advisor to the most powerful man in the world, his advice had to be carefully thought through.

"Nothing, sir. Don't tell her anything," Armstrong said. "We need to get our own hands on this substance as soon as we can, ally or not. While we're at it, we should also get rid of every bit of information about it. No one else can be allowed to get hold of it."

"What are you saying?"

"We could have a CIA team on site in two days. No one will ever find out about it."

Now it was President Samson's turn to think. He turned away from Armstrong and gazed out the window.

"No. Too risky. What would happen if something went wrong? Thanks to my fake-tanned predecessor, our relationship with the UK is already hanging by a thread. The last thing we need now is to get caught trying to run a CIA operation on British soil."

"But sir, what alternative do we have? We have to do something, and we have to do it fast."

Samson's position had taken Armstrong by surprise. He had never opposed black ops in the past. Why now, when the subject matter was so incendiary?

"We need one hundred percent deniability. We cannot allow ourselves to provoke an international incident. Not now. Leave it to me."

Armstrong looked at the president in disbelief. What did he mean by "leave it to me"? In all the years that Armstrong, one way or another, had served the office, no president had ever said anything like that.

"Thank you, Jordan," said Samson, preempting any further commentary that Armstrong might have felt the need to share. President Samson went back to gazing out the window as Marine One prepared to land in Arlington. Air Force One stood ready for takeoff on the tarmac, waiting to fly the president and his entourage to the WHO congress in London.

8

ABOARD A YACHT, ST. KATHERINE DOCKS, NEAR TOWER BRIDGE, LONDON, ENGLAND

Even now, Noah Pollock could hardly believe it. Again and again, he stood up and paced back and forth across the deck. Then he went downstairs to the luxury cabins and climbed up to the yacht's viewing platform, on the same level as the helideck. Everywhere he went, he kept looking down at his legs. The operation was already a few weeks behind him, but it still brought tears to his eyes. For years, he'd been stuck in a wheelchair. For years, he'd been a cripple, forced to watch others do his job for him. And in the course of those years, he had learned to hate the man whose fault it was: Tom Wagner.

It had been a joint operation, and Tom had gotten sloppy. Noah had been seriously injured and ended up in a wheelchair. Shunted aside. Condemned to sit at a computer in an office.

It was no surprise that he'd jumped at the opportunity when it was offered to him. No surprise that he'd grasped at a straw, that he'd been ready to do anything to be able to walk again. The organization had made him a promise, and the organization had delivered.

Now it was his turn to show the Leader his gratitude and humility. And once again, there was a lot riding on it. An ambitious plan, far more ambitious than the operations in Barcelona and Ethiopia had been. Certain steps had to be taken, decisions made, the right pieces positioned on the chessboard.

He saw the Kahle, his hairless skull striking even at this distance, approaching from the side of the City Quay luxury apartments that enclosed the exclusive harbor at St. Katherine Docks. During his time with Mossad, Noah had had dealings with the man, although back then they had been adversaries. And he had learned that it was not pleasant at all to have him and his brother against you.

Now, however, they were united, fighting together for the organization known as AF—Absolute Freedom—and for their Leader, whom Noah still had not met face to face. Noah's new team was unique in one glorious detail: they shared a common enemy, Tom Wagner. Not only was Wagner responsible for Noah's years in the wheelchair, he had killed the Kahle's twin brother. Wagner would pay. And everyone on his fucking team would pay with him.

The Kahle boarded the yacht and he and Noah nodded to one another.

"Drink?" Noah offered.

"No alcohol," the Kahle stated flatly, almost reproachfully.

Noah shrugged, and the two men took their seats at the round table on the deck, from which a monitor flipped up at the push of a button. Noah made adjustments to the terminal from his smartphone, and a few seconds later the monitor screen split into three sections. One showed the AF symbol, while the other two remained black.

"One minute," said Noah. "You'll be happy to hear that we've given our mutual friend Wagner a spot in the plan. But only at the end, so he can't screw things up."

The Kahle man's face showed no reaction. "I only want to avenge my brother. But don't worry, I won't let my desire for revenge get in the way. Work first, pleasure second."

The circular indicators in the right-hand corners of the screens, which had showed red until now, suddenly flicked to green: the three participants were now online and the speech distortion was functioning. Noah was redirecting the audio conference through hundreds of proxy servers located all over the world, and using highly complex algorithms to distort the voices of the participants in real time—no voice recognition software in the world would be able to identify them. It was one of the first things Noah had introduced when he joined AF, and he was damned proud to be able to stick it to the NSA and their cronies with his technological prowess.

"Let's get straight to business," said the Leader's voice. "This is a complex plan, and I hope you all know what needs to be done."

"Absolutely," Noah replied without hesitation. As he spoke, his icon changed color to green, signaling who had spoken. The other two participants, like Noah, also affirmed.

"Our first priority is the plant," the Leader went on. "We now know almost everything about it, but one thing isn't clear. We're still missing a crucial ingredient and we don't yet know how to get it."

"Leave that to me, sir," Noah said. "Count Palffy's papers can probably help, and I'll reactivate my old contacts in Vienna."

"Good. Friedrich, your job is to make sure we get our hands on the plant," said the Leader. "With the briefing I sent you today, that should not prove difficult."

"Consider it done," the Kahle said.

"Once all of that has been taken care of, Wagner is yours."

"I appreciate that, sir."

"Are things progressing in the White House?"

A voice with a broad southern U.S. accent drawled: "Yessir. As you know, we've been working on the implementation for some time. We're taking a long-term view; the web we're spinning won't be finished in a few days. Everyone's at their post and we've got our people in all of the administrative positions we need to make it happen."

"Then all that remains is the final step." Noah knew immediately what the Leader was referring to. "The situation has become intolerable and I will see to it personally that this is put right. It will be a hollow victory without all of our allies involved."

A second later, the Leader's indicator switched back to red. The meeting was over. Noah had gotten used to these abrupt endings; the Leader despised empty hellos and goodbyes.

"What did he mean at the end?" Friedrich asked.

"There's someone important he'd like to have on his side. That's all you need to know for now," Noah replied.

9

BAR IN KULIBIN PARK HOTEL, NIZHNY NOVGOROD

"Oh my God!" Hellen said. "That's Noah!"

Tom narrowed his eyes and moved closer to the screen. There was no doubt about it. It was Noah. The same Noah who had turned on them and almost derailed their mission in Ethiopia. But seeing Noah was not the only thing that astonished them.

"That's impossible," said Tom. "It's Noah, but he's not in his wheelchair."

Even as Tom spoke, he felt a pang of conscience. He knew he was to blame for Noah's confinement to the chair.

"How can that be?" Hellen asked.

Tom was over his initial surprise and pushed his emotions aside. The fighter was back. "If Noah's at the WHO conference in London, then AF is planning something."

"Aren't they expecting a lot of government heads? Even the U.S. president?" Hellen asked in disbelief.

"Yes. And the Austrian chancellor will be there, too. I have no idea what Noah and AF are up to, but we have to do something."

Hellen's expression clouded. "Tom, you promised my mother you'd fly to Vienna tomorrow and follow up on the El Dorado tip. She'll kill you if you get sidetracked again."

Tom scratched his head. "I need a drink," he said, and quickly searched the bar's selection of single malts. He found a bottle of Middleton 2010 Irish whiskey, raised his eyebrows in surprise, and poured two fingers into a whiskey glass.

"This is really a whiskey to be savored, but screw it," he said, and he tipped the contents back in a single gulp. "You're right. Your mother will blow her stack if we put this off again. But I can't just let it go. Noah's to blame for my uncle's death. He turned on us, and now he's working for AF. He's not there on vacation."

Tom refilled his glass and took another sip. "I have to go to London. If AF is there, people are in danger. And I have to do something about it in person—no one would believe us about Noah." He pointed to the screen, which now showed the ExCeL London convention center from the outside. Thousands of people were milling about. Hellen hated to admit it, but she knew he was right.

"I've got another bit of bad news, too," Tom said. He looked at Hellen, who had just finished her own drink, and lifted the Middleton bottle. She gave him a resigned nod and a few seconds later had a glass of whiskey of her own.

"Let me guess," she said. "You want to take the Blue Shield jet?"

Tom nodded sheepishly.

"She's going to have a fit. She'll throw us out. I'll never get a decent job as a historian ever again. I'll be lucky to get a job at the Vienna Goulash Museum, and they wouldn't hire you as a parking attendant. You know her. She'll really do it."

Tom had to grant Hellen that. He had come out from behind the bar and was now standing beside her. "You know I have to do this. People are in danger. I know how much this job means to you, but all the gold in the world can't outweigh that danger. And El Dorado isn't about to run away."

Before Hellen could respond, Tom had pulled her to him and kissed her. Taken by surprise, Hellen's first thought was *you son-of-a-bitch*, but her true feelings quickly won out. The kiss lasted a small eternity. They had never been closer than they were in this moment, not even when they had first come together after the hunt for the Florentine diamond, their first adventure together.

"I'll join you as soon as I possibly can. Remember Atlas, the joint European counterterrorism task force? I'm pretty sure they'll be in charge of security at the conference. I still know a lot of people there. I'll tell them about the danger and then I'll come find you, wherever you are."

Hellen looked into Tom's eyes and realized that he wasn't feeling nearly as cool as he was trying to look. The kiss had upended his world, too.

Deep inside, she knew he had to go to London if he was going to make anything happen. She'd already resigned herself to that. "Okay. I'll think of something," she said. "I'll come up with some kind of story for Mother tomorrow, don't worry. François will help."

"He's a much better liar than you," Tom said, and he pulled Hellen close again. "I'll be back before you can say 'El Dorado.'"

Hellen leaned her head against his chest and felt the beating of his heart. Tom breathed deeply, his arms wrapped tightly around her, one hand on the back of her head. Neither one of them really believed it would be that simple.

10

SECRET PRISON COMPLEX, NEW MEXICO

Ossana soon realized that something was different. They had traveled much farther than usual, going up many levels in the high-speed elevator before passing through a series of security gates and checkpoints. Now they entered a wing that looked more like a modern office building than a high-security prison. No guards at the door, no security cameras at thirty-foot intervals, and it seemed to Ossana that the security measures in place were designed to keep people out, rather than in. As they passed through another checkpoint with a retinal scan and voice recognition and finally stood before an office door with a sign that read "ADX Management," it was clear that this was not going to be the usual kind of interrogation.

The door opened and Ossana was led into a room that looked nothing at all like the interrogation rooms she knew. The windows offered glorious views of the New Mexico desert, and the furniture was far from the steel and concrete she had come to expect. The room looked like an early Victorian smoking lounge in an English castle: dark-brown shelves filled with old books, an enormous leather sofa, tapestries, a fireplace, Renaissance paintings on the walls, a billiard table, and an antique desk that would not have looked out of place at Buckingham Palace.

Ossana raised her eyebrows when the guards removed her shackles and left the room. The man sitting at the desk was a perfect match for the room: he was dressed in an anthracite-gray pinstriped three-piece suit, and from the left pocket of his vest hung the obligatory chain of a pocket watch. His burgundy necktie was tied in a double Windsor knot and held in place by a pearl-studded pin. On his right ring finger he wore a gold signet ring. His hair was parted neatly on one side, but without looking fussy. Mid-forties, Ossana guessed, as he stared at her with dark-gray eyes behind tortoiseshell spectacles. He radiated a cruel, almost cold-blooded charisma that Ossana found remarkably attractive.

"Please sit down, Ms. Ibori. I would like to apologize for your treatment in the last few weeks. I took up my post here only yesterday." He paused and sipped from a teacup. "My predecessor passed away unexpectedly, and I intend to make a number of changes to this facility. You will have to excuse me for not meeting you yesterday, but I had to get my office in order first." He waved one hand, indicating the interior furnishings. "Yankees simply have no taste. You have no idea what this room looked like before."

Ossana wanted to ask if the room had really been refurnished in just one day, but she kept the completely irrelevant question to herself.

The man stood up and went to a computer terminal set into the right-hand wall of the office.

"Come here, please, Ms. Ibori. I have to show you something."

Hesitantly, Ossana stood and went to the terminal. She saw that it, too, was equipped with a retinal scanner.

"Please keep your right eye in front of the scanner," the man said, as if it were the most natural thing in the world.

Again, Ossana hesitated, but then did as bidden. A second later, the screen changed and a message in her native language, Afrikaans, appeared. She quickly read the message and a smile flashed on her face. The man had turned away to allow Ossana to read in private.

"I do not know who you are, but as an inmate you are clearly different from the rest of the scum here. Shortly before my appointment was confirmed, I discovered a sizeable sum of money in one of my offshore accounts. Along with the money was a request: to pass this information on to you."

The man came across as simultaneously amiable and ruthless.

"Do not make the mistake of thinking you can exploit my goodwill because of this, however. You are a prisoner in the most secret and secure prison in the United States. I don't care why you're here. I don't care who you are. And just so we are perfectly clear: it doesn't matter how much money you or your friends throw at me, I always make my decisions with a view to my own advantage. Not yours."

Ossana's smile had vanished, but she now knew what she had to do. The man was vain, corrupt, venal, powerful and good-looking. She knew his type and she knew how to deal with them. Her next move came spontaneously, a gut feeling that surprised even herself. She had obviously been locked up for far too long, because she found herself succumbing to the man's sexual allure. A quick hand movement was all it took—Ossana opened her prison overalls and a moment later was standing completely naked in front of the man. If he was surprised, he did not let it show. He moved his head to the right, his eyes to the sofa. Ossana understood. She turned around, mentally preparing to feel him enter her, but without warning, an open hand crashed into her face, splitting her lip. Staggered by the force of the blow, she fell. Her head cracked against the stone floor and she found herself gasping for air.

"That will not work with me. I had one task, to make sure you received a message. You've received it. From this moment on, you are once again an inmate. With no rights whatsoever."

The door flew open and the guards entered. They pulled Ossana to her feet and snapped on the handcuffs and shackles again, leaving her overalls lying on the floor. They pushed Ossana naked into the corridor.

"Lead the prisoner through every floor," the man said, and the guards grinned.

One thing had become clear to Ossana. She had to find her way back to herself. She had to recover her instincts, her strength, her determination, and her cold-bloodedness.

11

FRANÇOIS CLOUTARD'S SUITE, KULIBIN PARK HOTEL, NIZHNY NOVGOROD

Hellen knocked on the door. "François! I need to talk to you."

She knocked again, harder this time.

"*Un moment*," she heard the Frenchman call from inside.

"It's important, François." Hellen was pounding on the door now.

She heard movement inside Cloutard's suite, and a moment later he breathlessly opened the door.

"What is it, for heaven's sake?" Cloutard croaked.

Hellen could barely hold back a smile. She had never seen the smug Frenchman like this. His hair stood on end; judging by the rings under his eyes, he'd hardly slept at all; his voice sounded as if he'd downed an entire bottle of his favorite cognac in one sitting; and even his mustache, usually so immaculate, stuck out in all directions.

Hellen pushed Cloutard back into the room and quickly closed the door. "We have to talk before we meet with Mother."

Cloutard looked at her in confusion. "Is that not exactly what the meeting is for? So that we can get answers to any questions we still have?"

Cloutard looked as if he'd been run over by a Russian tank. He slumped wearily onto the couch in the living area and downed a glass of water like Lawrence of Arabia after trekking through the desert for days. "*Merde!* These headaches are going to kill me. It's this abominable Russian vodka," he murmured, but quickly recovered himself. "Say what you have to say and then let me get back to bed. I need time to recover."

Hellen looked at him in amazement. He actually sounded surly, a far cry from the charming François Cloutard she otherwise knew. Even in their most dire predicaments, he'd always maintained his poise. She resolved to ignore his mood.

"Tom flew to London last night."

Cloutard's face did not change. He seemed not to have understood her words.

"Uh, excuse me? I think I did not hear you correctly. Tom is where?"

As the news sank in, his face turned pale and he looked anxiously over Hellen's shoulder. In a few words, Hellen told him what had happened the previous evening in the bar.

"And what is he thinking? That Noah is going to wait

until Mr. Wagner turns up in person in London? *Ta mére* is not going to be happy at all." As he said this, he glanced again over Hellen's shoulder in the direction of the bathroom door. Only now did Hellen recall that Cloutard had gone to dinner with her mother the night before. But he must have gotten drunk by himself—her mother hated losing her self-control; she was even more of a control freak than Hellen herself.

"We have to come up with a story we can tell Mother. Something plausible to explain why Tom will only be joining us later."

"You want to lie to your mother?" Cloutard asked doubtfully. "She is a walking lie detector! She will see through it in a second."

Cloutard's eyes were wide open now and he stood up nervously. He took Hellen by the arm and hustled her toward the door.

"If she finds out the truth, she'll fire Tom before we've even got our first official assignment," Hellen said.

"It is never a good thing for mothers and daughters to keep secrets from one another," François said. "You should tell your mother the truth. And I am astounded that you let Tom run off to London so easily. The man has to set priorities in his life. We will never be a successful team like this."

Cloutard was getting really wound up—Hellen could not remember seeing him so upset.

"I don't know about you," he continued, his eyes shut tight in exasperation, "but I need this job. Now go. Leave me alone. I need to freshen up."

Hellen was almost out the door again when she heard a noise from the back of the suite. Suddenly she realized why Cloutard was so nervous. And now she was annoyed. She pushed Cloutard aside, strode to the bathroom, and threw open the door.

"You can come out, Mother," she snapped, glaring angrily into Theresia's eyes. She, too, had obviously had a hard night. The Russian tank had not stopped with Cloutard.

12

ATLAS HEADQUARTERS, EXCEL LONDON CONFERENCE CENTER, ENGLAND

"We are witnessing an unprecedented event that started here in London yesterday," the CNN anchorman said. "It's the biggest World Health Organization conference in history. Medical experts and researchers from more than two hundred countries have gathered here together with representatives from the health care and pharmaceutical industries. Hundreds of forums, seminars and presentations have been planned. The conference highlight will undoubtedly be the meeting of the heads of the G20 states, here to ratify an historic agreement that aims to stabilize and expand health care around the world, a sorely needed initiative."

Tom shut off the news and leaned back. He hadn't seen Noah this time. Had he only imagined it? No, Hellen had recognized him, too. But he had to admit that a little doubt was beginning to creep into his mind. Was it really Noah he'd seen just a few hours ago? Yes, he was certain of it. And if Noah was here, it did not bode well. Everybody at the event was in danger.

The cockpit door opened and the pilot came back to him.

"Mr. Wagner, we have a problem. We were given clearance to land at London City Airport on our original flight plan, but we've just been rerouted to Bigging Hill. That's about an hour's drive south of London."

"We don't have time for that. There's nothing you can do? Tell 'em we're part of Atlas and have important info for the security of the conference."

"We tried. No luck," the pilot replied.

Tom thought for a moment. "How much time do we have?"

"We were supposed to land at London City in forty minutes," said the pilot, with a quick glance at his Breitling watch. He turned and went back to the cockpit.

Tom reached for the cabin telephone, called Cobra headquarters and had them connect him with London. The phone rang three times before someone picked up, and for a moment Tom was at a loss for words. He knew the surly voice on the other end far too well. In his old job, it had been his constant companion, but Tom had hoped fervently that he'd never cross paths with his old boss again.

"Maierhofer speaking!"

"Hello?" Tom's brain went blank for a second. "Yeah, hello, it's Wagner."

"Wagner?" Maierhofer sounded just as taken aback as Tom. A call from his former favorite troublemaker was probably the last thing he was expecting.

"Vahgner," Maierhofer said, deliberately mispronouncing Tom's name, as he always had. "What do you want?"

"What are you doing at Atlas HQ?" Tom asked in confusion. "Don't tell me they . . ." Tom stopped himself, but it was too late. Someone had obviously promoted Maierhofer to head of Atlas, so it made perfect sense that he'd be calling the shots. "Congratulations," Tom said, trying to salvage what he could, but if he knew Maierhofer, he was already too late.

"Wagner, what do you want? I don't have all day."

"Sure. Sorry. I'm in a plane on the way to London and we've just been redirected to Bigging Hill. We absolutely have to land at London City Airport. It's life or death. I've got vital security information about the conference and there's no time to lose."

"What are you mixed up in this time?"

"Believe me, Captain, I wouldn't ask if it wasn't serious. Get me permission to land and I'll explain everything face to face."

For a moment there was silence on the other end. Then Maierhofer said, "Okay. You'll get your clearance. But believe me, Wagner, if you're wasting my time, I'll bury you so deep not even your beloved chancellor will be able to dig you out."

Tom smiled. *I've got much more powerful friends these days,* he thought.

"Thanks. I'm not. I'll patch you through to the pilot. See you soon."

Tom transferred the call to the cockpit and sat down again. He hadn't even noticed that he'd been pacing up and down the cabin during the entire call.

Thanks to Maierhofer, the plane could now land at their original destination. Tom was glad to see the Atlas group's influence seemed to have increased in the last couple of years. At the start, they'd been no more than an informal amalgamation of thirty-eight separate special police units, one of which was Tom's old antiterrorism unit from Austria, Cobra. Thanks to Tom's efforts in Barcelona, the group's standing had improved considerably, and they'd been responsible for security at events of this magnitude across Europe ever since.

The Gulfstream jet touched down on time at London City Airport. The convention center was situated directly beside the airport, but a car was already waiting to pick Tom up—Maierhofer was leaving nothing to chance; he probably didn't want Tom running around the premises without a chaperone. The driver's face looked familiar to Tom, but for the life of him he could not put a name to it. His relationship with his fellow officers had always been rather cool. Tom was the lone wolf, had never been a team player. The only one he'd ever got on well with was the one he'd considered his best friend for years, Noah Pollock. But Noah had gone to the dark side.

After the short drive from the airport, Tom jumped out of the car and headed straight for the enormous semi-trailer that housed the Atlas mobile command center, a monstrous black beast equipped with the latest computer gear, surveillance equipment and communications. Tom jerked the door open without knocking, and, to the astonishment of everyone inside, walked straight up to Maierhofer and threw his arms around him.

"Thank you," he said. "You don't know how grateful I am."

Maierhofer pushed Tom off and glared at him. "What's got into you, Wagner? Come on, man, spit it out. What's so important?"

"First, my name's 'Wagner,' not 'Vahgner.' It's pronounced in English, 'a' as in apple." Tom inhaled deeply and went on when Maierhofer did no more than roll his eyes. "Noah Pollock," he said.

Suddenly, absolute silence fell. Everyone in the trailer held their breath. The tapping of keys instantly ceased.

"Noah Pollock. Your old best buddy, the one on the FBI's most-wanted list? That Noah Pollock?"

"Yeah. He's here."

"What do you mean, here? Here in London?"

"Yes. Here at the conference."

Tom quickly told Maierhofer about the anonymous phone call in Russia and the CNN report where he'd seen Noah.

"You're sure?"

"One hundred percent."

"And why do you think he's here?"

Tom grinned sheepishly. "This is where it gets complicated. I don't know." Tom could see Maierhofer's frustration growing. “Yet,” he quickly added. “I was hoping you could help me get my hands on him, and then we’d simply ask him.” Tom smiled and shrugged. “Because if he’s here, AF is also here and that can only mean that people are probably going to get hurt.”

“So this is a gut feeling, so to speak,” said Maierhofer sarcastically. “Wagner, do you seriously think I’m going to start a manhunt in the middle of the biggest WHO conference in history because you’ve got indigestion? If that’s all you’ve got, Mr. Vaaaaahhgner, then—”

“Well, actually, you’re not going to believe this, but . . .” Tom smiled meekly “Noah can walk again,” he added.

“Wagner, get out of my sight,” Maierhofer snarled and pointed at the door. The key tapping and murmurs instantly picked up where they’d left of.

Maierhofer pointed to the young officer who’d picked Tom up earlier and who’d been standing silently in a corner the entire time.

“Markus or Mark or whatever your name is, drive Mr. Wagner back to the airport and make sure he gets on a plane.”

Tom did not try again to persuade his ex-boss to help him. He’d gotten what he wanted. He turned around and left the truck, a smile on his lips.

13

PREMIER HIGH SCHOOL, TEXARKANA, BORDER OF TEXAS AND ARKANSAS, USA

He looked down and moved the scissors toward the red ribbon, opening them as if were about to slice through it, but then paused and looked up. And just then a storm of camera flashes went off. He smiled at the cameras like he always did and forced himself to look worldly-wise, as if he'd just co-signed a peace treaty between Israel and the Palestinians. Unfortunately, all he was doing was dedicating yet another gymnasium in yet another school somewhere in the boondocks, sponsored by one of the few Texans who actually supported the Democrats and who had therefore injected a sizeable amount of money into the president's election campaign. As vice president of the United States, it fell to him to attend dubious events like this.

When George Samson had asked him if he'd be available to serve as vice president, James J. Pitcock had been flattered. As a former Marine and Gulf War veteran, he'd risen rapidly through the ranks of the Democratic party to be one of the youngest congressmen in the United

States. He had never dreamed that he would advance as rapidly as he had. Nor had he imagined that the job of vice president would be so unspectacular, so boring and —at times—even humiliating.

Yet here he was again, shaking hundreds of hands, kissing babies, making small talk with third-rate politicians and mayors who all had a fistful of excellent tips for the president. So far, he could not name one thing he had done in his job that had really made a difference. But he was resolved to see out his term. He was a Marine, and he'd taken more than one oath on the flag of the United States to do everything in his power for his country and its citizens. And if that meant cutting yet another red ribbon, that was fine with him. His time would come. His values and views would be heard. The right moment to prove his competence and political talent would come his way. But he would not wait forever.

"Mr. Vice President, Miss Sorenson on the line."

One of the Secret Service agents, obviously bored, handed him the satellite phone. The agents knew as well as Pitcock that protecting the vice president was less dangerous than Black Friday at a Victoria's Secret outlet.

"What is it, Rita?"

"Mr. Vice President, excuse me for interrupting your important event, but I've just heard something that you need to know about."

Pitcock sighed. Rita Sorenson was his chief of staff, but she was also the biggest gossip in D.C. If she heard something important, it wasn't likely to be, say, a conversation between Russia and North Korea picked up by the NSA.

It was usually about which senator was in bed with which lobbyist, or which congresswoman had had the fat vacuumed out of which part of her body. And Pitcock didn't give a damn about any of that.

"I'm all ears, Rita," Pitcock lied.

"Our upstanding Mr. President has a new squeeze—Yasmine Matthews, CEO of NutriAm."

Pitcock could picture Rita's gleeful grin, and he smiled himself. Maybe it hadn't been such a dumb idea after all to hire a Desperate Housewife as his chief of staff.

14

EXCEL LONDON, ALOFT HOTEL

Markus, or Mark, or whatever his name was, was taken completely by surprise. His vision clouded, he stumbled, and finally his body went limp. Tom had grabbed the Atlas agent inside the hangar as soon as he climbed out of the car. Mindful of his duty, Markus was intent on escorting Tom all the way to the plane. But he didn't stand a chance: Tom's iron chokehold quickly sent to the land of dreams.

The pilot had trotted down the steps of the Gulfstream to help Tom, and together they carried the unconscious man into the plane. "Can I ask what this is all about?" the baffled pilot asked.

"Better not. Help me get him undressed," Tom said.

The pilot pulled off the man's jacket while Tom went to work on his trousers.

"One thing I'll say, Mr. Wagner: there's never a dull moment with you," the pilot said.

"Happy to oblige. Just don't say a word to Ms. de Mey about how much fun we're having, or I'll be out of a job before I've even started."

Tom pulled on the suit, clipped on the ID card and took a key card out of his jeans—the all-access card he'd stolen from Maierhofer earlier when he'd hugged him. He slipped it into the breast pocket of the jacket. They tied and gagged the unconscious man, carried him back outside and heaved his slack body into the trunk of the car. Tom got in and drove off.

He parked the car at the back of the hotel and made his way to an out-of-the-way back entrance to the curvaceous palace of blue glass where most of the meetings were taking place. He held Maierhofer's key card to the card reader and with a buzz the door opened. Tom was inside. *These security precautions are a joke*, he thought as he made his way along a corridor toward the lobby.

The noise swelled as Tom entered the overflowing hotel lobby. He needed a better vantage point if he wanted to find Noah. He climbed the designer spiral staircase beside the self-check-in counter to the first floor. From there he had a good view over the entire foyer. He leaned casually on the glass balustrade, scanning the room. Nothing.

Slowly but surely, the hopelessness of what he was trying to achieve dawned on him. How was he supposed to find Noah among all these people? He was probably holed up in a hotel suite somewhere, or maybe sitting in a conference room. Maybe he'd already placed a bomb and left London altogether. Tom wondered again if he ought to try one more time to get Maierhofer on his side and use

Atlas's considerable resources. All of these thoughts shot through Tom's head as his eyes flicked from one guest to the next.

Suddenly, an icy tremor ran down Tom's back. He turned around and froze. Noah Pollock was standing twenty yards down a hallway, talking with a man. Tom did not recognize the second man, who had his back to him. Tom stared in disbelief. Seeing his former best friend without his wheelchair was very, very strange. Slowly, instinctively, Tom's hand dropped to his hip, but he was not armed. Despite the milling crowd, Tom saw Noah hand the man a briefcase. Good. At least Tom was not too late. But what was in the case? A bomb? Or just a bribe? He had to get closer.

Cautiously, and as discreetly as possible, Tom edged toward the pair. He took out his phone to take a few photos for proof, but just as he clicked the shutter his iPhone was almost knocked out of his hand by a guest hurrying past. A sudden disturbance down in the lobby had drawn the curiosity of quite a few of the visitors, who began to crowd at the railing behind Tom to see what was going on.

"Get your hands off me! Let me go!" screamed a woman, lashing out with her feet as two security guards dragged her through the lobby. "I have to talk to the director-general. It's a matter of life and death!"

Like everyone else, Tom had turned away for a moment, distracted by the fracas. But when he turned back, Noah and the man had disappeared.

"Shit! Shit, shit, shit!" Tom cursed, jamming his phone into his pocket and zigzagging through the crowd. At the end of the hallway, he looked left and right. Empty. Noah was nowhere to be seen. "Goddamnit!" Tom cried.

He chose a direction and had taken two steps when he saw an agent from his old unit looking meaningfully at him and speaking into the microphone on his wrist, his other hand already on the butt of his Glock. Tom spun the other way, but stopped again. From the other side, another Atlas man was heading his way, and a third strode toward him along the hallway he'd just run up. He was trapped.

He had to act fast. He backed up, slowly, not letting the three agents out of his field of view, until he was literally standing with his back against the wall. The men closed in cautiously. Their first priority seemed to be not to cause a disturbance. As Tom leaned against the wall, he felt something pressing into his back. Installed on the wall was a little red box with a switch inside it—that was the solution. Not as elegant as he might have wished, but certainly effective. Tom smashed in the glass panel on the front of the box and pressed the fire alarm.

Seconds later, chaos broke out. Visitors ran like headless chickens for the stairways and exits. The deafening alarm wailed on every floor of the hotel. Doors flew open and people came streaming out of the conference rooms. Tom calmly dropped to his knees, laced his fingers behind his head and let the agents restrain him. He put up no resistance.

"You've really done it this time, Wagner. Snatching Maierhofer's key card was an idiot move," one of the men said as he searched him for weapons, taking everything Tom had in his pockets.

"You'll pay for that big time," said one of the others, a nasty smile on his face.

"Maierhofer will get over it," Tom said. He smiled. For the time being, he'd thrown a wrench in whatever plans Noah had, and all of the guests would get to safety.

15

FRANÇOIS CLOUTARD'S SUITE, KULIBIN PARK HOTEL, NIZHNY NOVGOROD

"Don't look at me like that. It's not as if I shut myself in a convent after your father died."

Theresia de Mey was standing in the bathroom in nothing but her underwear. She looked at her daughter with a mixture of guilt and annoyance, unsure how to react to the situation.

"Papa isn't dead. He's missing," Hellen said, hurt.

Theresia de Mey's face softened. She went over to her daughter and embraced her. "Hellen, how many times have I told you to accept things for what they are? You're right, of course: we don't know for certain that your father is dead. But he's been missing for more than ten years."

Theresia wanted to say more, but couldn't. The whole subject was as difficult for her as it was for her daughter. Since Hellen's father had disappeared, Theresia had never been able to fall in love with another man. And she feared it would be no different with Cloutard. But she swept aside her melancholy thoughts.

"We need to stop this. I have a right to a private life, too," Theresia said, gathering her clothes and getting dressed. "Far more interesting for me is the fact that Tom is once again doing his own thing, as I've just heard."

Hellen swallowed. She could forget the cover story she'd been planning.

"Tom had some news about Noah and—"

Theresia raised her hand. "Not another word. I don't know why you always defend him. Tom Wagner is selfish and irresponsible. He thinks about no one but himself. I'll probably have to find a replacement for him, and soon. Our situation is too precarious to rely on him."

"Too precarious?" Hellen asked with a frown.

"What your mother is trying to say is that UNESCO is considering cutting Blue Shield's budget."

Hellen glared angrily at Cloutard and ignored his answer.

"Maybe you've heard—the global economy is going through a recession," Theresia said, her voice growing louder. "And cultural financing, like it or not, is the first to suffer. We need to find something to justify our existence to UNESCO . . . something like El Dorado."

Hellen knew her mother. Once she got going, it was better to keep your mouth shut.

"And we can't wait around until His Lordship Tom Wagner finally decides to do his damn job."

"We will take care of it, Theresia," said Cloutard. "You do not have to worry about a thing. Hellen and I are a good team, as we have shown many times already."

That was before you jumped into bed with my mother, Hellen wanted to say. But for the sake of peace, she managed to hold her tongue.

"I assumed as much. You're flying to Vienna today," Theresia de Mey said, now fully dressed again. With her business outfit, her authority seemed to return.

"That . . . could be tricky," Hellen replied, looking at the floor.

Cloutard and Hellen's mother both knew instantly what she meant.

"You cannot be serious!" Theresia snorted. "Let me guess: Wagner took the Gulfstream to London."

Hellen nodded.

"*Quel connard*," Cloutard hissed, rolling his eyes.

"I'll sort it out. Make sure you're ready to leave. One way or another, this starts today," said Theresia.

She had picked up her handbag and was tapping furiously on her phone as she went to the door. Hellen had no interest in being left alone with Cloutard just now and also left. She had to figure out how to deal with her mother having an affair with a crook.

Cloutard wanted to say something, but he did not get the chance. The door had already closed behind Hellen and Theresia. "Without Tom, this will not be so easy," he said softly to himself. He could see his hopes going up in smoke once again. He had really wanted to be part of this team and, together with Tom and Hellen, to do at least a little good for UNESCO. For years he'd thought of no one but himself, after all. But maybe it had been stupid to rely on Tom. And maybe he himself, François Cloutard, wasn't made for this team. Maybe he was no more than a crook, and never would be. He made a decision. He went to the safe, took out his cellphone, and looked up Isaac Hagen's number. The former SAS man, who occasionally worked for AF, owed him a favor.

16

EXCEL LONDON, RECEPTIONISTS' BREAK ROOM

"Aren't you supposed to read me my rights? What about a phone call? I want to talk to my lawyer. I have rights!" Tom shouted, laughing, as his former colleagues departed, slamming the door behind them and locking it. Tom turned around and looked into the face of a surprised young woman—the same woman who had caused the disturbance in the lobby, inadvertently making Tom lose sight of Noah.

"Do you do this?" she shouted over the still-wailing alarm, waving her hand in the air overhead. When Tom said yes, she nodded, impressed.

"I saw you earlier. You put on quite a show," Tom shouted back as he rattled at the door handle.

"I'm a scientist with the Genesis Program. I was trying to warn the director-general about a new biological threat, but no one wants to believe me. What about you? Why all the fuss?"

"A biological threat? There's a lot going on here. I came to warn the security team about a terrorist, a guy they're looking for internationally. No one wants to listen to me either. That's why all the fuss." He also waved his hand overhead.

Just then, the alarm fell silent. Tom rubbed his ears with relief, then stepped toward the young woman.

"Wagner, Tom Wagner," he said.

"Dr. Sienna Wilson," the woman said, shaking his hand. "Nice to meet you."

"May I?"

Sienna nodded. Tom pulled up a chair and sat opposite her at the table.

"What do you think they'll do with us?" Sienna asked.

"Us? You'll probably get off with a warning. Me . . . hard to say this time."

"This time? You do this a lot?"

"Oh, yeah." Tom's laugh died in his throat. "Lately I've practically been a magnet for morons and trouble."

The door flew open and Maierhofer stalked in with two of his officers.

"Voilà," said Tom, gesturing toward Maierhofer as if presenting a new car.

"You may leave," Maierhofer barked at Sienna. "Don't let me see you here again. Next time, I'll hand you over to the local authorities. Have I made myself clear?"

Sienna nodded, and Maierhofer signaled one of his men to escort her outside. The officer took her by the arm and pulled her to her feet, and she did not resist as he led her to the door. "It was nice to meet you," she said to Tom. "Good luck!"

"Oh, luck isn't going to be much use to our dear Mr. *Vahgner* this time," Maierhofer said. The second officer shut the door behind Sienna and her escort, then turned and planted himself in front of it.

"Vahgner, Vahgner, Vahgner," said Maierhofer in a chillingly calm voice, pacing back and forth in front of Tom, who was still sitting at the table.

Tom raised a finger and shrugged innocently. "It's 'Wagner' . . ."

Every bit of color drained from Tom's face as Maierhofer slammed both fists onto the table.

"Have you completely lost your mind? Do you have any idea what you've just done? Can you begin to imagine the consequences of your actions? Count yourself lucky the G20 doesn't meet till tomorrow morning and most of the heads of state are still in their embassies. If you'd pulled this stunt tomorrow, I'd have had you summarily shot and they wouldn't have fished your body out of the Thames for days."

Tom was angry at himself. Tomorrow. Of course. The summit was taking place the next day. *Idiot, idiot, idiot*, he thought. That was why Noah was here now. Tom hadn't prevented anything. The briefcase was probably only the money for the assassin or something like that.

"Captain, listen to me. Noah was here. I saw him just now. He gave a man—"

But Maierhofer cut him off.

"Cut the crap. You've gone too far this time."

"Captain Maierhofer. Noah's *here*. And that means that AF is here."

"A . . . F . . ." Maierhofer pronounced the letters individually, dragging them out. "Absolute Freedom. You know, nobody has ever been able to demonstrate to me that this all-powerful terrorist organization even exists. Wagner, this isn't a Bond film. Noah isn't Blofeld," Maierhofer growled.

"I couldn't agree more, Captain. Noah isn't Blofeld. He's more like Dr. No. Because of the prosthetic hands . . . uh, legs, in his case. Also, he's not the leader of the organization," Tom said.

"Shut the hell up," Maierhofer seethed.

"I meant what I said earlier. I want to call someone. If you arrest me, I have the right to contact an attorney."

"All right, Wagner." Maierhofer turned and snapped his fingers. "Give me his phone."

The man handed the phone he'd confiscated when Tom was taken into custody to Maierhofer.

"Think hard about who you're going to call. I think you might have used up all your favors with the chancellor."

Maierhofer dangled the phone in front of Tom's face, but he was startled when it suddenly began to vibrate. Maierhofer looked at the screen, which read "POTUS."

"What's POTUS?" Maierhofer asked.

Tom's face instantly brightened. *My ticket out of here*, he thought, holding out his hand for the phone. "President of the United States," he said with a grin.

The phone continued to vibrate. "Don't mess with me, Wagner," Maierhofer snarled. Tom snatched the phone from his hand and took the call. Briefly, he explained his predicament. Then he ended the call and laid the phone on the table.

"Do you seriously expect me to believe you just spoke with the U.S. president? Wagner, you're even crazier than I thought."

"You don't have to believe me. Just wait a few minutes and we'll see who's crazy." Tom put his feet up on the table, folded his hands behind his head and grinned at Maierhofer.

"What's going to happen in the next few minutes?" Maierhofer asked.

"Well, the president's going to be speaking at the WHO event tomorrow, isn't he? Which means that half a dozen Secret Service guys from his advance security team are already here. Correct me if I'm wrong. You must have met them already, right?" Maierhofer's expression darkened. "A phone call from George and one of his men will be at that door any second." Tom used the president's first name to rile Maierhofer.

“I’ve had enough. Wagner, you’re officially under arrest. Get him out of my sight.” Maierhofer nodded to the officer by the door, who immediately came and dragged Tom to his feet.

“Oh, by the way,” Tom said as the officer snapped handcuffs around his wrists. “If you’re looking for Markus or Mark or whatever his name is, he’s taking a nap in the trunk of his car. It’s parked out back of the hotel.”

Maierhofer opened the door, but was startled to find a man in a black suit standing outside, holding an ID card for Maierhofer’s to read.

“U.S. Secret Service,” he said.

17

RIVE DROITE BEACH, ÈTANG DE THAU LAGOON, MEZE, FRANCE

Isaac Hagen dug his toes into the warm sand, enjoying his *pastis rouge*. He did not particularly like the French, but he had trouble resisting the anise cocktail. The area did not offer the best of French culinary delights, nor would anyone compare the Ètang de Thau lagoon to the Cote d'Azur. But Hagen loved the region nonetheless, for one reason: he could relax and no one would get on his nerves. So he kept coming back. Traditionally, the people who lived on the Ètang de Thau lagoon earned their living from fishing, and brought in a little money with salt production. Since the mid 20th century, oyster farming had also played an important role. There was some tourism, certainly, but it had never really taken hold. Hagen didn't mind that at all—it was one of the reasons he loved the region so much. He could sleep easily and didn't have to spend his days worrying about waking up with a pistol pointed at his head. He could drive his car without having to check it first for bombs, and he would not run into anyone from his decidedly sordid past. The region was simply too run-down for that. It wasn't the kind of place you'd expect to find a high-strung Briton like Hagen.

Hagen had given up active service in the SAS years before. These days he was a freelancer, as he liked to call it. "Mercenary" and "contract killer" were such uncultivated terms for the work he did, a métier he'd elevated almost to an art form.

"Another *pastis*, Monsieur?" asked the waiter at the only decent bar Hagen had found along this godforsaken beach.

Hagen nodded. He put a fifty-euro bill on the bar.

"Keep 'em coming until that runs out," he said, gazing thoughtfully out over the lagoon. "And leave a good tip for yourself, too."

Only a few boats bobbed out on the water. The waterfront promenade was almost empty, though it wasn't unusually hot for the time of year. Hagen was enjoying his time here. He'd get decently drunk on pastis before nightfall, then stroll into town, have dinner at one of the fish restaurants, where the food was unbelievably plentiful, good and cheap. Then he'd take a cab to the neighboring town of Marseillan and go in search of Giselle, who would make him forget whatever was on his mind with a mixture of tenderness and ferocity, as she always did. Hagen was so lost in his daydream that he did not notice the old man with the three-day beard, Persol sunglasses, and crumpled straw hat who sat down on his left at the bar.

"I'll have what he's having," the man said in French, pointing to Hagen's drink. Then he, too, turned and gazed out over the lagoon.

"You have to take care of something for me, Hagen."

The sentence struck Hagen like a punch in the face. He almost turned and looked at the man, leaning against the bar just a few feet away, but he was professional enough not to. It took him a heartbeat to regain his composure. They sat in silence while the bartender brought the old man's pastis. After a while, the old man reached into a dirty linen bag that he'd been carrying on his shoulder. He laid an envelope on the counter and pushed it a few inches in Hagen's direction, just far enough for Hagen to be able to see it out of the corner of his eye. The old man finished his pastis, stood up and signaled the barkeeper.

"The drink's on him."

Hagen could only assume that the old man had pointed in his direction, because he had not taken his gaze off the waters of the lagoon. He straightened up slowly, leaned a little to the left, and collected the envelope. He wouldn't be getting drunk that night after all, nor would he be eating well or forgetting his troubles with Giselle. He was on duty.

18

U.S. EMBASSY, LONDON

The two uniformed Marines posted on either side of the U.S. Embassy driveway stopped the black SUV. They checked the passengers' IDs and one of the men rolled an inspection mirror beneath the car, checking for bombs. Out the window, Tom peered up at the architectural monstrosity, which looked more like a Borg cube from Star Trek than an embassy building. *Appropriate*, he thought. The often blind loyalty of Americans to God and country reminded him a little of the hive-mind behavior of the Borg.

The car rolled down the ramp into the basement garage and stopped in front of the underground entrance. The agent in the passenger seat jumped out and opened Tom's door, and Tom climbed out of the SUV and followed him. Once they were past the ultra-modern security terminal, they rode the elevator up. The agent led Tom into a plain waiting room.

"Please take a seat, sir. It may take a little while, but the president will see you soon," said the Secret Service agent, his face impassive. He closed the door, positioned himself in front of it, and gazed into space. The agent's cool, military rigor amused Tom a little. He went to the window and looked out. The Stars and Stripes fluttered atop an enormous flagpole in the embassy garden.

Tom's thoughts drifted and he gleefully recalled Maierhofer's face when he'd come face to face with the Secret Service agent less than an hour before.

"Sir, the president would like a word with Mr. Wagner. I'm here to accompany him to the U.S. Embassy."

At first, Maierhofer had tried to object, but the uncompromising and exceptionally direct agent had nipped his dissent in the bud. Finally, Maierhofer admitted defeat and had personally unlocked Tom's handcuffs.

"I still have a bone to pick with you, Vaaaahhgner. When the Americans are done with you, you're mine. I don't care what friends you have, what you did today will not be swept under the carpet."

"Put it on my tab," Tom had said, slamming the door in Maierhofer's face.

President George William Samson emerged from his office and nodded to the agent, who replied with an almost imperceptible head movement, then turned and left the room. Samson shook Tom's hand and asked him to come into his office.

"Have a seat. Thank you for coming," Samson said, waving toward one of the two sofas in the room. Tom sat down and Samson took a seat on the sofa opposite.

"Thank you, Mr. President. Your call came at just the right time. What can I do for you?"

Tom's eyes swept the room. It wasn't the Oval Office, but it was definitely the office of the U.S. president: flags stood behind the desk and the presidential seal was embossed on the carpet between the two sofas.

"Yes. I hear you were responsible for some confusion in the hotel."

Tom told the president everything that had happened since the anonymous phone call in Russia.

" . . . and now I'm here. Just another typical Tuesday morning."

"I see. So Noah Pollock is in London," Samson said thoughtfully. "But I don't think AF is planning to attack the conference. The NSA and the CIA haven't picked up anything in that direction. AF is careful, but we would have heard something. I suspect it's about this." Samson handed Tom the file that he'd received from his chief of staff. "What the NSA overheard here is no less unsettling, I'm afraid."

Tom opened the file, and the first thing he saw was the photograph of Sienna Wilson.

"I know her. She was at the conference. She was trying to warn everyone about some kind of biohazard. She got herself arrested, but Maierhofer let her go. I think he was more interested in me."

"That biological danger is what this is all about. We believe Dr. Wilson extracted a substance from a plant she brought back from Central America, a substance that can easily be weaponized."

"You're probably right that Noah and AF are after that. How can I help?"

"I'd like you—unofficially, of course—to obtain this substance and all of the documentation that goes with it for us, before it falls into AF's hands, and to destroy all evidence on site. I can't officially approve any black ops on British soil, you know." He paused for a moment. "I couldn't even have gone to your uncle with this request. But you are not a U.S. citizen. If anything should go wrong, God forbid, our already rocky relations with the U.K. won't suffer any further damage."

"Plausible deniability," Tom said.

Samson nodded. "You've got it. I assume, of course, that the job will go smoothly. A contact will take over afterward, and your part's done. And if you can sort out our little problem with Noah Pollock while you're at it, all the better."

"Of course, Mr. President."

"The lab complex is about 270 miles southwest of London. It's part of something called the Genesis Program. The details are in the file. We've already found a car and equipment for you through a middleman, so you can get started right away."

"Thank you, Mr. President. I won't let you down." Tom stood up, shook hands with Samson and turned to leave.

"Rupert will bring you to your car."

The door opened and the Secret Service man who had escorted Tom this far entered the office.

“Mr. President,” he said in greeting, then turned to Tom. “If you would follow me, please.”

“And Tom . . .” Samson said.

Tom stopped and looked back.

“Good luck.”

19

PLAZA IN FRONT OF THE ALBERTINA MUSEUM, VIENNA, AUSTRIA

There had been a time when Hellen would have given her eye teeth for a job at the Albertina.

The museum was named for Albert Casimir of Saxony, Duke of Teschen and son-in-law of Empress Maria Theresia. Founded in 1776, it was considered one of the world's great art collections. For more than fifty years, Albert had exploited a network of art dealers and auction houses across Europe, amassing fourteen thousand drawings and two hundred thousand old master prints. Many of the pieces—including Michelangelo's male nudes, Dürer's "Young Hare" and Rubens's portraits of children—were among the most famous works in the history of art. The Albertina collection was so massive that the custodians, like those at the Vatican, had catalogued only a fraction of what they had. No one really knew what treasures lay slumbering in the depths of the various ultra-modern high-bay warehouses and deep storage facilities.

"Do you feel it?" Cloutard asked as they rode up the escalator, passed the Albrecht fountain, and entered the museum. "We have been so intimately involved with long-lost artifacts and treasures of late that a museum like this has lost most of its appeal."

Hellen was still a little put out with François, but she smiled and nodded. It did not feel like very long ago at all that she had curated her first exhibition at the Museum of Fine Arts, just a few hundred yards from the Albertina. That was also where she first met Tom. Everything had started with the Habsburgs' Stone of Destiny, the Florentine diamond. Since then, she had felt as if she were riding on a rollercoaster through history. And now here she was, doing it again.

"I know what you mean. Dürer's 'Young Hare' has got nothing on El Dorado," she said with a laugh as they approached the ticket counter. To the woman at the desk, she said, "My name is Hellen de Mey and this is François Cloutard. We're here on behalf of Blue Shield and UNESCO and we'd like to speak with Director Richter, please."

"Richter is the director here now?" Cloutard asked. "Wasn't he also your boss at the Museum of Fine Arts?"

"He certainly was. And the Florentine affair gave his career a big boost. Now he's running both places," Hellen replied.

The woman at the counter, meanwhile, had picked up the phone to announce Hellen's arrival.

"Have you thought about how we will get access to the documents? Officially we do not even know they exist," said Cloutard.

"Simple. Before he left for London, Tom called the chancellor and the chancellor assured him that he would take care of it. The documents are probably already prepared and waiting for us."

Cloutard had no time to respond, because Director Richter's assistant appeared just then in the foyer to escort them to his office. When they arrived, she opened the door and ushered them inside. When Director Richter saw Hellen and her companion, however, his face was a stony mask, and Hellen knew immediately that he was not happy to see them at all.

"Good morning, Ms. de Mey. To what do I owe the honor?" Richter asked, his tone as cold as the look in his eyes. Hellen could see which way the wind was blowing. Cloutard, too, knew that something was going on.

"The chancellor must have told you we were coming? It's about the newly discovered documents concerning the Spanish line of the Habsburgs. On behalf of Blue Shield, we would like very much to examine them."

Director Richter removed his glasses and placed them carefully on his desk. He stood up and went to the window, which offered an impressive view of the Vienna State Opera. "Yes," he said. "The chancellor informed me you would be coming," he said, his back to them as he gazed out the window.

Hellen exhaled. False alarm.

"And I told the chancellor that we are not at UNESCO's beck and call here. I don't know what makes you think we have found any new documents at all."

Hellen swallowed. Director Richter was still not particularly well disposed toward her. He had been promoted following the Florentine diamond affair, but most of the credit had gone to Hellen and the Museum of Fine Art. Hellen had given dozens of interviews and received even more job offers from all over the world, which had infuriated Director Richter at the time. Clearly, he still hadn't gotten over it.

"Director . . ." Hellen began, but her voice faltered. She had no idea what to say. The director's temper did not improve.

"The audacity you display is the very height of impertinence," Richter continued. "Presumably, these documents have been under hidden away here for centuries. We are in the process of analyzing them ourselves, under the tightest security. Most importantly, the documents must be handled with extreme care. This is our find. *Our* find. And—"

"*Excusez-moi*, Monsieur," Cloutard interrupted him. "I have the feeling that this conversation might take a while. If you don't mind, I have to pay a quick visit to the restroom." He stood up without waiting at all for the director's reaction and left the office. Hellen, bewildered, could only sit and watch him leave. But she did not have time to wonder about it for long; Director Richter barely paused in his tirade.

"And you, Miss UNESCO, don't even begin to think that you can get your boyfriend to call the chancellor and then come waltzing in here with your aging art thief. Batting your eyelashes won't make me or the Albertina researchers bow or roll out the red carpet for you."

"I would certainly have expected at least a little more respect among colleagues," Hellen shot back.

"Respect? *Colleagues*? You've practically just stumbled out of university, and now you consider us colleagues? Respect is earned, my dear. Over many, many years."

The director's phone rang and he picked it up. Hellen knew that he normally instructed his assistant not to pass through any calls when he was in important meetings, which meant this was no more than a show of strength. He wanted Hellen to squirm. The call lasted almost ten minutes, and the director didn't seem to mind making Hellen wait.

Hellen had rarely been as angry as she was by the time he finally hung up. Her standing as a scientist had been denigrated. She'd done more pioneering historical work in the last year than this pencil pusher had in his entire life.

"As an official delegate of Blue Shield, you cannot treat me like this," she began. But that was as far as she got.

"Can't I? Can't I? You'll see what I can't do!" Richter's face was beet red as he stabbed a button on his intercom. "Security, please come to my office!"

"How dare you!" Hellen stammered in disbelief.

"Having you thrown out is my pleasure. UNESCO and Blue Shield have never lifted a finger to help us, and if you think I'm going to roll over the minute we find something you think is interesting, then you'd better think again. Over my dead body! You can apply for access like anybody else. And when the bureaucrats are through with your application, and you've dotted all the i's and crossed all the t's, you'll have your access. In six to nine months. Now, if you'll excuse me, I have more important things to attend to."

The door opened and two security officers stepped into the office.

"Escort Ms. de Mey off the premises."

Hellen jumped to her feet and was stalking furiously out of the office when she received a WhatsApp message from Cloutard.

"I am sitting in the Palmenhaus. The *melange* here is fabulous," she read. Hellen hurried down the escalator, turned left and walked about two hundred yards down the Hanuschgasse and entered the Burggarten park. She quickly spotted Cloutard sitting in the pavilion fronting the Palmenhaus. The left wing of the Art Nouveau complex contained the Butterfly House, while the right wing was still used as a greenhouse; between them was a café and brasserie, popular with tourists and Viennese alike.

"I need something stronger than a *melange*," Hellen sighed as she dropped into a chair beside Cloutard.

"Champagne, perhaps?"

"That's nice of you, François, but I don't really feel like celebrating just now."

The Frenchman held out his iPad to her. "You might soon change your mind about that."

20

U.S. EMBASSY, LONDON

His cell phone buzzed. He put the file on the desk, reached for the phone and took the call.

"Yes?" he said.

"It's Rupert, sir. Tom Wagner is on his way. He's taken the assignment. He's due in Ambrose Street tomorrow morning, London time."

"Thank you, Rupert. Keep me up to speed," said Chief of Staff Armstrong, and put the phone aside again.

Rupert was a loyal man, personally recruited by Armstrong at the start of President Samson's term. As chief of staff to the most powerful man in the world, it was essential that Armstrong know what the president was up to when he wasn't around. Armstrong could only ensure the smooth operation of the West Wing if he knew the president's every step. And no one was better positioned to tell provide him with that information than the president's personal Secret Service agent. It was

Rupert, too, who had told him about Samson's liaison with Yasmine Matthews, the NutriAm CEO.

So he really did it, Armstrong thought. Samson had entrusted this risky job to an outsider. He picked up the file again and opened it. The CIA file on Tom Wagner was impressive. Nephew of a four-star admiral. Antiterror specialist, recently recruited by UNESCO for Blue Shield. Saved the Pope's life and defused an atom bomb in a highly unconventional manner. And together with his team, he had discovered the Library of Alexandria. But why the hell wouldn't Samson not send his own CIA people to secure a biological weapon? Why give the job to an outsider? To avoid problems with the British? That seemed a specious argument at best. *We've done a lot of other things behind the backs of the British. Something else must be going on*, Armstrong thought.

He stood up and went to the window. He needed help with this. Since Samson had started his affair with Yasmine Matthews, he'd been resistant to all advice. Armstrong had to do something—it was completely against his convictions, but right now he saw no other option. His mind made up, he picked up the phone and dialed a number.

21

GENESIS PROGRAM, CORNWALL, ENGLAND

Tom climbed out of the car and stretched. Several hours at the wheel of the uncomfortable Vauxhall the U.S. Embassy had given him had left their mark. He'd parked the car some distance away from the official parking areas, on a secluded forestry road. Before he could risk breaking into the research lab, he had to familiarize himself with the area. The Genesis Program grounds lay under a blanket of fog in the crater-like remnant of an old, open-pit china clay mine. Tom walked around the car, unlocked the trunk and opened the small flight case they'd put at his disposal. He lifted out the laser-sighted Sig-Sauer P226, chambered a round, slid it under his belt, and flipped his shirt over it. The spare magazine and utility knife went into his back pockets.

He grabbed the dossier and closed the trunk. Moving around to the front of the car, he called up Google Earth on his phone. After getting an overview of the surrounding area, he spread the contents of the folder on the hood and studied them in detail. It was a little terrifying just how much information the NSA could put together about someone or something at short notice, Tom thought, looking at the photo of Sienna Wilson. She was the key, and she could definitely be useful to him. Dr. Wilson had already shown that she did not want the dangerous substance to fall into the wrong hands. He closed the file, returned it to the car, and headed for the Genesis Program entrance.

A short way down the street, a winding, covered path led from the parking area to the visitor center. It was just after five o'clock, and the gates would close in an hour. A horde of children, laughing and jostling, squeezed out through the exit as Tom stepped into the foyer. He bought a ticket and headed directly for the enormous domes built inside the old clay pit. Connected by a flat building, the two biodomes hugged the former mine face. With their honeycomb-like construction, the domes were essentially oversized greenhouses, unique in size and shape. The rear dome housed the largest indoor rainforest in the world, while the smaller, in front, was dedicated to the flora of the Mediterranean. The research complex was in the forest above the larger dome.

Tom entered the entry building, lush with greenery, that connected the two domes. He turned left, heading for the rainforest, and when the automatic door slid open, it felt like walking into warm soup: the temperature was almost ninety degrees, with ninety-nine percent humidity. It literally took his breath away for a moment and made him forget that he was on a mission. A fascinating world unfolded in front of him, and he could easily imagine a dome on Mars looking something like this. A high waterfall, small streams, rope bridges, wooden huts, and simulated weather. High overhead, near the top of the 180-foot dome, one could look out over the five-acre rainforest from an observation deck, and above that was a smaller service platform.

Tom followed a winding path through dense tropical gardens, past other visitors slowly making their way toward the exits. He was heading for the northernmost section of the dome, directly beneath the research center. He did not know what he was expecting to find there, but if there was a direct connection between the two structures, that's where it would be.

From the corner of his eye, he noticed someone behaving in an exceptionally suspicious manner. He turned around casually and saw a woman in sunglasses, with her eyes lowered and a baseball cap pulled low over her face. Sienna Wilson.

Why the masquerade? Tom wondered. She works here. It said so in the dossier, and she'd mentioned it herself the first time they met. She practically jumped when a passing employee almost bumped into her, and she quickly turned away and pulled the cap even lower. With all her efforts to appear unremarkable, she was achieving the exact opposite. She was up to something.

Tom followed the attractive scientist for a while to find out what was going on, but quickly decided it was taking too long. Looking ahead, he saw that he could speed things up substantially. Moving faster, he caught up with Sienna, grabbed her by the arm, and pushed her into one of the cool-rooms beside the path: the small, air-conditioned wooden huts offered visitors respite from the tropical climate.

"Hey! Let me go! Who do—" Sienna stopped short when she recognized Tom.

"Out!" Tom ordered the two other visitors already in the hut; indignant, they left.

"You're that crazy guy from London who set off the fire alarm. What are you doing here?"

"My guess is, the same as you."

Sienna looked at Tom in astonishment. "I work here. What's your excuse?"

"If you work here, why the masquerade?" Tom lifted the baseball cap off her head and held it in front of her. Sienna snatched it back and crammed it into her back pocket.

"What do you care? You didn't answer my question. What are you doing here?" She pulled off her sunglasses.

"I'm here to prevent your 'biological danger'"—Tom made air quotes with his fingers—"the one you want to warn the world about, from falling into the wrong hands."

"What? Why?" Sienna said, struggling for words. "What do you know about the 'danger'?" she asked, with air quotes of her own.

"Two years ago, you found a very special plant in Central America. In your research, you discovered that it could quite easily be transformed into a biological agent. Then you overheard a telephone call and found out that your boss was trying to sell your research to mysterious buyer." He let his words sink in a moment. "How am I doing so far?"

Sienna was speechless. "Who . . . who are you and what do you want with my plant?" she finally stammered.

"You know my name: Tom Wagner. Officially, I work for Blue Shield, a department of UNESCO, but I also freelance on the side. Sometimes for the pope, today for the U.S. president. He would also love to get his hands on your discovery." Tom had no time to fool around and he'd decided to go with the truth from the start. But even as he spoke, he realized how absolutely crazy he sounded, and Sienna confirmed his fears.

"Oh, of course. And on weekends you have tea with the Dalai Lama." Sienna snorted derisively and tried to push past him. He held her back.

"No, but I *was* doing shots with the Russian president yesterday." He straightened up in front of Sienna and tried to win her over with his most charming puppy-dog face. "Look, we can help each other here. I'm one of the good guys."

"I don't need help from a James Bond wannabe. Now let me go or I'll scream."

Tom moved aside and Sienna stormed out of the little hut. Tom followed a few seconds later, but she had vanished.

22

KRANICHBERG CASTLE, FOOTHILLS OF THE AUSTRIAN ALPS, ABOUT 50 MILES SOUTH OF VIENNA

"I still can't believe anyone swallowed your story. Why would anyone believe you're a serious historian from the Louvre?"

Hellen thought it was the funniest thing she'd heard in a long time, and she laughed while Cloutard steered the Smart car up the winding mountain road. "Well, that got me inside. Once I was in, our mole on the inside helped me find what I needed."

"What mole?" Hellen held on tightly to the door handle of the Smart—Cloutard was taking the curves perilously fast.

"At our first briefing, your mother told us that Blue Shield had a contact inside the Albertina. Fortunately, it happens to be the same individual who has assisted me in getting into various Austrian museums in recent years. All I can say is: Cellini salt cellar . . ."

Cloutard smiled mischievously.

"*You* stole the Cellini salt cellar from the Museum of Fine Arts?" She punched him in his side. "But we got it back again. You're lucky no one caught you."

"First: no one has *ever* caught me. And second, just between us: the salt cellar you got back is a forgery. But it does not matter. To make a long story short, my contact, who understandably would prefer to remain anonymous, allowed me to photograph the documents."

Hellen was about to say something when Cloutard braked hard. A big truck came rumbling down the narrow mountain road in the opposite direction, and Cloutard steered the Smart close to the shoulder. Although they were still a long way from the High Alps, Hellen's fear of heights made itself felt. To distract herself, she focused on Cloutard's iPad, going through the photographed documents once again.

"I hope we're going to the right place," she said. "Kranichberg Castle was one of the Habsburgs' oldest possessions, and my gut feeling tells me we're about to get lucky. It says here that they kept their emergency cache of treasure deep in its cellars. And one of the rediscovered inventories lists a large number of artifacts that originated in Central America."

"The name Cortés is also on that list. But there is one thing that bothers me," Cloutard said, looking up the mountain, where the top of the watchtower already loomed over the treetops. "Why has no one ever found the old Habsburg vault?"

"Because until now, there were no documents pointing to it. No one has ever looked for *anything* here. I mean,

Cortés, El Dorado and an old, empty castle south of Vienna? Who'd ever make the connection?"

Cloutard swung around the last curve and they drove through a narrow arch onto the castle grounds. They climbed out and looked around. This high in the hills, it was deathly quiet. Cloutard pointed to the building on the left of the castle.

"That looks like a hotel," he said.

"It was a fancy spa hotel a long time ago, apparently. But things did not work out financially and these days it's empty."

The passed through a second arch and could now see the rear of the crumbling hotel. An overgrown terrace, smashed windows, ramshackle balconies and graffiti-covered walls—it was a sorry sight.

"I did some research while you were driving. The castle and all the land around it was bought up cheaply a few years ago. There were big plans for it, but so far nothing's been done."

"Which means we will have to find our own way inside," said Cloutard, rubbing his hands together.

"How convenient that I've brought along a professional burglar," said Hellen, only half joking. She would not soon forget that Cloutard had been sharing a bed with her mother just a few hours earlier. They ignored the "private property" and "trespassing prohibited" signs, and climbed over the fence, Cloutard's still-healing bullet wound slowing him down a little. He examined the castle's weathered entrance door and whistled softly through his teeth.

"I think we should go in through the old hotel. The door will be easier to open and there is bound to be a connecting passage. This entrance does not look like anyone has opened it for years."

They went back to the hotel and Cloutard checked the entrance for any security safeguards. He grinned.

"A hardware-store alarm system," he said. He reached into his backpack and pulled out a set of lockpicks. Seconds later, the door swung open and the alarm beeped, a sign that the countdown had started. "We now have fifteen seconds to deactivate it."

23

HOPE AND ANCHOR BAR, EL PASO, TEXAS

"Goddamnit, Jonathan, you can't do that!" The woman was getting loud, and the barkeeper was starting to get worried. "Are you out of your fucking mind? You cheated on *me*, motherfucker! How could the court give you custody of Dylan?"

The barkeeper looked directly at the woman and raised his hand, signaling to her to keep it down. The woman ignored him.

"Dylan's all I've got. You can't take him away from me . . . what do you mean, I can't take care of him? What? You don't even have to pay alimony? What the actual fuck?"

The barkeeper was starting to lose his patience. The bar was busy and the karaoke session had just started, but more and more faces were turning to the woman shouting into her phone at the bar. He was about to wave the bouncer over when the woman burst into tears and slammed the phone onto the bar. The display shattered and part of the phone broke off and flew at the barkeeper, who dodged it like a boxer dodging a straight jab. The woman buried her face in her hands and sobbed bitterly.

"Give the lady a double scotch. On me," said the man at the end of the bar, who'd been following the woman's distraught conversation the entire time. The barkeeper poured the whiskey and set the glass in front of the woman, her face still buried in her hands. Suddenly, she felt a touch on her shoulder. She raised her head and saw an unbelievably good-looking man holding a glass of whiskey.

"Good scotch heals all wounds," he said, and his mischievous smile made her face flush red. She threw back the drink, then took a few moments to really look at the man. She could see right away that he didn't belong here. He wore jeans, like all the other guys in the bar, but his fit perfectly and looked new, not like the scuffed, grimy jeans you normally saw in El Paso. Also missing was the flannel shirt and Stetson that usually completed the outfit. The man was clean-shaven, he looked after his hands, and to top it off he actually smelled good.

"What's your name?" he asked.

"Shelley," she said, and she knew the man wasn't from El Paso. There probably wasn't a man on either side of the border as attractive as he was, with his charisma and that gorgeous accent.

"I know a good divorce lawyer in the city. Dylan will be back home with his mother soon enough, where he belongs." Shelley liked what she was hearing, but she was also surprised. "I couldn't help overhearing you just now," the man explained, and he ordered two more whiskeys.

Shelley nodded and her eyes again filled with tears.

"A boy shouldn't have to grow up without his mother," the man said, and Shelley saw a sad look in his eyes, too. "My own mother passed when I was a child," he whispered, then turned his face away for a moment. Shelley laid her hand on his arm and the man smiled at her.

Christ, he sure is pretty when he smiles! she thought.

"Can you sing?"

The unexpected question took Shelley by surprise, and without thinking she said, "Of course I can."

The man handed her a fresh whiskey, and they downed their drinks together. Then he led her away from the bar.

"Then let's see if we make a good duet."

Only then did Shelley realize she was in a karaoke bar. Two high-school girls were just finishing Whitney Houston's "Greatest Love of All," and judging from the wild cheering from the other patrons, they were ready to go straight on to "America's Got Talent."

"Oh my God! I've never sung in front of other people," Shelley managed to stammer, but she was too late. The man grasped her around the waist and lifted her onto the stage. He went over to the DJ and came back with the microphone. With two whiskeys inside her, Shelley could feel her inhibitions dissolving. But the alcohol was only partly to blame. The rest of the credit went to the man who'd managed to make her forget her problems with Jonathan in the blink of an eye. Seconds later, she heard the opening notes of the Righteous Brothers' "You've Lost that Lovin' Feeling."

The man crooned: "You never close your eyes anymore, when I kiss your lips . . ."

And a moment later, Shelley joined in, and they sang their souls out together. With only one microphone to share, they stood close together. Shelley didn't know if it was the whiskey or the man's aftershave, but she simply tuned out everything around her and had more fun than she'd had in years.

The audience whooped and whistled, and Shelley was not surprised at all when the man kissed her as the last note faded.

Then everything happened as if they were in a film. They drank, laughed, kissed, and before Shelley knew it, they were lying in bed in El Paso's most luxurious hotel, the Camino Real. Shelley had never had a one-night stand in her life. And she'd never been with a foreigner. She had no idea the British could be so passionate in bed.

24

KRANICHBERG CASTLE, SOUTH OF VIENNA

Cloutard took out his phone and calmly opened an app. He scrolled through it until he found what he was looking for.

"*C'est bon*," he said, as he tapped a numerical code into the alarm system, which instantly shut down.

"Don't tell me there's an app for that," Hellen said, astounded.

"Cheap alarm systems always have a standard code, like an electronic skeleton key. And yes, someone made an app that lists every manufacturer's code."

Hellen shook her head. "You're a dangerous man, François."

"Your mother said the same thing," Cloutard remarked without thinking, regretting it immediately when he saw the look on Hellen's face.

The interior of the building was a mess. Like a hotel in a ghost town, the lobby looked as if it had been abandoned from one day to the next. Behind the reception desk the keys all hung in neat rows beneath their respective room numbers, old newspapers lay on tables, and the bar on the way to the overgrown terrace was still stocked with glasses and bottles. But all of it was covered with a thick layer of dust. "I've seen photos of 'lost places' like this on the internet," Hellen whispered, "but I didn't know it would be so creepy." Huge cobwebs stretched across everything, and the moldering wood, musty air, buckled floorboards, and an unnerving silence all added to the atmosphere.

"Why are you whispering?" Cloutard asked. "We can talk perfectly normally here. We are not disturbing anyone."

But a loud crash suddenly sounded from a floor above. The stairs were still intact and there were footprints on the steps.

"This would be the moment when Tom would head upstairs with his gun drawn," Hellen said, her voice trembling.

Cloutard rummaged in his backpack and came up with an old Walther PPK pistol. "As much as I detest weapons, I thought we might be able to use this, considering our John Wayne is not here," he said with a smile, raising his eyebrows twice. Another noise from upstairs made both of them jump, and now they could hear voices.

"Hello?" Hellen called. "Is anyone there?"

Cloutard rolled his eyes. "Hellen, you are acting like the blonde victim in a horror movie. If someone is up there, then they are here just as illegally as we are and they are not simply going to announce their presence."

"Hey, cool, more guests for our party!" they heard a voice say from the floor above. Then they heard steps and two young women were suddenly standing in front of them.

"You don't look like cops," said one of them. She was wearing a tank top and jeans, had shoulder-length black hair, and wore practically no makeup. Both arms were covered in delicately interwoven tattoos. "Hey! Maybe we can use them in our photo shoot?"

The other girl was holding a camera with an impressive lens. "Maybe just the guy. Yeah, with that ''stache, hat and walking stick . . . a fossil like him fits perfectly in here."

"*Excusez-moi?*" Cloutard said, a little aggrieved, looking at the woman with the camera.

Hellen, more on the ball, said, "You're urban explorers, aren't you? You're on a shoot for one of those 'lost places' websites."

The girl with the tattoos smiled at Hellen. "It's actually for Insta, but you're basically right. So are you, like, fetish types who like to get it on in creepy old buildings?" She looked from Hellen to Cloutard. "Isn't he a bit old for you, lady?"

Hellen was glad Tom wasn't with them. He would have loved this. She could see him talking trash with these girls, in a race to the bottom of the barrel.

"We're scientists."

"Oh, right," said the photographer. "And I'm Annie Leibowitz."

"I dunno, Mel. I could believe it. I mean, they look kinda stuffy."

"Look, we don't want to interrupt your shoot," Hellen said, not wanting to lose any more time. "We're looking for the connecting passage to the castle."

"I mean, we're not tour guides . . . but we can help you out with that," said Betty. Mel was still eyeing Cloutard. She seemed to really think he'd look good in their pictures. "Go up to the second floor, then turn right and go down the corridor 'til you—"

She stopped when they heard a noise from the courtyard out front. Judging by the crunch of gravel, several cars were pulling up outside. Cloutard suddenly realized what had happened.

"How did you get in here?" he asked.

"We climbed the mountain from the other side, then came over a busted balcony into a hotel room," Mel said.

"What about the alarm?" asked Cloutard.

"Alarm?" Betty asked, shocked.

Hellen understood. The girls had tripped a silent alarm. She could already hear steps approaching.

"Shit. The cops've never caught us this fast before," Mel said, packing her camera away.

Hellen and Cloutard ran upstairs to the second floor. The higher they went, the more rickety the stairs seemed to get. Before Hellen could warn Cloutard, he'd already broken through. One leg had disappeared to the knee and he was stuck fast in the staircase.

25

GENESIS PROGRAM, CORNWALL, ENGLAND

Where had Sienna vanished to? She could not have gone very far. Was there a service tunnel nearby connecting the dome with the research center, as Tom suspected? He went back down the path a short way, searching the slope for an entrance. Nothing. He tried the other direction and found what he was looking after just a few yards. On a curve behind a large information panel explaining the cooling effect of rainforests on global climate, an unobtrusive, narrow path branched off. A sign dangling on a rope across the path read "Authorized Personnel Only." Tom climbed over the barrier, but stopped halfway when he heard a voice.

"Hey! What are you doing? Can't you read?" A man dressed like a hippie hurried over to Tom. "We're closing. You need to head to an exit, right away."

Tom, thinking fast, said, "It's my son, Eric. He ran back there. I was just going to get him. He's been monkeying around the whole day." Tom turned down the path and called, "Eric! You better get back here right now!"

"You can't just go back there."

"Do you have kids?" Tom asked.

"No. Not yet." The man smiled a little and seemed sympathetic to Tom's plight.

"Then take my advice: don't. It's nothing but headaches." Tom pointed along the path as if to underscore his point.

"Follow me," the man said, climbing over the rope. "He can't be very far." Tom followed.

"You don't look like a security guy," Tom said.

"I'm not. I'm a biologist here in the Genesis Program. I was just checking on a couple of my seedlings."

"Where does this path actually lead?"

"It's just to an entrance to our research labs. Eric!" the scientist shouted, calling to Tom's imaginary son. "You've got a very stubborn boy there."

"I've got a confession to make," Tom said. "I don't actually have kids at all."

The man had no time to react. Tom grabbed him from behind in a chokehold, cutting off the blood supply to his brain. After a few moments the biologist slumped, unconscious. Tom dragged him into the bushes and searched him, taking his key and key card. "Sorry," he said as he laid a large leaf over the man's face. Then he hurried ahead to the entrance.

The gray steel door had a small window in it and was surrounded by climbing plants. He pushed them aside to reach the terminal hidden behind them, then let out a groan: the door was secured with two-factor security, the key card plus a retinal scan. *You need to check these things out* before *you knock out the only man who can open the door for you*, he growled at himself.

Tom dragged the biologist's limp body out of the bushes and up to the door. He heaved him up and placed his head on the chin rest of the retinal scanner. Holding him in place with one arm, he slid the key card through the card reader. Then he tried to open the man's eye.

It didn't work the first time. *Of course not*, Tom thought. *That would have been way too easy*. He tried again. Still nothing. The man's body was getting heavier by the second and Tom's arms were starting to ache. *At least Larry had help when he dragged Bernie all over the place for a whole freakin' weekend*, Tom thought. But on the third attempt, the door buzzed and opened.

Wedging the door open with his knife, he dragged the biologist's unconscious body back into the bushes and out of sight.

Tom didn't have much time left. The man's little snooze wouldn't last much longer, then he'd wake up with a hammering headache and call the cops. Tom grabbed the knife from under the door and ran down the long service passage. Pipes and cable ducts lined the ceiling. At the end of the passage was an open elevator. "Laboratories" read a label beside one of the elevator buttons. Tom pressed it and the elevator shot upward. A chill brought goosebumps as he stepped out of the elevator. *Overdoing it with the air-con, aren't you?* he thought. Thank God the research center was not particularly big. There was just a handful of laboratories; the other floors were dedicated to management and administration.

Tom soon found something he wasn't expecting: a door which appeared to have been opened with a crowbar. He stepped inside the lab, and the startled Sienna screamed and threw a handful of papers that she'd just collected from the laser printer into the air.

"You again?" she said, annoyed. "I told you, I don't need your help. Now get lost before I call security." Sienna crouched and started collecting the papers, and Tom went over and helped her.

"Sorry, but it's like I said: I've got a job to do."

"I thought you were kidding."

"Is that what I think it is?" Tom asked rhetorically, straightening up. Beside Sienna's monitor stood a small, silver transport case with a handcuff and a digital lock. The case was open, and inside it, bedded in foam, lay a cylindrical, stainless-steel container with a little window built into the side. It contained a green liquid. Pages were still emerging from the printer. "What are you going to do with it? Who are you planning to give your research results to? Or are you just trying to get them as far as possible from here? Do you even have a plan?"

"Look, my boss wants to sell this stuff on the black market. You were right, okay? How you knew about it is another question. He fired me to get rid of me, and he threatened to end my career to shut me up. Good men have already died for this substance and I'm not going to sit by idly and watch a money-hungry asshole get rich off my research."

"Let's not forget that someone could turn it into a biological weapon," Tom added.

Sienna took the last of the pages from the printer and added them to the ones she'd just picked up. She clipped them all into a folder, then put the folder in the case with the container.

"I can't let you do that. My orders are to secure the research results and destroy everything here. And that's what I'm going to do."

The copying finished, Sienna pulled the USB stick out of her computer. She tapped a few keys on the keyboard.

"You can save yourself the trouble. I've just erased everything on here and on the server, including the backups." She held up the USB stick. "This is the last copy." She tossed it into the case, which she immediately closed.

"Give me the case. It'll be in good hands, I promise."

"Then you'll run off and give my research to the Americans. No thank you."

"I don't have time for games." Tom didn't want to do it, but he was running out of options. He whipped out his pistol. "Please, Sienna, give me the case."

"What if I don't? You'll shoot me? I hardly know you, but you don't seem like the type."

Sienna snatched up the case and snapped the handcuff around her wrist.

"Where this case goes, I go." She picked up the handcuff key, made a show of placing it on her tongue, and swallowed it.

"Aaahhh, lady, are you crazy?" Tom jammed the pistol back under his belt. "You have no idea what you're getting yourself into. There are some *very* unpleasant people after your research, the kind who'll stop at nothing."

"Then you'd better do a damn good job of looking after me."

Tom grabbed Sienna by her hand and led her out of the laboratory. "How did your boss know so much about your research? He seemed to find a buyer pretty fast," Tom asked off-handedly as they stepped into the elevator.

"Shit!" Sienna jabbed at the third-floor button several times and ran out as soon as the elevator door opened.

"Wait! Where are you going?" Tom shouted after her, holding the elevator door.

"My boss still has copies of my work."

She jerked open an office door and disappeared inside. An anguished scream echoed through the floor. Tom ran.

26

KRANICHBERG CASTLE, SOUTH OF VIENNA, AUSTRIA

Hellen picked her way back down the few steps to Cloutard and helped him pull his leg free. He groaned in pain—it was the same leg he'd injured in Russia. He gritted his teeth and hobbled on.

Hellen, in front, looked back down the stairwell. "They haven't spotted us," she said. "They've gone after the girls." She pointed ahead, "Come on, François, there's the hallway that leads to the castle."

Between them, they heaved open a medieval portal and suddenly found themselves in another world. Everything here had been abandoned for years as well, but it all made more sense. Where the hotel had seemed spooky and neglected, everything inside the walls of the centuries-old castle seemed infused with history. Hellen was in her element. Cloutard closed the heavy door behind them and they both caught their breath.

"They're not following us," Cloutard said.

Hellen, a few steps ahead, had found an arrow slit

through which they could see the castle courtyard. "They've caught the girls," said Hellen. She watched as the two urban explorers were bundled into separate police vehicles. "Give me your iPad. I'm pretty sure one of the documents describes the route to the strongroom."

Cloutard handed her the tablet and together they searched the photos.

"Here," said Cloutard, tapping the screen.

Hellen nodded and looked around. "Okay. We have to get down to the ground floor. A stairway goes from there down to an old armory. There's a hidden passage from there to the strongroom."

Cloutard had already retrieved two Maglite flashlights from his backpack. "They did know how to build things solidly back then," he murmured as they made their way downstairs to the ground floor and continued on to the armory. Reaching its door, Cloutard pulled out a crowbar and pried it open.

"Judging by the smell, no one's been down here for decades," Hellen said. The narrow corridor led past several doorless and empty chambers before coming to a dead end. "According to the drawings, there's a kind of bolt in the last chamber that we have to slide across." Hellen pointed to the iPad. "That should open a passage."

They went into the last chamber and quickly found what they were looking for: mounted low on the wall in one corner was a large bolt, like the one used to secure a heavy gate. It took their combined strength to slide it from left to right, but from outside, they heard a grating squeak, and a moment later discovered that a small recess had opened in the wall. Behind it was a tunnel no more than eighteen inches across.

"Now I am glad that the food in Russia was so terrible," said Cloutard. "I would not have fit through here otherwise."

Minutes later they found themselves standing in a spacious square room, at least thirty feet across. The walls were completely lined with shelves from floor to ceiling—all empty.

Cloutard frowned and took his hip flask out of his backpack. "It looks as if the Habsburgs used up their reserves after all," he said, taking a belt of cognac.

Hellen sighed and held out her hand for the flask. "I need a little of that myself."

The agreeable warmth of the cognac revived their flagging spirits. With the flashlights, they probed every inch of the shelves, but found nothing. Cloutard rattled every shelf, trying to pull them forward, but it was impossible. Hellen inspected the base of each section, knocking on the wood, pushing and prodding, trying to lift them out. Nothing. Finally, they both got down on their knees and examined the floor beneath each of the shelves—all in vain.

"A dead end? Already?" Hellen sighed.

"The shortest trail we have followed yet," said Cloutard.

They stood in the empty room a few minutes longer, discouraged and unable to believe it. This couldn't be the end of their search.

“Mother’s going to kill me,” Hellen groaned. Cloutard looked at her but didn’t say a word. “I guess there was nothing to it all along.”

Hellen trudged back to the tunnel. Cloutard followed, shoulders sagging. Just before she left the room, she swung her flashlight around a final time, hoping to spot something she might have missed. But there was nothing.

Disappointed, they squeezed back through the tunnel to the armory. Suddenly, Hellen stopped in her tracks and raised her index finger.

27

WHITE HOUSE, WEST WING, WASHINGTON, D.C.

"Thank you for taking me into your confidence, Mr. Armstrong," said James J. Pitcock, vice president of the United States. "You've done the right thing," he reassured the president's chief of staff. Pitcock could practically feel Armstrong's discomfort through the phone; the chief of staff didn't enjoy having to discuss such an indecorous subject. He leaned back in his chair. "So Samson has a girlfriend," he repeated. Rita had told him about it just that morning, and he'd used the flight back from Texarkana to think about how he could use that bit of news. In Washington, rumors were certainly worth something, and now that Armstrong had confirmed the affair, it was pure gold.

The wheels in Pitcock's head began to turn as he played through various scenarios. Armstrong, with astonishing naiveté, had just handed him a trump card that he could use to rid himself of Samson forever.

"But the affair is not our main problem right now," Armstrong said.

"So we're back to the issue with Tom Wagner?"

"Yes. Essentially, the president has assigned a foreign agent to secure a biological weapon and deliver it to our CIA safe house on Ambrose Street. Imagine the shit-storm if that gets out."

"You're right, of course. But isn't Wagner the nephew of a highly decorated admiral, the late Scott Wagner?"

"That's true, but—"

"And wasn't Scott Wagner the go-to guy for the last two presidents' dirty laundry?" Pitcock continued.

"Also true. Still, it's a strange move. And everything comes back to this woman, Yasmine Matthews. Since she came on the scene, the president no longer listens to a word I say."

Pitcock thought for a moment. "If that's the case, then *we* have to sort this out. If not, he can kiss his presidency goodbye after one term," he said. He paused for effect, then added, "And we'll be out, too."

"I agree," Armstrong said. "We have to work together if we want to get Samson back on track. This affair is going to damage him—and by extension, it's going to damage us. And if wind of Tom Wagner's involvement hits the media, we're through." He was on his feet now, pacing back and forth through his office.

"Settle down. If we stick together, I'm sure we'll come up with a solution."

"Thank you, Mr. Vice President. I trust we can keep this between us for the time being."

"Of course, Mr. Armstrong," Pitcock said. He smiled to himself and ended the call. Then he dialed an internal number.

"Rita, would you come into my office for a minute?"

"Sir?" Rita Sorensen, Pitcock's chief of staff, said as she entered the office.

"Let's get back to that new squeeze you mentioned . . ." Pitcock began. Rita smiled and closed the door behind her.

28

KRANICHBERG CASTLE, SOUTH OF VIENNA

"When we slid the bolt across, there was a hollow in the wall behind it, wasn't there?" Hellen asked, remembering, and she ran into the last chamber without waiting for Cloutard's answer. She knelt down and shone her flashlight into the space behind the bolt.

"There's something inside!" she cried gleefully. She hesitated for a moment, then overcame her aversion and, grimacing, reached in among the cobwebs and spiders. She grabbed the object inside and pulled it out: it was a small metal casket. Sweeping cobwebs and creepy crawlies off her hand, she placed it on the stone floor and squatted in front of it. Cloutard followed her example, his eyes riveted on the casket. Hellen brushed away centuries of accumulated dust, revealing a coat of arms underneath: a shield divided into three horizontal bars of red, white and red.

"It's Austria's old *Bindenschild*," she said in awe.

"And what is that?" Cloutard asked, pointing at the lid. With a little scratching, he loosened more of the old dirt and uncovered a keyhole. Beside it was a combination lock engraved with letters.

"It's an old wordlock," Hellen said, her eyes widening. "So the Habsburgs also used them to protect their documents . . ."

"Something like Leonardo Da Vinci's 'cryptex,' you mean?"

"I see you've read *The Da Vinci Code* too!" Hellen said with a laugh. "Wordlocks like this date back to an Italian engineer named Giovanni Fontana—in 1420, in fact, more than thirty years before Da Vinci was born. This particular box, obviously, was doubly secured. You need a key *and* the right combination of letters. And this metal looks solid. If you try to open it by force, you'll probably damage whatever's inside."

Hellen lifted the small casket up and turned it around several times. She could hear some kind of light object moving inside.

"We need the key," she said. "Without that, we can't even move the letters on the cylinders."

Cloutard grinned. "I think I might be able to help with that. I wouldn't be François Cloutard," he said, digging into his backpack, "if I didn't pilfer a little something from every museum I visit." Triumphantly, he produced an ancient lever-lock key that looked to be made of the same metal as the casket. Hellen grinned from ear to ear.

"It was just lying around with the documents in the Albertina. I thought it could not hurt to bring it along," Cloutard said cheerfully.

Hellen snatched the key from his fingers, inserted it into the keyhole and turned it counter-clockwise. There was a click, and the letter cylinders moved freely.

"And now? What is the combination?" Cloutard said.

Hellen frowned intently at the casket. "Strange," she said. "Normally, wordlocks and cryptexes have six cylinders. This one only has five."

Hellen's mind was working feverishly. Suddenly, her face brightened, and Cloutard watched as she turned the cylinders to read "AEIOU." The lock sprang open.

"*Austriae Est Imperare Orbi Universo*," said Hellen.

"*Austria Erit In Orbe Ultima*," said Cloutard.

"And dozens of other interpretations of the Habsburgs' motto, all saying roughly the same thing: the world belongs to Austria."

Cautiously, Hellen opened the lid, and she and Cloutard almost cracked their heads together as they leaned over the casket. Inside was a sealed envelope. Hellen opened it carefully, removed a sheet of paper from inside, and quickly scanned the first lines.

"François, do you know what this is?" Hellen said. Cloutard could see the excitement in her glowing eyes. "It's the fifth letter!"

"But of course, the fifth letter! So . . ." he counted on his fingers. "E?"

"Hernan Cortés, the conquistador, sent four letters to Charles V, the Habsburg emperor. In the letters, he talked about his experiences in Central America. For hundreds of years, rumors have persisted that a fifth letter must exist, one in which he talks about El Dorado. I think we've just found that letter."

"Then I suggest that we get out of here before someone also decides to arrest us for 'urban exploring' or whatever it is called," said Cloutard.

Hellen nodded. She grabbed the letter and the casket, and they ran back to their car the same way they had come. They checked that no one was waiting for them there, and minutes later they were back in the Smart and Cloutard was racing back down the mountain road. Hellen, in the meantime, read the letter more closely.

"My Spanish is a little rusty, but the letter seems to have been written after Cortés's last journey, a sea battle where he fought beside Charles V and Andrea Doria off the coast of Algeria. The Knights of Malta and the Knights Templar were also involved."

Cloutard looked up. "The Knights of Malta?" he asked. "The ones with the sword?"

"Yes. But that's not the exciting part. He writes that he couldn't even begin to carry back all the treasure he found in El Dorado. What he brought to the Spanish court was just a fraction of the gold he left behind."

"*Magnifique*," said Cloutard breathlessly.

"Cortés writes that there is not only immense wealth in El Dorado but also an object of immense power. He tells the emperor that whatever might befall the Habsburgs, with what they find in El Dorado they can rule the world forever."

"*Austria Est Imperatrix Omnis Universi*," Cloutard murmured.

"Oh my God!" Hellen suddenly shrieked, giving Cloutard such a shock that he almost drove off the road. "Cortés says he drew a map for the emperor showing the exact location of El Dorado!"

"With a red 'X' to mark the spot? Like with One-Eyed Willy's treasure in 'The Goonies'?"

"So now that Tom's not here, you start coming at me with movie references? I have no idea if the map has an 'X' marking the spot." She looked across jubilantly at Cloutard. "But I do know where to find the map."

"The suspense is killing me. Where?"

"In Alcazar."

"The Spanish royal palace in Seville?"

"Exactly. According to this letter, Cortés had the plan hidden in the head of the emperor's bed."

Cloutard stomped on the brakes.

"Then it might as well be in the White House or Buckingham Palace or the Kremlin in Moscow."

"You're right. Alcazar is the summer residence of the Spanish royal family. We can't just waltz in."

Cloutard leaned back in his seat with a self-satisfied smile and began to whistle "La Marseillaise."

"And that is why you have me, French master thief François Cloutard. Because we can just waltz in—and I know how," he said, smiling across at Hellen.

"How? Don't keep it to yourself, François!"

"First, Geneva," the Frenchman said, and he stepped on the gas again.

29

GENESIS PROGRAM, CORNWALL

Tom had seen this kind of thing before. Still, he could understand Sienna's reaction. Rigid with fear, she stood in the center of the office, her arms wrapped tightly around the small case, her fingers clawing at the cold aluminum. Her entire body trembled.

Tom stepped cautiously around the desk and surveyed the scene. Dr. Emanuel Orlov was dead. He was slumped in his leather chair, head tipped back and mouth open, with a hole in his forehead. His arms hung loosely at his sides. The contents of his skull were splattered across the wall behind him. *A damn good Jackson Pollock imitation*, Tom thought. The killer had cut out one of Orlov's eyes. His computer lay on its side on the floor, the hard drives torn out. They were definitely too late, but by how much?

Rigor mortis had not yet set in, which meant that he had not been dead very long. The killer might still be close by, Tom knew, and he had no desire to find out if that was the case. Sienna's scream had probably alerted everyone in the building—she was definitely up there with the great big-screen scream queens.

“Come on, we’ve gotta go,” Tom said. But Sienna didn’t react. She was in shock, staring at her dead boss in horror.

Tom stood in front of her and grasped her arms gently, looking intently into her eyes. “Sienna,” he said. He knew what she was going through. What she’d experienced in the jungle would have fazed the strongest man. According to her file, she’d been struggling with PTSD ever since, and the sight of her boss had just set her progress back by months.

“Sienna,” he repeated, louder, shaking her softly. No reaction. With no warning, he slapped her across the face. *Sorry*, he thought, but it worked: she snapped out of her trance. “Are you with me?” he asked. He looked into her watery eyes. Sniffling, she wiped away her tears.

She nodded. “Yes. I’m all right.”

“We need to go. The killer could still be here.” Sienna nodded several times, then pushed Tom aside to take a final look at her boss.

“He was a back-stabbing bastard, but I would never, ever, have wished this on him.”

“You’re too nice. In my world, he got off way too easily.”

Tom took her by the hand and led her to the door. Pistol drawn, he peeked carefully down the corridor.

"The coast's clear. Which way to the stairs?" In situations like this, he preferred the stairs. More options. In an elevator, you were trapped.

"Last door on the left." Sienna said, nodding in that direction.

They ran down the corridor and Tom opened the door, keeping Sienna close behind him and making sure she only moved when he told her to. His gun followed his gaze, first up, then down. The stairwell was empty. Sienna stayed near, still hugging the case like a favorite stuffed animal.

When they reached the ground floor, Tom looked out carefully into the research center lobby. He saw nobody. Everything seemed calm. *Too calm*, Tom thought. He had to double-check.

"Wait here," he said. He settled Sienna into a corner of the stairwell, then dashed out, ducking low, pistol raised, moving silently through the lobby. At reception, he leaned over the counter.

"Shit." The security guard lay in a large pool of blood beside his chair. A small TV was tuned silently to a sports channel.

He heard a *ping* and spun around. An elevator had just arrived at the ground floor. The door slid open. A man with slightly tousled hair stepped out. He was wearing a white coat and tinted glasses. *What's wrong with this picture?* Tom thought. It wasn't just the military boots and the cargo pants he could see beneath the white coat. The man's posture and body language looked familiar, but he could not say immediately where he knew them from. He had no time to think about it, because a split second later all hell broke loose. From under his coat, the man whipped out a fully automatic, silenced Glock with a high-capacity magazine and started firing. Tom sprinted back toward the stairwell, ducked low, returning fire without looking back. Bullets zinged overhead and stitched a line into the wall behind him.

Tom flung himself at the door to the stairs and, with more luck than good aim, managed to dodge the line of fire. He slammed the door behind him, whipped out his knife, and wedged it under the door, jamming it in place with a kick. Sienna was cowering in the corner where Tom had left her, her eyes squeezed shut and hands pressed over her ears. Tom grabbed her and hauled her to her feet, and together they ran as fast as they could down the stairs.

It was a long way down, the equivalent of descending the stairs of a sixteen-story building, and there was only one exit: through the rainforest dome at the bottom. Above them, the gunman kicked and pounded at the jammed door, the noise reverberating down through the stairwell. When they were a third of the way down, he got through. Sienna screamed as the killer fired down at them, but the bullets flew wide.

"Almost there," Tom said. They were taking the stairs two and three at a time, and when they reached the bottom, Tom jerked open the door and they ran into the long corridor leading directly to the biodome. But they came to an abrupt halt at the end: the exit used the same two-factor lock from this side, too.

"How did you get inside?" Tom asked. He'd been

thinking about it the whole time. "I've got a card, but the guy who loaned me his eye is lying unconscious in the bushes out there," he added.

Shaking, Sienna fumbled out her card and placed her chin on the scanner. The door buzzed and opened. The small success renewed her hope and raised her spirits a little. "Our brilliant security guys literally walked me to my car yesterday, but nobody took my key card and nobody deleted me from the system. They just canceled my access to the lab," she said.

"Bureaucracy at its finest," Tom said. Relieved, he pulled open the door and they stepped out into the biodome. Tom glanced into the bushes, but the hippie had disappeared.

"He's coming," Sienna cried. "He'll get through the door, too. He's got Dr. Orlov's eye. There's no way to lock it."

Tom turned and fired two shots at the retinal scanner and card reader. "That should slow him down."

Tom looked through the small window in the door and saw the gunman running toward them. He grinned at the man and raised his pistol, aiming straight at him. The man snarled, tore off the toupee he was wearing, and threw it aside. Now Tom knew who he was dealing with: Friedrich von Falkenhain—the Kahle, or as Tom liked to call him, Mr. Clean. Without the slightest hesitation, Tom pulled the trigger.

30

TOP FLOOR OF NUTRIAM TOWERS, ARLINGTON, VIRGINIA

"Howard, don't bore me with details. Can we skip the logistics?"

Yasmine Matthews stood up from her desk and gazed out over the Potomac River and Theodore Roosevelt Island. It was a glorious day, and it occurred to her briefly that she could go for a walk in the sun instead of wasting her time with idiots. Why had she dedicated the last ten years of her life to a job that, she was realizing more and more, meant nothing to her? She was one of the most powerful, most highly paid managers in the United States. She had achieved things most people could only dream of. And yet she felt empty inside.

"Yes, you understood me correctly. I want to know if it is possible to take every batch we produce in Belize and which we would otherwise sell in Central America, and distribute it all here in the States."

Howard launched into his reply, and Yasmine could see instantly where it was going. If she did not stop the man in the next three seconds, he'd lecture her on NutriAm's entire supply chain. She had no interest in that at all.

"Howard, stop. I want a simple yes or no."

The door opened just then and her assistant entered the office. She had hired him straight out of Harvard, and at his job interview she had thought to herself that he could easily work as a model instead of being stuck here, topping off her coffee and taking the minutes of meetings. But to each his own.

"Ms. Matthews? The White House is on line two."

Yasmine smiled. "Howard, I have to take care of something. Let's talk later. Between now and then, you have one simple task, which is to prepare a yes or no answer to my question. I'm sure you can guess which answer I want to hear."

She had no intention of waiting for Howard's reaction. She hung up and pressed the button for the incoming call, and her body language changed instantly. The lines of her face softened and she transformed from a hard-as-nails CEO to a tender, adoring woman.

"Hel-loo," she purred into the telephone. She was very happy indeed: it was unusual for George to call her at work.

"Good morning, Ms. Matthews. This is Vice President James Pitcock."

Silence. It took a moment for Yasmine to realize it was not her lover on the line. She shook her head as if to shake off the daydream that had formed in her mind and return to dismal reality.

"Mr. Vice President," she said, and she swallowed audibly. "To what do I own the honor?"

Yasmine was once again the sober CEO. The pause at the other end of the line was longer than it needed to be—Pitcock wanted her to know who was in charge. An uncomfortable suspicion rumbled inside her, only to be confirmed an instant later.

"Some information has come my way, Yasmine, that I would like very much to discuss with you."

Yasmine cleared her throat, abashed. "I'd be glad to. May I ask what it's about?"

"The matter is . . . sensitive. Too sensitive to discuss on the telephone. I have a secure line, certainly, but after the espionage scandal last year, I have to assume that the NSA are not the only ones listening in on yours."

Yasmine nodded, then realized that her caller could not see a nod at all. "As you prefer, sir. I'd be happy to come to your office sometime in the next few days," she said quickly.

"I'd prefer somewhere neutral. No one else needs to know that we have anything to discuss," said Pitcock. Yasmine did not like his tone at all. "When I was a boy, my father used to take me fishing to down to Dyke Marsh. You can park in Belle Haven. That's just a short hop from your headquarters. The Secret Service will pick you up there and drive you to my favorite fishing hole. We can discuss the matter there without being disturbed."

Pitcock paused for a moment as if to give Yasmine an

opportunity to say something. But just as she was about to answer, he interrupted her and went on: "Tomorrow would work for me. Oh-seven-hundred. I'm an early riser, you know – once a Marine, always a Marine."

The sentence sounded to Yasmine more like an order than a suggestion. Of course, the vice president could not tell her what to do, but she felt it would be prudent not to enter into a long discussion.

"Of course, sir," she simply said.

"Great! Then I'll see you tomorrow morning."

Pitcock hung up. *What the hell does he want?* she asked herself. Was it about her affair with the president, or the re-election? Would he support the plan? She couldn't read Pitcock at all. She did not know how far he was willing to go to win the next election, and what she had in mind was audacious indeed. She decided not to brood on it any further. She would find out in the morning anyway. Working her way to the top of NutriAm hadn't been a walk in the park. It had taken a lot of tact, hard work, and negotiating skill for Yasmine to get where she was. She could handle the vice president . . . but forewarned was forearmed. She pressed a button on her phone and her Harvard boy appeared in the office a second later.

"Get Hudson here, fast."

Aaron Hudson was her head of security, and had also taken care of one or two delicate matters outside the company on her behalf. Yasmine had learned to hedge her bets. It couldn't hurt to document her discussion with Pitcock.

31

IN FRONT OF THE RITZ-CARLTON HOTEL, GENEVA, SWITZERLAND

"I know you like to have your secrets, but could you finally tell me what the hell we're doing here?" Hellen was in a rotten mood. Cloutard had insisted on keeping her in the dark about why they had to fly to Geneva first, when their actual destination was the Alcázar of Seville.

"All right," Cloutard sighed. "We need to get into the Alcázar, right?"

"Right."

"And we need someone who knows the palace."

"Right."

"And someone who can get us into the king's bedroom."

"Right."

"Enough 'rights' for now, please . . ." Cloutard shook his head in amusement. "But it does not matter. There is only one person who can do all of that, one person who can help with this absurd scheme: the former king of Spain, José Rodrigo I."

Cloutard was grinning as if he'd won the lottery. Hellen just stared back with incomprehension. "The old Spanish king? The one who abdicated and fled Spain amid reports of money laundering? Wasn't he living in exile in Dubai?"

"Exactly. Except, he is not in Dubai. That is just what people are supposed to believe." Cloutard pointed up to the top of the balconied façade of the Ritz-Carlton Hotel. "In reality, he currently resides in the Grace Kelly suite on the top floor." He looked at his watch. "*Mon Dieu*, we have to hurry. We have an appointment with His Royal Highness in two minutes."

Cloutard took the utterly baffled Hellen by the arm and pulled her with him into the hotel lobby.

"The king has done a little business with me in the past and owes me a favor."

"So it's true? The king really was getting his hands dirty?"

Cloutard pinched his thumb and finger together and drew them across his lips as if closing a zipper. "My lips are sealed. The presumption of innocence is sacred."

He went to the elevator, exchanged a few words with the bellboy, and slipped him a banknote.

"Madame de Mey, the king awaits," said Cloutard, ushering Hellen into the elevator. She stepped in hesitantly. "Don't worry. A king is as human as you or me," said Cloutard in an attempt to reassure her, with only moderate success.

The elevator opened onto the luxurious hallway in front of the Grace Kelly suite. Cloutard went to the door and knocked, and it opened a moment later.

"François, *viejo ladrón*!" exclaimed a man of around eighty, his hair combed back rigorously. The former king exuded the charisma that only an aristocrat can, and he rose slowly to his feet and waited for Cloutard to come to him. Then Jose Rodrigo I glanced past Cloutard to Hellen and, paying no more attention to the Frenchman, shuffled over to her. He took her hand and kissed it.

"*Bienvenido* to my modest home. Whom do I have the undeniable pleasure of receiving?"

Hellen blushed and stammered out an introduction.

"What are you doing with this old crook, *señorita*?" the king said, glancing back at Cloutard. "He is certainly not the best company you could keep."

"I am sure you are a much better influence, Your Highness," Cloutard replied archly.

"Let's get down to business," the king said. "Come into the salon."

They went into a different room, this one decorated entirely in white, gray and gold: white walls, a highly polished white conference table, gold-framed pictures and mirrors on the walls, armchairs upholstered in mottled gray. The window offered a stunning view over Lake Geneva.

"We need to get into the Alcázar," Cloutard said. "To be more precise, we need to get into the royal bedroom."

Jose Rodrigo leaned back and nodded knowingly. "Ah. You're after the El Dorado map," he said.

Cloutard and Hellen could only stare back in surprise.

"What did you think? That the royal family knew nothing about it? We've known about the map for centuries, and we have tried many times, with the map as our guide, to find El Dorado. But we never found anything in that green hell."

Hellen spoke up. "But Your Highness, Cortés's letter is very clear. He drew a map for Carlos V showing where El Dorado lies."

"Cortés was a first-class swindler. After his return, he was not treated well by the Habsburgs and presumably did whatever he could to crawl back into the emperor's favor. But the fact is, everything Cortés brought back with him from El Dorado has long since been spent, down to the last gold coin. The map is worthless."

"And where is it now?" Cloutard asked.

"Let us make one thing perfectly clear, François: after this conversation, we are finished. Understood?"

"*Bien sûr*," François said.

"Good. I have no faith whatsoever in the treasure map, so I am happy to tell you. The map is still hidden away behind the headboard of the bed, as Carlos V ordained. It is no longer the same bed, to be sure, but it has become a ritual to pass the map from generation to generation and to hide it on the back of the headboard, though we know it is worthless."

“I would still very much like to see it,” said Hellen.

“And for that we need access to the royal bedroom in the Alcázar,” Cloutard repeated.

José Rodrigo sighed and glanced out the window.

“All right. But only because I will be rid of you forever, François. I still have many friends at court, and one of them lives in the Alcázar.”

The door to the lounge opened and a servant entered.

“Your Highness, I am terribly sorry to interrupt your conversation, but something distressing has happened.”

32

CAMINO REAL HOTEL, EL PASO, TEXAS

Shelley opened her eyes. It took her a few moment to realize where she was and what had happened the night before. A smile spread across her face. She could not remember the last time she had felt so free. Singing, dancing, laughing, drinking, the whole night long. And then there was this man, this man who managed effortlessly to flip the switch inside her—the switch that, for a few hours, turned off the stressed-out, care-ridden, frustrated single mother and brought out the fun-loving, positive, confident woman she used to be.

And the sex that followed . . . although she almost hesitated to describe what had happened the night before with a word as cheap as "sex." It didn't even come close to what she'd experienced with this man. Shelley's smile stretched into a grin and she had to admit to herself that, right now, she wouldn't mind at all being taken by him again the way he'd taken her the night before. Deep down, in fact, she hoped that he would do it not only today, but tomorrow, too. And the day after that. She was ready for him. Dreamily, she rolled over. But the other half of the bed was empty.

"Oh," she murmured to herself, disappointed. She lifted her head and looked around. The evening before, she'd had no chance to actually look at the room, so she hadn't noticed that it didn't really look like anyone was living there. In fact, there was no sign that anyone but her was still there now. She got out of bed, picked up her panties and bra, and began to put them on, but then changed her mind. *Maybe he's in the shower,* she thought. If so, she would join him. On the way to the bathroom, she dropped her underwear on the couch. She opened the door and her shoulders slumped. There was no one, not even any personal effects. She was alone.

But just then somebody knocked at the door. Shelley turned around. That would be him; he must have gone out for a minute and forgotten his key.

"Room service," she heard a second later.

He even took care of breakfast, she thought with a smile, pulling on her underwear and the dressing gown she found in the wardrobe.

She went to the door and opened it. A waiter pushed in a serving cart. Shelley took no notice of all the delicious food stacked on the cart, because the whole situation suddenly made her feel a little queasy.

"Where is Mister . . .?"

Shelley paused. Only then did she realize that she did not even know the man's name.

"The suite was booked by a Mr. Isaac Hagen," the waiter said.

"Was?"

"Yes. Mr. Hagen checked out early this morning. According to his instructions, we were to bring you breakfast in the room and give you this envelope."

The man reached into his jacket pocket and handed Shelley a brown envelope. Shelley was crushed. Men were just scum. How could she have thought that a guy who picked her up in a bar and with whom she'd screwed drunkenly half the night might be a dependable, responsible man? She sighed. The waiter excused himself and Shelley poured herself a cup of coffee. It was fantastic. She could always rely on coffee to soothe her soul. She picked up the cup and sat down on the couch. Then she opened the envelope. She took a second mouthful of coffee as she slid the photos out of the envelope. The coffee cup clattered to the floor. The liquid spread across the white carpet. Shelley struggled to breathe. One glance at the photos and her whole world came crashing down.

33

GENESIS PROGRAM, CORNWALL, ENGLAND

The wired glass deflected Tom's shot. Mr. Clean had ducked for cover below the window and was crouching out of sight against the door.

"Tom, we have to go!" Sienna plucked at his shirt and pointed up at the dome. The sun was starting to set, and flashing blue lights illuminated the curved structure in the twilight. They were surrounded by police. *And Mr. Clean's gotten away again*, Tom thought angrily.

Staying low, they crept along the service trail until they reached the main path. From their slightly raised position, they had a good view over most of the rainforest. The first cops were entering the biodome and fanning out. Tom and Sienna soon discovered who had called them.

"He was back there," the hippie said, pointing in Tom's and Sienna's direction.

"We'll take it from here, sir. Please stay back," the officer instructed the man, sending him back outside.

We're sitting ducks if we stay here, Tom thought. *Hot, sweaty ducks*. For now, he wanted to keep that from Sienna. Maybe he'd have a flash of inspiration in the next five minutes. The dome only had one main entrance. Presumably, there were also a few emergency exits, but if his local colleagues were halfway competent, they would already have those secured. They needed an exit that didn't look like an exit and would therefore be unguarded. They crept on cautiously, putting as much distance between them and the police as they could, at least for the time being. At an information board, Tom briefly studied a map of the entire area. And, in fact, an idea started to form in his adrenaline-junkie brain. He looked up at the arching dome overhead.

"That's where we have to get to," he said to Sienna, and pointed to the center of the roof. The small service platform could be reached via a series of steps leading up from the rock face.

"What do you have in mind?"

"Simple. We fly." Tom took off at a run, Sienna close behind. They had a solid head start on their pursuers now. The dome was more than two hundred yards long, with numerous interwoven paths and nooks and crannies where a person could hide. Searching all of them would keep the cops busy for a while. Only one obstacle stood between them and their destination: the long rope bridge that led to the foot of the steps. Keeping low, they crept across the wobbly construction, trying to stay as quiet as possible, but the wildlife and the rushing water inside the biodome covered the little noise they made.

Suddenly, Tom's fist shot into the air, a signal to stop. Tom turned back to Sienna, a finger placed to his lips. Directly beneath them, a member of the local constabulary appeared, assault rifle at the ready, searching the winding path. Sienna stared back at Tom, her eyes wide. She held one hand pressed over her mouth, stopping herself from making the slightest sound. When the man moved on, so did they.

They climbed the steel stairway cautiously. The view from 160 feet in the air was breathtaking. Nobody looked up, and why would they? No one in their right mind would see an escape route in the star-shaped hatch in the arched roof, allowing the service team access to the outside of the dome. Luckily, Thomas Maria Wagner was not in his right mind.

In a small cabinet on the service platform, they found ropes and climbing gear. "Ever heard of Australian rappelling?" Tom asked, grinning, as he pulled on a harness. Sienna, watching him wide-eyed, shook her head. "It's easy. You run face first down a building with the rope holding you. Tom walked his fingers down his arm to demonstrate.

"You're kidding me," said Sienna with a dubious frown. "No, no, no! Can't we just turn ourselves in? We haven't done anything. All we wanted was to stop something worse." She held up the case.

"If we turn ourselves in, we'll spend the next few days in custody trying to justify ourselves, and we'll have no control over what becomes of that lethal stuff," he said, nodding toward the case. He hooked the rope to the top of the dome. "Your turn." He helped a reluctant Sienna climb into a harness.

They climbed outside.

"It's very simple. You hold the rope in your hands in front of you like this, and you lean forward. The rope will hold you." He demonstrated a few steps for her. "Then you just take one step after another.

The elements were definitely on their side: a layer of fog still blanketed the entire area. *Three cheers for English weather*, thought Tom. "Stay on the frame. Don't step onto the plastic panels," he said.

Tom let Sienna go ahead. At first slowly, then faster, she walked forward down the honeycomb structure. Tom slackened his brake and followed close behind. Trying to manage both the rope and the case, however, Sienna lost her balance on one of the last thirty-foot-high honeycomb sections and slipped, her foot breaking through an octagon. The sudden noise alerted the police inside. Tom, close behind, helped her pull her foot free.

"Up there!" shouted one of the policemen, pointing up at Sienna, his attention drawn by the noise. "Stop! Don't move!"

Sienna screamed in panic as bullets suddenly flew around her, one actually ricocheting off the case.

"Keep going," Tom shouted, when Sienna was free again. He returned fire, not trying to hit anyone. He just had to make the cops duck for cover, and it worked. For a few moments, the firing stopped.

Seconds later, they reached the bottom. With solid

ground beneath her feet once again, Sienna hugged Tom with relief.

"If no one's shooting at you, that can be a lot of fun," Tom said, unclipping both of them from the ropes, and they ran into a small patch of woods next to the dome.

"Where to now?" Sienna asked.

"I thought you worked here. Don't you know your own park? You've got the longest zip line in England right here."

Sienna remembered. With everything else going on, her mind had gone blank.

"And I figure, seeing as I'm already here, I've just got to try it out."

Another fifty yards and they saw the wooden tower where the zip line started, rising high above the surrounding trees. "Unless I've miscalculated badly," Tom said as they ran up the stairs, "this thing should fly us right over the top of the police lines."

Tom snapped Sienna into a harness on one of the trolleys and himself into the other. The twin cables dropped hundreds of feet, crossing both biodomes and the entire park complex surrounding them. "Now or never," he said, and they kicked off from the platform and soared like Superman across the park. Tom was in his element as they shot through the fog and they reached the other end without incident. Shrugging off their harnesses, they ran to Tom's car, still parked on the nearby woods road.

"See? Piece of cake. We're out!"

Tom and Sienna jumped into the car and Tom pulled out onto the road. But they didn't get far. A single bullet hurtled through the rear window, passing through Sienna's seat and her torso before burying itself in the dashboard.

34

GRACE KELLY SUITE, RITZ-CARLTON HOTEL, GENEVA

The servant whispered into José Rodrigo I's ear and the former king paled.

"François, Señorita de Mey, I'm afraid we have to postpone our conversation to a later date. Unfortunately, I have to leave."

The king was already on his feet and leaving the salon. Cloutard and Hellen shared a look of incomprehension, shook their heads, and followed him.

In the living room, everything was in an uproar. Two young women—the king's servants, apparently—were gathering and packing whatever they could get their hands on. José Rodrigo himself had quickly gotten changed and was now barely recognizable: he had donned a long-haired wig and a tattered t-shirt. An old, crumpled hat sat on his head. He put on a pair of sunglasses and left the suite.

"Can someone tell me what is going on?" Cloutard shouted, but no one took any notice of him. The servant who had come in before was emptying the safe, stuffing documents indiscriminately into a briefcase. He looked up fearfully at Cloutard and Hellen. "Interpol," he said, and returned his attention to the safe.

"But we don't yet know who our contact is for the Alcázar!" Hellen cried.

"*Merde!* We have to go after the king," said Cloutard.

Together they ran out of the suite, where they saw the king, flanked by two security staff also dressed in thrift store clothes, getting into the elevator at the end of the hallway.

Do they really think they'll be less conspicuous dressed like that? Hellen wondered, running ahead of Cloutard. *In Geneva?* The elevator doors were already closing, but she managed to get her foot between them just in time. The doors slid open again and the king stood and glared at them.

"You forgot one little detail, Your Highness," Cloutard said as he and Hellen joined them in the elevator.

One of the security men pressed the button for the garage several times. The king obviously had no intention of leaving through the lobby. The elevator descended, all eyes watching the display.

Then Cloutard pressed the stop button. "We need our contact, Your Highness." Cloutard's voice was uncompromising. José Rodrigo looked at him angrily. He was clearly not used to being spoken to like that.

"All right. Go to Café Citroën in Seville. Between 8 and 9 a.m. is best. Ask for—" The king stopped and pointed at the elevator buttons. “Can we move on, François? As you can see, we’re in hurry.”

Cloutard released the stop button and pressed the button for the garage.

“Thank you. Ask for Eloisa Arebalo. She always takes her breakfast there,” the king continued. “She will be told to expect you. She has remained loyal to me, and she will find a way to get you into the palace.”

Hellen nodded warily—getting inside was only half the battle.

“How you get into the royal couple’s apartments is up to you,” said the king, as if reading Hellen’s thoughts.

Just then, the elevator doors opened and the two security men looked out cautiously.

“No one in sight, Your Highness. We can escape up the ramp. On the corner is an old VW microbus. We will get you to safety in that.” The king nodded. “Pedro goes first and scouts the situation. You follow, and I bring up the rear,” the man continued. The king nodded again, but his face was ashen. He seemed tense and shaky. This level of stress couldn’t be healthy at his age.

“What about us?” Hellen asked.

“You are planning to break into a royal palace. I don’t think you need our help to get away from here.”

Cloutard pushed Hellen back into the elevator. “We will go up again,” he said. “Being seen with the king now would not be advantageous.”

Hellen nodded. They watched for a moment as the

monarch and his two security men made their way through the garage. Then the doors closed and Cloutard pushed the button for the top floor. The elevator started to rise. Holding their breath, Cloutard and Hellen stared at the display, but the elevator stopped unexpectedly at the ground floor. Hellen and Cloutard shared a look.

"Easy, Hellen. We are just regular hotel guests," Cloutard said.

The elevator doors opened and they found themselves staring down the barrels of four pistols, two held by plainclothes men, two by men in Swiss police uniforms.

"Interpol. You're under arrest for aiding and abetting the escape of an internationally wanted criminal."

Seconds later, handcuffs snapped shut around their wrists. They were grabbed by their arms and pushed into the back seat of a police car. Minutes later, they saw the king also being led away in handcuffs.

"I though Tom was a disaster magnet," Hellen snapped at Cloutard. "But you're really giving him a run for his money. Great plan, François. Now we're accomplices of a money launderer."

"But at least we have the right to a phone call, do we not?" Cloutard asked.

35

BELLE HAVEN PARK, DYKE MARSH WILDLIFE PRESERVE, VIRGINIA

Yasmine Matthews turned her silver GMC Yukon off the George Washington Parkway at Belle Haven Park and pulled into the sailing school parking lot. As she climbed out, she could already see two men in black suits and sunglasses, wearing the obligatory earpieces. One of them waved to her. She locked her car, the shrill chirp of the alarm slicing through the early morning silence. Even here, just a few miles from the United States Capitol, it was as if she had stepped into another world.

Yasmine had an uneasy feeling about this meeting. An empty parking lot. No one else around. A few hundred yards away was a housing development, the Belle View Condos, but no one there was likely to take any notice of them.

"Morning, ma'am. Vice President Pitcock is expecting you. It's not very far."

"All right," Yasmine said, but in truth, nothing felt right to her at all. She did not believe that anything would happen to her, or that Pitcock could do anything to her with the Secret Service around, but she felt acutely uncomfortable. The two men escorted her onto the Dyke Marsh Trail, which soon turned along the shore of the Potomac River. The trail soon became one of the wooden boardwalks so common across the U.S., built to prevent the trail being washed away by high water.

She saw Pitcock ahead when she was still some distance away. He had stepped away from the boardwalk and was sitting on a tree trunk close to the shore that had been washed up in the last storm. He was leaning down and picking up stones and tossing them into the water, lost in thought. When he saw her coming, he straightened up and brushed the soil off his hands.

"Good morning, Yasmine. Thank you for coming. Shall we take a little stroll?" he said, stepping up onto the boardwalk again.

The two agents stayed at a respectable distance, too far away to hear what they said.

"I'll cut to the chase," Pitcock said, and he reached into the inside pocket of his sport coat. Casually, almost as a matter of course, he held the photograph out for Yasmine to see. The picture had been taken at Camp David. Yasmine turned pale. In it, she was naked, sitting astride the president. Both her face and the president's were clearly recognizable.

"Where did you get that?" she asked.

"Yasmine, please don't insult my intelligence. You and I both know that I'm not going to reveal my source.

Anyway, it's beside the point. If this falls into the Republicans' hands, Samson can kiss a second term goodbye."

Yasmine swallowed, but she was not about to buckle so easily. "But why? The president is a widower and I'm as good as divorced."

"Ma'am, George Samson isn't the president of Sodom and Gomorrah. This is the United States of America. People don't take well to their president jumping from one bed to another."

Yasmine's breath caught in her chest. She wanted to know what he meant by "one bed to another," but let it be.

"I have no intention of hindering the president's re-election. On the contrary, I'm working to guarantee it." Pitcock stopped in his tracks and looked at her intently. A small victory for Yasmine: she had piqued the vice president's curiosity.

"And how do you expect to do that?" Pitcock asked calmly.

"I've got a plan."

Pitcock laughed so loudly that it made Yasmine flinch. His ringing laughter sounded diabolical, especially in the morning silence.

"Oh, you've got a *plan*. I didn't realize you'd switched careers. So you've hung up your CEO suit and joined the spin doctors? Don't you think we have strategists in this country more qualified to plan the biggest and most important election campaign in the world?"

She couldn't care less about Pitcock's opinion, but his tone of voice was so disdainful that Yasmine was actually hurt. "This is not just some campaign plan. It is a strategy that will guarantee George's re-election—and yours, too."

"Then let's hear it."

"It's not something I can talk about right now. But I can tell you this: I have the absolute backing of the president. He's given me a free hand to put my plan into action. And he's willing to do everything in his power to win re-election."

"I am not particularly surprised to hear you have the president's support, to be honest. Especially not when you're doing a Monica Lewinsky on him at Camp David."

"I would have expected a little more discretion from you, Mr. Vice President. A little more decency. But this has nothing to do with my relationship with the President."

Pitcock had stopped walking again. He looked at Yasmine now with annoyance. "Ma'am, you have two options. Either you tell me right now what you're up to and what this plan is that has the president's support, or this picture will be on the front page of tomorrow's Washington Post."

Yasmine looked at Pitcock and realized she had no choice. "We're engineering the election in our favor," she said.

Pitcock raised his eyebrows and looked around. The two agents were still far enough away. The vice president said nothing, but he looked at Yasmine and slowly raised his eyebrows, a clear signal for her to continue. Yasmine nodded.

"The president *cannot* find out that you know about this," she said, and she began to explain the plan to him in detail.

36

THE CUSTOM HOUSE PUB, EXCEL LONDON CONFERENCE CENTER

"Here's to an almost perfect first day, Captain." A small group of Cobra officers had gathered around Captain Maierhofer, each with a pint in their hand, and they raised their glasses in a toast. "A masterpiece of coordination! Pulling off the biggest event in the history of the WHO practically without a hitch is a feat that won't soon be matched."

Captain Maierhofer knocked back a large swallow of Guinness, ignoring the sly allusion to the minor disturbance Wagner had caused that morning, and tipped his head back to release the tensions of the day. Wagner was the Americans' problem now, and this event was truly among the high points of his career. Ever since he'd taken over command of the European Atlas antiterror unit, he'd been put to the test several times. But another was still to come—never before had all the European heads of state and the U.S. president been gathered at a WHO event. But he already had the troublesome Secret Service agents under control, and now the first day was over. There would be more to deal with tomorrow, of course, but most of the work was behind him. Everyone on his team knew what they had to do, and the machine was up and running. He smiled and was raising his glass to his lips once again when his cell phone rang.

"I'm off duty, damn it," he joked. "Leave me alone." It couldn't really be anything very important. He looked at the display. It was a number he didn't know.

"Maierhofer," he said brusquely, taking the call.

"Captain, I apologize for calling you in the middle of a stressful event, but I have to talk to you. It's Theresia de Mey speaking. I'm the president of Blue Shield."

It took Maierhofer half a second to realize what this was about. Blue Shield was the organization that Wagner's little girlfriend worked for. And wasn't Wagner part of their new special ops team? Now he was curious.

"What can I do for you, Ms. de Mey?" he asked, sipping from his glass with satisfaction.

"You know Tom Wagner, don't you? I believe he used to work for you, with Cobra?"

"Oh, I know him, all right. And I'm damned glad to be rid of him. Frankly, the ten Biblical plagues are a walk in the park compared to Tom Wagner. The man caused so much trouble that it wouldn't fit into his personnel file."

"That's exactly why I'm calling. I let my daughter talk me into handing Wagner command of our Blue Shield special ops team."

"Good God, really? Probably not a wise decision, ma'am. If Stallone and Schwarzenegger had a love child, it'd be subtler than Wagner. You might as well put Chuck Norris in charge of a royal wedding." Talking about Tom Wagner always got the captain got worked up quickly. His face turned beet red, his pulse surged to a hundred and eighty, and he prowled through the pub like Reinhold Messner on his way up Everest.

"Let me guess," one of the Cobra officers whispered to another. "Maierhofer's talking about Wagner." The other man nodded and they both grinned.

"I am also getting the impression that Wagner isn't particularly reliable," Theresia said.

"'Isn't particularly reliable'? *That*, Ms. de Mey, is an understatement. Kim Jong-un is a choirboy next to Wagner. There's one incident I remember very clearly. Once, when he was on air marshal duty, Wagner put an entire aircraft and its passengers in danger. Then he drove at speed through the middle of a Vienna pedestrian zone and crashed into St. Stephen's Cathedral. He concealed evidence. He shot the Imperial Treasury at the Hofburg to smithereens. And as a grand finale, he commandeered a horse-drawn carriage! And if that's not enough for you, we found a flight attendant dead in his houseboat the same day. All in less than twenty-four hours. The man's a walking curse."

Captain Maierhofer was in a rage. Theresia let him catch his breath before she spoke again. "Captain," she said cautiously. "I have a large favor to ask of you."

"Go ahead. I hope I can help."

"I want a replacement for Wagner. I need someone I can rely on, someone who can lead the team with good judgement, without starting World War III in the process."

Maierhofer nodded. He could understand the president of Blue Shield only too well, and he was glad that he himself no longer had to deal with Wagner.

"Ms. de Mey, I think I can help. I have a quite a number of reliable, experienced, highly decorated colleagues amongst my team."

"It would be wonderful if you could put your feelers out and recommend someone you feel would be a suitable candidate."

The captain smiled to himself. Destroying Wagner would almost be better than Christmas, running Atlas, and winning the lottery all rolled into one.

"I'll be in touch soon," he said. "I have a man in mind who'd be the perfect replacement."

37

COMMUNITY HOSPITAL, ST. AUSTELL, ENGLAND

Sienna didn't scream. The shock was too great. In the first moment, she felt no pain at all, just a sensation of burning in her belly. She looked down in amazement at her blood-smeared hands. The bullet had passed through her stomach. She coughed a gout of blood onto the windshield. Another bullet zinged through the rear window, then smashed through the windshield and kept going. Tom turned around. The Kahle had appeared out of nowhere, racing after Tom's car on foot. Tom stomped on the gas and the Kahle fell back and gave up the chase.

"You've been hit. Hold on," Tom said. He was shaken, but he kept his cool. He grabbed his jacket from the back seat and handed it to Sienna. "Here. Press that onto the wound."

Sienna's adrenalin level slowly dropped and the pain set in, making her groan with pain. "Oh, God, I don't want to die," she cried.

Speed limits and road rules cast aside, Tom raced along the country road. His eyes switched from Sienna to the street ahead to the GPS navigation as he tried feverishly to find the nearest hospital.

Finally. "Turn around at the earliest opportunity," was the first thing the electronic female voice said. Tom wasted no time, swinging the wheel and sliding into a 180 degree turn in the middle of the street. He tried to push the gas pedal through the floor again. According to the navigation system, the nearest hospital was five miles away.

"You have to stay awake, Sienna. Look at me. Hold on." He grasped her hand, and she raised her head and looked at him. A tear rolled down her cheek.

With an effort, she fished a small key out of the pocket of her trousers and opened the handcuff. "Magic," she said, forcing a smile. She coughed up more blood and cried out in pain. She looked at Tom, knowing that she would not survive the day. She closed the handcuff around Tom's wrist. "Take care of this," she said. Then she lost consciousness. Her hand went limp in Tom's.

"AAAAAHHH!" Tom screamed, and he beat his right fist furiously on the steering wheel. Tom gave the Vauxhall all it had as he shot along the A390 toward St. Austell, passing one car after another, leaning on the horn the whole way.

His driving, of course, did not go unnoticed, and a police patrol car was soon on his tail. Blue light flashing and siren wailing, it raced after the Vauxhall. But Tom ignored it. Tires squealing, he slid left into Porthpean

Road and turned in to the hospital a quarter of a mile farther on.

"Sienna! Wake up! Don't do this to me. Sienna!"

He screeched to a halt at the entrance, leaped out and ran around to the passenger side. Carefully, he lifted Sienna's limp body out of the car and carried her into the hospital. The case with the biological essence dangled from his left wrist, the handcuff digging painfully into his skin, but right now that was the last thing on his mind.

"Hey! I need help! She's been shot," Tom screamed as he pushed into the emergency ward. The nurse at the front desk jumped as if stung by a bee when she saw Tom carrying the blood-covered body of the young woman.

Tom heaved Sienna onto an empty gurney. He stroked her face with his bloody hand to sweep a few hairs aside.

"Sienna, you've got to hold on," he said softly.

A doctor suddenly pushed Tom aside. "What happened?" the man asked as he checked Sienna's vitals.

"Her name is Sienna Wilson. She's been shot. The bullet passed straight through, I think her stomach," Tom replied with military precision.

"I'm hardly getting a pulse. We have to get her into surgery. Wait here," the doctor ordered, and he ran off after the gurney, which was being pushed by two nurses through the double doors toward the operating room. Tom stood without moving for a moment, staring at the doors, which swung back and forth a couple times before coming to a stop. Then a sudden commotion behind him snapped him out of his trance.

"Hands in the air and turn around," a policeman shouted. A shocked murmur rumbled through the waiting room.

———

Just a few miles away, still close to the Genesis Program, the Kahle sat listening to the local police radio band. When he heard a report about a high-speed pursuit and an injured woman in a local hospital, he stomped on the accelerator and sped away.

———

"I'm not going to say it again. Put your hands in the air!" The trembling in the officer's voice was not lost on Tom. He obeyed the order, raising his hands slowly, holding the case by the handle in his left hand.

"Drop it," the second cop shouted.

Tom obeyed that order, too. But the case didn't fall far. The handcuff caught it and it swung in the air.

"As you can see, I can't drop it."

"Down on your knees," the first cop ordered. Terrified, the few patients already in the waiting room could only sit and watch the drama playing out in front of them. The small town would be talking about this for years.

Tom slowly dropped to his knees and reached both hands out in front. With the case on his wrist, he could not easily put his hands behind his head. He had to come up with something fast. He was in a serious mess this time, and shooting his way out was not an option. The two policemen wouldn't be too great an obstacle, but there were too many civilians in the room to risk it. For now, he decided to play along and see where things led. He could always escape later.

"Who are you and what's in the case?" the first officer asked. The man was clearly extremely nervous. He'd probably never been part of anything this exciting in his career. His colleague, meanwhile, edged around to the other side of Tom.

"My name isn't important, what's in the case is none of your business, and you wouldn't believe my story anyway."

"You're the guy all that stir's about down at the Genesis Program. You killed all those people there, didn't you?"

The people in the waiting room held their breath.

"Sorry to disappoint you, but that wasn't me."

"Hands behind your back!" The second officer was now standing behind Tom.

"Full disclosure: I've got a gun tucked in the back of my belt," Tom said, making the cop pause for a second.

"Don't move." He approached Tom as he might a snake ready to strike at any moment. First, he took Tom's gun away, then the two officers put him in an armlock and dragged him outside. The waiting patients applauded with relief.

"We've got him! We've got the guy from the Genesis Program," the second officer announced gleefully on his radio when they reached the parking lot.

The first officer had time to say, "We'll get a promo—" before he was cut off by the bullet passing through his head.

The second officer tried to draw his gun, but a second bullet to the head instantly killed him, too.

Nobody heard the two shots from the silenced pistol, but Tom found himself staring down the smoking barrel of Friedrich von Falkenhain's gun.

38

OFFICE OF PRISON ADMINISTRATION, GENEVA, SWITZERLAND

A black Audi A8 sedan and an armored police van, both with Dutch license plates, rolled along the Chemin des Corbilletes and, at the junction with the Chemin des Coudriers, turned at the traffic circle into the parking lot of the F-shaped brick building. The prison was located in a surprisingly nice part of the city, surrounded by parks, well-tended gardens, modern office buildings, an embassy, and a cultural center—not the kind of places one would normally associate with a prison. The passenger door of the A8 opened. A man in a black suit and sunglasses climbed out and opened the rear door, and an elderly woman, elegant in a dark-gray business outfit, stepped out of the back. Flanked by two men in dark suits, she made her way to the prison entrance.

At the first security checkpoint, the woman and the two men escorting her showed their identification papers.

"*Bonjour*. I am Antonia Bolovatto, from Europol headquarters in the Hague," she said in flawless French. "I would like to speak to Warden Lanchet."

The man checked the woman's papers in his computer, making the necessary confirmations: Antonia Bolovatto, Deputy Director of Europol's Organized and White Collar Crime division. The officer reached for the telephone and informed the warden of her arrival, and the electronic door latch buzzed. "You're in luck. He's still in the building. Take the elevator to the second floor. Warden Lanchet's assistant will meet you there."

Passing through additional security points, Antonia Bolovatto was soon seated in the warden's office. She came straight to the point.

"I'm here because of a Red Notice concerning a Hellen de Mey and a François Cloutard. I am here to transfer both prisoners to Europol headquarters. Cloutard is an international art smuggler, a man we've been after for years. Madame de Mey is working with him, and we have reason to suspect she is connected to the man behind the incident at the WHO conference."

Bolovatto handed Lanchet the file. He leafed through it, raising his eyebrows repeatedly and nodding. Beside the warden's desk, a bank of twenty-five monitors displayed the most important sections of the prison. One of them showed the parking area, and it was this monitor that Lanchet now pointed to.

"I see I don't need to provide you with a vehicle."

Bolovatto shook her head. "I would like to take both prisoners for interrogation as soon as possible."

"Of course, of course," the warden said, scanning the transfer papers again. He pressed a button on his desk telephone. "Stephanie, bring me a transfer form, please."

Lanchet smiled at Bolovatto. "Every time the same old paperwork."

"Every 'i' dotted and every 't' crossed," said Bolovatto.

A few minutes later, Bolovatto was back in the parking area. She watched as Cloutard and Hellen were led out to the armored van. A prison guard removed their handcuffs, and Bolovatto personally snapped new cuffs on. Then she opened the back of the van. Hellen glanced fearfully at Cloutard, who also seemed nervous, and they both climbed inside.

"We're innocent," Hellen blurted, her voice loud and shrill. Her whole body was shaking. "We are UNESCO employees, for God's sake! Where are you taking us?"

"You will find that out soon enough."

One of the officers climbed into the armored van and Bolovatto slammed the door closed and locked it. She looked across the parking lot and up to where the warden stood at his second-floor window. She raised her hand in farewell, then climbed into the back of the A8. Both vehicles began to roll.

"My God, François! We're in big trouble. Europol! Handcuffs! Armored cars! I'm starting to feel like an actual criminal," Hellen said, staring angrily first at the Europol officer and then at Cloutard.

Neither of the men said a word. Hellen's mind raced. She should have insisted on calling her mother and not left their one post-arrest phone call to Cloutard. Whoever it was he'd called, it obviously hadn't achieved anything. But Hellen could not think about it any longer: the van was already slowing to a stop again. The Europol officer stood up and unlocked first Hellen's and then Cloutard's handcuffs. Uncomprehending, Hellen could only sit as the door opened and the elderly woman glared reproachfully at Cloutard.

"Your father would roll in his grave, Francesco. How many times have I had to spring you from jail?" she said in Italian, and Hellen was fairly sure that she could detect a Tuscan accent.

Meekly, his shoulders slumped, Cloutard raised his hand and indicated the severe-looking woman.

"Hellen, I would like you to meet my foster mother."

39

SOMEWHERE IN THE SOUTHWEST OF ENGLAND

"So what's the plan for me?" Tom asked, and he glanced to the left at the man in the passenger seat. Friedrich von Falkenhain, also known as the Kahle, kept his automatic pistol trained on Tom as Tom drove the SUV through the darkening twilight toward London.

"You'll find out soon enough. For now, you drive. I'll tell you when to turn," the Kahle replied. His excitement at the chance to torture his brother's killer at his leisure, then finally send him slowly and painfully to the after-life, was palpable. His instructions had been clear enough, but now that he had Tom Wagner in his power, he didn't give a damn about the instructions. Just days before, powerless to intercede, he had watched as Tom had brutally murdered his twin—his best friend, his other half. All that mattered to Friedrich now was avenging his brother's death.

The silence was getting unbearable. Tom had to think of some way to get clear of the car without Friedrich shooting him full of lead from his Glock. "That was you in London with Noah, wasn't it?" he asked, breaking the silence. "Before I set off the fire alarm. He hired you to get this stuff, didn't he?" he rapped on the case, still attached to his left wrist and lying in his lap. Tom was glad, at least, that Cueball's car was an automatic. Changing gears on a stick shift with the case cuffed to his arm would have been a challenge. The Kahle ignored him.

Samson was right, Tom thought. *It was never about the WHO summit. Maierhofer will be happy*. The oppressive silence continued. *This bastard's stubborn*.

"You're better off without a wig, you know. The bald look suits you better. But I don't really get the eyebrow thing. If you ask me, you shouldn't keep shaving them off," Tom said, running his fingers over his own eyebrows. He knew perfectly well that the Kahle had a genetic defect that kept him from growing hair at all. Maybe Tom could use it to get him riled up.

"Shut up," the Kahle replied, and he pressed the Glock to Tom's temple. "Keep driving."

"Are you taking me to Noah so *he* can kill me?"

The Kahle laughed out loud. "No. I'm not going to share that pleasure with anyone. Mr. Pollock's only interest is what's in that case, which I'm going to cut off your dead hand when I'm finished with you," he said confidently, almost with delight.

"See, that's what I find hard to believe," Tom said, with impudent nonchalance. "If I know Noah, he's got something special planned for me." After a short pause, he added, "I hope so, too. For his sake. I'd take it very badly if he just left me to an idiot like you. No offense. But after all he and I have been through, I feel I've earned better."

"Just shut your fucking mouth."

Slowly but surely, Tom was getting to him. All he needed now was the right place. They were just coming into the port city of Plymouth, and in the distance he saw what he'd been waiting for.

"Should I tell you something? Your brother cried like a baby before he kicked the bucket." That was the last straw.

The Kahle pressed his gun hard against Tom's head and roared at him: "Pull over, right here. I'll show you here and now what I'm going to do to you." The Kahle unfastened his seat belt to get out as soon as the car stopped. That was Tom's cue. He'd secretly deactivated the passenger airbag via the on-board computer and activated sport mode. He jammed his foot on the accelerator, and the SUV lurched forward. The inertia swung the Kahle's arm swung back. The Glock fired, but the shot went through the rear side window, just before the speeding car slammed into the upright of an overpass spanning all four lanes.

Tom hit the airbag, but the Kahle was thrown into the windshield. Blood poured down his face, but he wasn't dead, just stunned. Tom struggled to free himself from the airbag, and once he'd managed to get clear of the car, he ran for the bridge across the Tamar River, just ahead. A backward glance showed him that the Kahle was already after him—hobbling, to be sure, but he had the gun. Tough guy.

"WAAAAGNER!" the Kahle screamed, and he fired a salvo in Tom's direction. But the blood pouring down his face affected his aim. "I'll kill you, Wagner!" Blind with rage, he staggered on after Tom.

Cars flew past Tom and the Kahle, horns blaring, blinding the Kahle with their headlights. Tom climbed over the bridge railing. It was a long way down and he had no idea how deep the water was, but he had no other choice. It was either that, a bullet, or Cueball's torture chamber. He took a deep breath and dropped into the darkness. Straight as an arrow, the case pressed to his chest, he slammed feet-first into the icy water. Bullets fizzed into the dark water around him. He'd done it. He was alive. But he couldn't surface yet. Handicapped by the case, Tom battled his way toward the central pylon of the railway bridge that ran parallel to the automobile bridge. Protected by the pylon and the structure overhead, Tom surfaced and waited.

Furious, the Kahle staggered into the middle of the road and stopped a car. Being covered in blood, looking insane, and carrying an automatic weapon were enough to make anyone stop and run for their life. He dragged a panicked woman out of her car, jumped in and raced away.

After a while, Tom swam slowly through the night. A hundred yards upstream was an offshore mooring where several boats lay at anchor, and Tom climbed aboard one of the larger motorboats. He hot-wired the ignition and deactivated the GPS, then steered the boat down to the mouth of the Tamar and into open water. He puttered east, following the coast. After about two hours, he turned the boat into the bay at Newton Ferrers, a coastal village east of Plymouth in the county of Devon. Steering the boat into a dark corner, he dropped anchor close to the forested shoreline. Through the trees, he'd spotted a large number of wooden huts, and he soon found what he was looking for. One of the huts stood some distance off the path, hidden by a thicket. It looked as if no one had been there in quite a while. He smashed a pane of glass with his elbow and slipped inside. Exhausted, he dropped onto the bed and immediately fell asleep.

40

CAFÉ CITROËN, SEVILLE, SPAIN

"Your foster mother is really a charming person," Hellen said.

She and Cloutard had just stepped out of the taxi that had brought them from the airport. The Café Citroën was just a stone's throw from the Alcázar royal palace. The medieval complex boasted a long history that stretched back to the rule of the Moors. Originally designed as a Moorish fort, it was later extended several times to become the present-day palace, and was one of the most imposing examples of Mudéjar architecture. Constructed under Christian rule, the buildings were nevertheless influenced by Islamic styles and motifs. Later monarchs, expanding the palace, had added Gothic elements and impressive parks and gardens.

Cloutard frowned. "If you say so. She still treats me as if I am a little boy."

"If the only time you call her is when you're in trouble, then I'm not surprised. I didn't realize that it was also her who got you out of jail back when you first met Tom."

Cloutard could clearly hear the mocking edge to Hellen's voice. She was enjoying this—a little payback for his affair with her mother.

"Please do not rub it in. She still keeps bringing that up."

"You'll have to tell me sometime how you came to be brought up in an Italian mafia family. But for now let's focus on finding Eloisa," Hellen said.

She squeezed between the crowded tables on the terrace, which offered a view of the palace, and headed for the bar. Cloutard watched from a distance as the waiter pointed to a table beneath the trees, where a petite elderly woman with a voluminous, elaborately pinned-up hairdo was sitting. Her hair was pitch black and obviously dyed—Cloutard estimated that she had to be almost seventy years old. Hellen waved to him and pointed him toward her table.

Hellen was about to introduce herself when the woman cut her off. "You're the two crazies who want to break into the Alcázar," she said disapprovingly.

From one dominatrix to the next, thought Cloutard, his mother's imperious tone still ringing in his ears.

"Sit!" Eloisa commanded, pointing to two free chairs, and Hellen and Cloutard immediately did so. Eloisa's tone was more suited to a drill sergeant than to the frail old woman she appeared to be. "His Royal Highness has already instructed me. It's all coming together nicely. I can certainly use both of you today."

Cloutard and Hellen looked at each other in confusion.

"*Use* us? What for?" Hellen said. She could see that Cloutard did not feel comfortable asking questions.

"The royal family is currently in residence in the palace, and a gala dinner is taking place today in honor of . . ." her voice faded and she appeared to think. "To honor . . . oh, something. We celebrate non-stop and don't even know why. As long as they manage to spend all our tax money as quickly as they can. Things would be different if I had any say in it."

Hellen cautiously raised her hand and repeated her question despite the old woman's anger. "Señora, you have not told us what you need us for."

Eloisa looked daggers at Hellen. She was obviously not used to people interrupting or questioning her.

"I am the royal family's chef, and today I can use every hand I can get." She looked at her watch. "We don't have much time. The *mise en place* is already well underway and, as always, we are going to be extremely pressed for time."

She waved to the waiter and he signaled back that Eloisa did not need to pay for her breakfast. Hellen and Cloutard were still confused. Eloisa had already stood up and was preparing to leave. Cloutard had to smile, because although Eloisa was now standing, she was at eye level with him—she stood no higher than four-foot-six.

"Well, what are you waiting for? Do you want a special invitation? I'm slipping you in as catering staff. For the next few hours, you will help me. And I hope you're not complete nincompoops!" Hellen and Cloutard both looked at her in horrified surprise. "Once the dinner is running nicely, you can do whatever you want."

Eloisa was already stalking along Avenida el Cid toward the Alcázar. Hellen and Cloutard had to move fast to catch up with her.

"How is it possible for someone with such short legs to walk so fast?" Cloutard asked, panting. Eloisa was setting a very good pace.

"You'll help in the kitchen," Eloisa said to Hellen. "And you look like a waiter. I'll need you in the banquet hall."

Affronted, Cloutard glared at the little dictator, but he dared not contradict her. They walked through the staff entrance and were inside the medieval walls of the Alcázar.

41

AN OFFICE IN A SECRET PRISON COMPLEX, NEW MEXICO, USA

Shelley could not get the images out of her head: pictures of her son, Dylan, bound and gagged, staring despairingly into the camera, his eyes red from crying. No matter what she tried, the images were burned into her mind.

She would do anything to get him back. Anything.

So she had not hesitated for a second when she read the accompanying letter. She'd fallen headlong into the Englishman's trap and revealed her greatest weakness to him. She'd served up her son on a silver platter. But she'd make up for it. She had to fight back her tears and pull herself together more than ever before just to make sure no one noticed, but she would meet every single one of the Englishman's demands. She would do what he wanted, and she would be able to hold her son in her arms again.

She'd been sitting in the office for several minutes, waiting, marking time until she finally summoned up the courage. One more deep breath and she was ready. She stood up. She reached for her handbag and took one final look at the photographs. A moment later, summoning her strength, she left the office. She locked the door with her ID card and made her way along the corridor. She was one of the first to arrive at work that morning, and the office wing was still deathly quiet. Every step she took sounded like an rifle shot. She kept picturing someone coming around a corner any second and discovering what she was up to.

But she knew it was just her mind playing tricks. She could do this. Shelley was the warden's assistant and her ID gave he access to every part of the office, without exception. If she was smart, no one would ask any questions, no one would notice what she'd done. She would get the Englishman what he wanted.

And she would save her son's life.

42

NEWTON FERRERS, FIFTY MILES EAST OF THE GENESIS PROGRAM

Tom's arm was hurting like hell when he woke up. The small case lay on the floor beside the bed, still cuffed to his wrist. It took less than a second for Tom to remember where he was and everything that had happened. It all came flooding back: Sienna, the Kahle, the police, the bridge. His head was pounding. He rubbed his face, sat up, and looked around the hut. No phone, no computer, no Internet, just an old TV in one corner—he'd fallen through a hole in time and landed back in the good old days. At least the place had a shower, and he found some clothes that would probably fit. His own were crusted with dried blood.

A shooting pain in his left arm made him wince and forced him back onto the bed. He grimaced as he rubbed the chafed, raw wound on his wrist. He had to get the damned cuff off. Like a bird with a broken wing, he grasped the case by its handle and stood up. He searched the entire hut but found nothing. No saw, no bolt cutters. A paperclip was all he could find that might do the job, so he set to work with that. Contrary to what the film industry tells us, handcuff locks are not easy to pick. It felt like forever before he finally got it open. *Lucky for me it's not an official police cuff*, he thought. *Probably something from a sex shop*. Tom turned on the TV in the corner, then jumped under the shower.

His mind turned to Sienna. Had she made it? Tom's conscience was bothering him. It had taken a while, but just when she'd started to trust him, she'd been all but torn from life. Tom put his destructive thoughts aside. He climbed out of the narrow shower stall when the hot water ran out, dried himself, and pulled on the clothes he'd found: a pair of jeans and a strange t-shirt featuring the logo of some small-time heavy metal band. *Beggars can't be choosers*, he thought. He turned on the TV and the local news caught his attention. He turned up the sound.

"Leading today's news, a grisly incident at the Genesis Program in Cornwall yesterday evening. Popular with locals and tourists alike, the botanical park was the scene of a terrible crime. An unknown man"—an identikit image, which fortunately looked nothing like Tom, flashed on the screen—"forced his way into the complex at around six p.m. local time and murdered the head of the research institute, Dr. Emanuel Orlov, and a security guard. The man then took botanist Dr. Sienna Wilson hostage as he fled the scene. Dr. Wilson died late last night of serious injuries sustained during the incident. The fugitive also shot two local police officers who tried to stop him. Both officers died instantly. Whether the man stole anything from the laboratory is not known at this time." Tom hurled the remote control across the room and sank onto the bed in disbelief. Sienna was dead.

"Fuck, fuck, fuck," her murmured to himself. "Next time, no more hesitation. Next time, asshole, you die," he said aloud. There was an interview with the hippie guy, then a report about the tragic journey to Central America during which Dr. Wilson's colleagues had perished. The usual "reward for any information leading to . . . etc." followed. Tom stood up and switched the TV off.

He had to get the case to his CIA contact as soon as possible, then make sure the real murderer was brought to justice.

He pulled on a baseball cap and his expression clouded over: the baseball cap reminded him of Sienna and her miserable attempt at going undercover to retrieve the substance she'd developed. Then Tom grabbed the case, slipped a pocketknife he found in a drawer into his pocket, threw the windbreaker hanging in the closet over his shoulder, and left the hut.

He followed a narrow path back down to the water, where he'd left the motorboat at anchor the evening before. But his plan to take the boat along the coast to Newhaven to avoid possible roadblocks was a nonstarter. A police launch was bobbing alongside the motorboat, and one of the officers was just calling through his discovery on the radio. *Cops are fast here*, he thought. *And I thought yesterday was bad . . .* He turned back and disappeared into the woods, following a walking path called Passage Road toward the southeast. In five minutes, he reached the end of the little patch of woods and was back in civilization.

He needed to find wheels, fast. Something fast, maneuverable and inconspicuous. Then his eyes fastened on something: a Ducati Scrambler 1100 Sport Pro. A beauty of a motorcycle. Okay, the Ducati was far from inconspicuous—two out of three would have to do. It stood in the small front yard of a house. He looked around, but there was no one in sight. He ducked beneath the arching gateway and looked the motorcycle over. To his surprise, the key was still in the ignition. He smiled. Every biker, at least once in their life, had done that. It was one of the main reasons bikes went missing. Hot-wiring a modern motorcycle was actually next to impossible. He strapped the case to the pillion seat with his belt. To avoid immediately alerting the owner to the theft, he rolled the Ducati out onto the street before firing it up.

43

KITCHEN AT THE ALCÁZAR OF SEVILLE, SPAIN

The large kitchen during a banquet lay somewhere between a war zone and a Black Friday sale. People swarmed everywhere, hurrying back and forth with knives and other implements, shouting to each other, working feverishly on a thousand different things at once. Deadlines had to be met. Everyone depended on everyone else. They were simultaneously a team and lone warriors, all ultimately under the command of a sergeant who had to keep track of everything and everyone. In this kitchen, Eloisa Arebalo, the *chef de cuisine*, was that sergeant. Her voice rose above the countless sous-chefs, sauciers, junior cooks and dishwashers, and everything ran like a well-oiled machine.

Hellen and Cloutard had spent the last several hours helping out wherever they could. Cloutard was wearing a waiter's livery and had helped with the *mise en place* in the banquet hall, folding napkins, setting out cutlery, distributing bread baskets, draping vases, and lining up countless glasses in neat rows. Hellen had been put to work as a kitchen assistant and, with about twenty others, was busy setting up all of the ingredients, herbs, spices, and utensils in the optimal order for the cooks. Cloutard, the perpetual gourmet, was familiar with these kinds of gastronomic processes, but Hellen was deeply impressed when she caught a glimpse of the countless checklists with which Eloisa worked.

"I thought the exhibition I curated at the Museum of Fine Arts was complicated, but that was nothing compared to this," she sighed, sweat pouring down her face. She had spotted Cloutard amidst the confusion and had left her post to join him, and they both stood and watched the organized chaos for a moment, impressed. But Eloisa had seen them and stalked grimly in their direction.

"We're going to get chewed out for standing around," Hellen said, glancing at the time. The gala dinner would start soon, and they could focus on the real reason they were there: to find the map of El Dorado.

"Change of plan," Eloisa said, and she looked Cloutard up and down. "It has not escaped my attention that, as a waiter, you are not completely ignorant. One of my men has just injured his ankle and is out of commission." Cloutard and Hellen looked at each other, both knowing what was coming. Eloisa pointed at Hellen. "You I can do without. You can go and do whatever you like. But you," she said, whacking the flat of her hand so hard against Cloutard's chest that he had to take a step back, "will serve in the banquet hall. The whole thing is planned from start to finish. If I am one man down, nothing works anymore."

"But I can't—" Cloutard began, but Eloisa cut him off.

"No discussion. You help, or I blow your cover."

Eloisa glared at them, and both Hellen and Cloutard knew she meant exactly what she said.

"Well, then. I did work as a waiter in my youth," said Cloutard, and immediately put on a supercilious servant's face. "Let me see your *carte du jour*." Unbidden, he picked up one of the checklists that laid out the evening's menu. He began to recite as if he were reading for the role of King Lear.

Salmorejo andaluz
Lobster medallions with shrimp and a spinach-lobster sauce
Périgord truffles à la Savarin
Toulousian quails à la Souvarov
Beef Wellington in a red wine sauce
Potatoes with red pepper and sel de mer
Strasbourg foie gras supreme à la francaise
Rhine wine jelly with mandarin
Lemon tart with mango-passion fruit ragout and Cornish clotted cream

"Your menu is a little all over the place, don't you think? I know you are only a Spaniard, so I am willing to overlook an occasional culinary *faux pas*, but are you sure you want to serve the *foie gras* after the beef Wellington? That will confuse the palate mightily ahead of the Rhine wine jelly."

He took a second sheet of paper, this one listing the wines for the evening, and his eyes widened. "*Mon Dieu!* And who chose the wines? The Pingus 2004 with the beef Wellington is already dubious, but a Spanish white wine with the quail?" he shook his head and screwed up his face as if he'd bitten into a lemon. "A Domaine Baron Thenard Montrachet Grand Cru chardonnay is the only acceptable wine to have with Toulousian quail."

Hellen looked first at Cloutard and then at Eloisa, whose pulse was probably just topping two hundred just then.

"You insufferable *frog*! Shut your mouth this instant and start serving the aperitif, or I'll personally call the Palace Guard and you'll both be in prison before you can say *Français vaniteux*!"

Cloutard looked as if he were about to reply, but thought better of it.

"By the way," Eloisa said. "Australian white wine is far superior to French."

Cloutard sniffed indignantly, but he turned to the trays of vermouth glasses and joined the line of waiters. Hellen saw that as her cue to leave. She grabbed a tray as well, but hers held plates of snacks—a little camouflage, at least—and she left the kitchen. Eloisa had already explained how to get to the royal apartments on the top floor, and had told her where she could expect to find guards posted. There were only two that she would need to get past. With everyone gathered for the banquet, the palace was completely deserted.

44

CIA SAFE HOUSE, LONDON

The ride to London passed without incident—no roadblocks, no increased police activity. When he reached the London suburb of Bermondsey, not far from the Tower Bridge, he parked the motorcycle between a tree and a trash container at 17 Ambrose Street. His grandfather, a Jimmy Stewart fan, would have been delighted at the address. According to Tom's briefing, the CIA safe house was above the barber shop. Tom's intuition kicked in, however, and he made an spur-of-the-moment decision.

He trotted up the outside stairway to the first floor and rang the bell. The fish and chips smell rising from the Elite Fish Bar next door was mouthwatering. The unobtrusive security camera above the white door swung its electronic eye toward Tom, and a tinny voice spoke through the intercom.

"What's the password?"

"The blue hummingbird with pink feathers flew over the cuckoo's nest." Tom rolled his eyes as he spoke the silly security phrase out loud.

A moment later, the door buzzed and Tom pulled it open. Before he was even two steps into the entryway, he heard laughter ring out. A man in his mid-forties, still chuckling, came out of the office and shook Tom's hand happily.

"Sorry. We do that to all the new contacts. Come on in. I'm Jack and the guy back there's Anthony. We spend hours thinking up stupid passwords. There's not a great deal to do here most of the time. You're the highlight of the month."

In one corner stood a bank of high-tech surveillance and computer equipment, in the other an old sofa where Anthony was sitting. Empty pizza boxes and beer cans littered a small side table. "Call of Duty" had just been paused on the sixty-inch TV. *The exciting life of a CIA agent*, Tom thought ironically as he shook Anthony's hand.

"Nice to meet you," Anthony said.

Tom looked around and went to the window.

"So you've got something for us?" Jack asked.

Tom pushed the curtain a little to one side and peeked out. "This isn't quite what I expected," said Tom, turning back to Jack.

"We hear that a lot. Thank you, Hollywood."

"I don't have it on me." He'd hidden the case outside before he went into the safe house. "It's been a rough twenty-four hours. I figured it's better to play it safe. Okay?" Jack nodded. "Have you got a phone for me? Mine's dead."

"Sure thing," Jack said. He crossed to a steel cabinet, took out a white box, and handed it to Tom. "Fully charged and the PIN's in the lid."

Tom took the phone out, switched it on, and slipped it into his pocket. "Thanks," he said, and he glanced out the window again.

"Don't keep us in suspense," Anthony said. "What was so important that you had to shoot the shit out of a research center to get it?"

"It's close by. And I didn't shoot the shit out of anything," Tom said absently. His attention was on the brown delivery van that had just pulled up across the street. "Grenade launcher!" he screamed, as the side door of the van slid open and Tom recognized the Kahle. Tom turned from the window and ran toward the exit on the opposite side of the apartment, but he didn't get very far. The shock wave from the explosion tore him off his feet and sent him flying into the steel cabinet. Part of the ceiling fell in, and for a brief moment Tom lost consciousness.

45

AN OFFICE IN A SECRET PRISON FACILITY, NEW MEXICO

Shelley had worked with Terrance Zane for years, but the man was still an enigma to her. And though she had been inside his office countless times, she still felt uneasy every time she went in. She'd heard what Zane had done just recently with that black woman they were holding. He'd hit her, apparently, then humiliated her. He sent her out of his office naked, exposing her not only to the eyes of the guards but also of the other prisoners. And in a prison of this kind, that did not bode well at all.

"What is it, Shelley?"

His voice, and indeed his whole demeanor, made Shelley shudder every time. Zane looked up at her intently from behind his Victorian-style desk.

Don't get nervous now, she chided herself.

"HR sent the papers for the new guards. I've gone through everything with them. You just need to sign."

Warden Zane slowly reached for his spectacle case and removed a pair of vintage-looking reading glasses with an amber frame, the color matching the grain of the desk perfectly. Shelley wondered for a moment what it would be like to be married to such a pedantic perfectionist, before deciding she didn't want to know.

Zane sighed and reached for the seven files that Shelley had prepared.

"The first page of each file is a summary. You just need to sign on the bottom right."

Shelley's pulse raced. She felt herself getting warm and feared that her face was turning bright red. He would notice. He would see that something wasn't right. Zane opened the first file and looked up reproachfully at his assistant.

"You call this a 'summary'? Goddamn it, Shelley, your job is to save me time. It's going to take me forty-five minutes to read all these so-called 'summaries.' It's out of the question. Do I look like I have the time to read job applications?"

"Excuse me, sir, but HR and I have already double-checked everything. You don't need to read them. Trust me."

Fuck! she thought. She'd used the trigger word. If there was one personal trait that Warden Zane lacked, it was a capacity to trust anyone. She knew she'd screwed up. Now he'd go through everything in minute detail and spot the deception. And her son's life was on the line. Just then, the security door opened with a beep and a guard named Coby Chapman entered Zane's office.

"Excuse the interruption, sir. We have a problem in section 12."

"And you can't take care of it yourself?" Zane sounded irritated. Shelley seized her chance.

"HR is waiting for the paperwork, sir. The staffing situation is getting unsustainable." She looked at her watch. "If these doesn't go back today, with the holiday season coming, we're going to have a real problem."

"Shelley's right," Chapman confirmed.

"Why do I even have staff if I have to do everything myself?" Zane snorted.

He reached for his Montblanc fountain pen and opened and signed the files quickly, one after another. Then he stood up and strode past Chapman. "Let's go solve a problem," he said.

The door fell closed and Shelley was alone. Her heart was racing and it took a few moments before she realized that she had done it. She'd gotten into the human resources department, taken the job applications, changed the details as the Englishman had instructed, and organized Zane's signature. She had done everything he'd demanded of her. She left the office and went back to HR. There was still no one in the office yet, so she left the paperwork. HR would inform the new employees tomorrow. And she'd get Dylan back.

46

THE ALCÁZAR OF SEVILLE, SPAIN

On the way upstairs, Hellen ran through her plan one more time. She was doubly grateful to Eloisa for her tips. She had just reached the top of the stairwell, decorated with Moorish tiles, and had stopped to orient herself when she saw the first guard standing at the end of the long corridor. He immediately turned in her direction. Hellen walked toward him as confidently as she could, although her knees were trembling and she was afraid she'd go sprawling, tray and all, at the man's feet. He looked at her suspiciously at first, then his face lit up when he saw what was on her tray.

"Eloisa sends greetings from the kitchen," Hellen said. Her Spanish was good, but far from perfect. But during her studies she'd spent a summer on Majorca, where she acquired a little *mallorquí*, the dialect of the Balearic island. She hoped it would be enough to avoid detection. The guard noticed nothing out of the ordinary, and simply took a big bite of the beef Wellington sandwich. Hellen smiled at him and lifted the second plate.

"This one's for your partner," she said.

The man nodded, munching happily. Hellen turned left and passed through a series of stunningly decorated rooms. She had spent a good deal of time in Schönbrunn Palace and other such edifices that had been turned into museums, but it was rare for a royal family to still use the museum as a residence. And even though she was there on a secret mission, she could not switch off her inner historian. She admired the beautiful arched hallways and the evolving range of styles that had been in the various additions and renovations over the centuries. In a room with delicate ceiling frescos, she even caught herself standing, staring open-mouthed in awe. It was almost physically painful for her not to be able to stop and study the Mudéjar architecture more closely. She came to a wide corridor where she saw the second guard at his post. Now everything depended on whether Eloisa's tip would really work. With her sweetest smile, she handed the man the plate, and he bit into his sandwich as enthusiastically as the first guard had.

"The queen's having another one of her migraines," Hellen said, as if it were the most natural thing in the world. "And of course she's forgotten her medicine again."

Eloisa had told Hellen that the queen was constantly forgetting her migraine tablets, and one of the servants would always be running through half the palace to fetch them for her.

The guard was silent for a moment. He looked at Hellen, looked at the plate with the sandwich, looked at Hellen again. He shook his head, at first serious, but then he began to smile. "She's never going to remember, is she? She forgets her pills all the time," he said. He was smiling broadly now, and Hellen realized that the man was exceptionally good looking.

What a crappy job I've got, she thought. *A palace. Fabulous architecture. Dashing Spaniards . . . and instead of actually enjoying it, I'm stealing a treasure map.* The guard took another bite and Hellen disappeared into the royal bedroom.

The room was so impressive that she had trouble focusing on her goal. This was the Mudéjar style at its finest, combining construction concepts and decorative forms from Islamic architecture—horseshoe arches, honeycomb vaulting, Moresque and stucco ornamentation, majolica vases and pottery—with the stylistic repertoire of the Romanesque, Gothic and Renaissance periods. Hellen saw a magnificent *artesonado* wooden ceiling with the vaulted dome typical of the Mudéjar style, with ribs passing beside the apex of the vault, allowing it to open at the top into a lantern-like recess.

With a heavy heart, Hellen ignored all of it and went straight to the head of the bed. She pushed her hand between the headboard and the wall and immediately felt the light leather folder tucked away there. A few seconds later, she had taken it out and concealed it under her apron. She already had the door handle in her hand, ready to leave, when her heart almost stopped. The tablets! Hellen turned back, whipped open the nightstand drawer, and took out the small box. Then she left the room, waving the box like a trophy under the nose of the chewing guard. As soon as she was out of the man's line of sight, she ran, only slowing down again when she came to the first guard. She sidled past him, then ran down the stairs to the bottom, where she turned toward the kitchen.

Cloutard, just returning from the banquet hall, saw her. She waved to him and Cloutard nodded. Eloisa was nowhere in sight—time for them to go.

47

CIA SAFE HOUSE, 17 AMBROSE STREET, LONDON

Tom, momentarily stunned by the blast, coughed and shook his head. The air was thick with dust. *Lucky*, Tom thought, *just a few scratches.* He scrambled to his feet. Devastation wherever he looked: cables dangled from the caved-in ceiling, and the back of the apartment had been partially torn off.

"Jack? Anthony?" Tom shouted. At first, he got no response, but then something moved in the haze. A groan. A cough. A cry.

"I'm here. I'm pinned," Jack gasped. "Where's Anthony?" Tom picked his way cautiously through the apartment. The whole place looked like it might collapse at any moment. Then he saw a section of the sofa and Anthony's hand protruding from beneath a large chunk of concrete that had crashed from the floor above. Anthony hadn't made it.

"He's dead," said Tom, and he stumbled through the destruction toward Jack's voice. He heaved pieces of rubble aside and finally found the injured CIA man.

"Fuck, Wagner, what kind of goddamned amateur are you? You led 'em straight to us."

Jack was on his back with a piece of rebar through his thigh, literally nailing him to the floor.

"Believe me, that's impossible. I was careful. No one followed me." But the man had a point. *How did Cueball know where I was? How did he know about the safe house?* Tom had to hurry. The Kahle could show up any second to finish the job.

"Forget about me. Finish your mission. Looks like it's pretty important after all. Just get me a gun." He nodded toward the next room. Tom had to climb over a fallen beam to get inside, but the destruction was not as complete in there. The gun cabinet had tipped over onto its front and was buried under several pieces of concrete. Clearing them aside, Tom suddenly heard a noise from the room he'd just left. He stopped what he was doing and quietly took cover.

"Where's the case?" he heard the Kahle ask. Tom peeked cautiously around the corner. The assassin was leaning over the injured agent.

"What case?" Jack said, coughing and grimacing. Every movement he made seemed to cause him extreme pain.

The Kahle crouched and gripped the iron bar sticking out of Jack's thigh. He gave it a shake, and Jack's scream cut Tom to the bone.

“The case Wagner was supposed to drop here,” the Kahle said with frightening calm, almost fondly, in his German accent.

Tom thought feverishly. He couldn’t reach the guns, not now. Turning the cabinet over would make too much noise.

“Kiss my ass, you fucking Nazi.” In a final rush of courage and rage, Jack spat in the Kahle’s face.

“Have it your way.” The assassin stood up, wiped away the spittle, and fired two shots at point blank range from his assault rifle into Jack. Then he turned away, disappeared into another room, and began hunting for the case. This was Tom’s chance. He grabbed the gun cabinet and, with all his strength, heaved it onto its side. He whipped open the door and took the first gun he found: an StG77, a standard-issue Austrian assault rifle. The noise alerted the Kahle, of course, and a hail of bullets immediately flew past the cabinet, where Tom had taken cover. Tom grabbed a Glock, too, jamming it under his waistband before returning fire.

“Is that you, Wagner?” the Kahle shouted from behind a wall. Tom heard him reloading, and used the moment to move to a more secure position.

“Yep. How’s the head? I’ll bet hitting the windshield like that left a mark,” Tom said in his best smart-ass voice. He swung around the corner and fired a few quick rounds at the Kahle’s hiding place.

“Give me the case and I’ll make it short and painful. Or don’t—and I’ll make it last.”

"Keep dreaming," Tom said. This time, the Kahle fired, but neither his shots nor Tom's had any effect. Stalemate. "We can play this game until one of us runs out of ammo. Or we can settle it like men," Tom suggested.

The Kahle thought for a moment. "Okay. On three, we throw our guns away and come out," he said confidently.

"Deal," said Tom. He counted down from three, then tossed his rifle around the corner. The Kahle did the same. "And no tricks," Tom added innocently.

Slowly, Tom stepped into the open. The Kahle appeared from behind the opposite wall. Grinning, he stalked toward Tom, taking out a huge knife as he moved.

"Gotcha. Only you would bring a knife to a gunfight," Tom said, and he drew the Glock and emptied the magazine into the Kahle's chest. The force spun the man around and he lay where he fell, unmoving.

Tom took a deep, relieved breath and pushed the gun back under his waistband. He had to hurry. He could already hear sirens wailing in the distance, and the way things looked, he'd better be as far away as possible before emergency services showed up. They'd try to pin this mess on him, too. He grabbed a few spare magazines from the gun cabinet and left. Outside, he grabbed the case from where he'd hidden it in the trash container, swung onto the motorcycle and roared away. Not a moment too soon: a fire engine, paramedics and police screeched to a halt at the front of the building. He had to contact the president as soon as he could.

48

HEATHROW AIRPORT, LONDON

Tom quickly restored his phone book from the cloud and dialed the president's number. *Let's hear it for the Internet,* he thought. *Who remembers phone numbers anymore?*

"Who is this?" Tom asked, when the connection went through.

"Rupert, sir," replied the president's secret service agent. It was the same agent who'd taken him to Samson the day before. "The president's in a WHO conference right now. He will call you back when—" But Rupert did not get to say anything else, because just then Jordan Armstrong snatched the phone out of his hand.

"This is Chief of Staff Armstrong. Who am I speaking to?"

"Wagner, sir. Tom Wagner," Tom said, puzzled.

"Wagner." Armstrong lowered his voice and moved a few steps away from Rupert. "When we heard about the CIA safe house, we feared the worst. Where are you now?"

"Where's President Samson? I'm only speaking to him," Tom replied.

"The president won't be reachable for the rest of the day. He asked me to look after you." After a short pause, Armstrong said, "Have you got it?"

Tom thought for a second. Could he trust Armstrong? Someone had tried to feed him to the wolves, and he had to find out who. His options were very limited at the moment, but he knew he had to get out of London. As far away as possible, ideally out of the country. He had no interest in trying to solve his problems from inside a prison cell.

"I've got it. But someone else is after it, and whoever it was knew exactly where I would be. I have to get off the street as fast as possible."

"I'm not surprised, after the chaos you caused in Cornwall and here in London."

"First of all, that wasn't me. That was Friedrich von wherever-the-fuck, one of AF's assassins. I haven't killed anyone except him, and I only got him *after* he blew up the CIA safe house."

"Okay. Then you'll come with us to D.C. We'll sort it all out there. Sound good?"

It did sound good, in fact. And there was no way he was going to turn down an offer to fly in Air Force One. "Okay. Where do I go?"

"Rupert will give you the details. And Tom, keep your head down and don't go destroying any more buildings. The British are our allies, you know."

"Yes, sir."

Then Rupert was back on the line, and as promised he told Tom all he needed to know. When Tom hung up, he took a deep breath—this was the first good news in the last forty-eight hours. His tension eased a little, and his mind turned for the first time in a while to Hellen and Cloutard. And to the fact that he'd presumably sacrificed his job at Blue Shield. This was the second time he'd left Theresia de Mey stranded, not to mention his team, and it was highly doubtful that Theresia would give him a third chance.

Tom looked at the phone that Jack had given him less than an hour before. Jack . . . he didn't even know the man's last name. *Ironic*, he thought, recalling that fallen agents were honored with no more than a star on the wall at CIA headquarters, in the George Bush Center for Intelligence in Langley.

He had to get in touch with Hellen and tell her everything that had happened. Her phone rang, but no one picked up. Disappointed, he put the phone away again and headed for the meeting point he'd agreed upon with Rupert.

49

GARDEN OF THE ALCÁZAR OF SEVILLE

Hellen and Cloutard were still out of breath. They had left the palace in a hurry, exiting into the walled Jardin de la Danza and passing 16th-century fountains and columns with satyrs and nymphs in the dark, until they reached one of the exits leading to the outer gardens. Hellen looked around nervously.

"We'd better hide," she said, "in case someone's followed us. We need to find a way out of here without being seen. There are guards everywhere." Her voice betrayed her uneasiness.

"I have never in my life been caught on one of my . . . sorties. And that is not going to happen tonight, either. But you are right. We need a hiding place," Cloutard said.

"Yes. Then we can take a closer look at this map." Hellen pointed ahead. "There's a labyrinth that way. No one will disturb us there."

They jogged on about a hundred yards and came to the entrance to the labyrinth, which had been added to the gardens only in the 20th century.

"Are you sure about this?" Cloutard asked, looking dubiously at the sign marking the entrance.

"It's the only place in the gardens where the lights don't reach," Hellen said, pointing to the two spotlights slowly sweeping the gardens.

"Considering how strict the security is, we got inside very easily," Cloutard said.

"Well, maybe you and I understand 'easily' differently," said Hellen, heading down the first path into the maze. Cloutard still hesitated. "François, don't worry. You're with a scientist. I'm not a mathematician, I admit, but I know the strategy for getting out of a labyrinth," she said, and she beckoned Cloutard to follow her.

He tilted his head left and right and finally decided to ignore his misgivings. They turned a few corners, then Hellen stopped, sat down on the ground and unrolled the map. Cloutard turned on the flashlight on his phone, and they examined the map together.

"Hmm. I think we're going to have to rethink the history of the Spanish conquistadors," said Hellen.

Cloutard narrowed his eyes, clueless. "By which you mean . . .?" he asked.

Hellen took out her phone and opened the maps app. "This," she said, pointing first at the Cortés map and then at her phone's display. "This is the coast of Belize. It's generally believed that the conquistadors arrived here in

1525, when they encountered descendants of the Maya. But that doesn't actually seem to be true, because this map was drawn by Cortés himself in 1524. Look, he added the date here." She pointed to a year handwritten below the title.

"You mean Cortés visited the region first and found El Dorado there? And then deliberately rewrote the history of his own explorations?"

"I wouldn't go so far just yet. But he and his men were certainly in the area. And that makes this a brand new starting point. If I'm reading the map and the scale correctly, then Cortés's map shows this area . . ." Hellen showed the approximate region on her phone.

"Somewhere between Orange Walk Town and the Rio Bravo area," Cloutard said.

"Yes. And it would make sense. Several Mayan ruins have been rediscovered around Orange Walk Town, so it's absolutely possible that there are more undiscovered Mayan sites farther inland."

"But isn't El Dorado supposed to be somewhere else completely? This is the first I've heard of it being anywhere near modern Belize."

"That's true," said Hellen. "Which would also explain why no one has ever been able to find it."

"There's some handwriting on the back," Cloutard said.

"Yes. Let's take a closer look."

Cloutard stood up for a moment and peered over the top of the hedges, but he saw nobody. Hellen allowed herself a little time to translate the lines on the back. "This is Cortés's own handwriting, I'm sure of it," she murmured. She read on, and suddenly her eyes widened and she covered her mouth with one hand, as if to stop herself from repeating the horrors she had just read.

Cloutard noticed instantly that something was wrong. "What is it? What does it say?"

"This might explain why we know nothing about Cortés ever being in Belize. He writes here about a drug or a drink that sent his men completely mad."

"What kind of 'mad' does he mean?" Cloutard asked.

"I'm not really sure. Some of the lines are hard to read. As far as I can tell, they took gold from El Dorado, but then most of his men killed each other. He writes that they were 'no longer themselves.'"

"*Merde* . . . is that the element of immense power that was supposed to ensure the Habsburg's eternal empire? What Cortés wrote about in his fifth letter?"

"Presumably," Hellen said. "Because according to this, El Dorado is more than just a hoard of gold. Cortés is convinced that the death of his men was connected inextricably to El Dorado itself."

"Then we should make sure we find this powerful element before anyone else does," said Cloutard.

"We're going to need Tom, I think," Hellen said. "Dealing with bad guys who are after this kind of thing is what he does best."

"First things first," Cloutard said. "We have to get out of here. It will be easiest if we return to the banquet. The way we are dressed, we will blend in, and we can leave the palace when the rest of the staff go home."

Hellen nodded, but her thoughts were elsewhere.

"We have to go to Belize whether we reach Tom or not. Cortés describes how to get to El Dorado here very clearly. And he talks about what he calls a 'Golden Path' that's supposed to show the way to a trove of gold inside a Mayan pyramid. This is our job, François. This is what Mother hired us for. We have to get to Belize, pronto."

Hellen got to her feet. Putting her phone back in her pocket, she noticed that it was still on silent mode. One second later, it began to vibrate.

50

AIR FORCE ONE, SOMEWHERE OVER THE ATLANTIC

The first thing Tom heard was a skeptical "Hello," but it was a voice he knew very well indeed. Hellen hadn't recognized the number on her screen, of course, but she had answered nevertheless. *Finally*, Tom thought.

"It's me," he said.

"Tom! You won't believe what we've just found," Hellen said, and she was off. It had only been forty-eight hours since they had last seen each other, but for Tom it felt like an eternity. The last two days had been a real trial, but Hellen was so excited that he didn't want to bring her down with his story. He let her talk.

"We've got our hands on a treasure map from the Alcázar royal palace in Seville, a map hand-drawn by Hernán Cortés himself. It shows the location of El Dorado." She lowered her voice to a whisper and continued, "And Tom, you're never going to believe this . . ." But Tom knew exactly what was coming, and his lips soundlessly formed the same words as Hellen spoke them: "X marks the spot! El Dorado is in Belize!"

Tom smiled. He could picture Hellen's elated face, though he was a bit disappointed that he could not be there with her.

"Sorry, I'm babbling," she said. "How is England? Did you find Noah?"

"Yes and no. Long story. I'll tell you all about it next time we meet. Right now, I'm sitting in Air Force One on my way to D.C."

"Sorry, did you say Air Force One?" Hellen asked, taken completely off guard.

"Also part of the long story. You're heading to Belize? Then come to D.C., pick me up, and we can fly down together. If you're in Seville, then D.C. is practically on your way."

Tom heard Hellen and Cloutard conferring on the other end of the line. Finally, Hellen came back on.

"Okay. The earliest we can reach D.C. is tomorrow, around noon. And Tom, say hi to Samson for me."

She ended the call. Tom returned the handset to its cradle and leaned back in the comfortable seat. It was even more luxurious than the seats on the Blue Shield Gulfstream, he thought, and he closed his eyes.

A gentle shaking roused him. He was still holding Sienna's case containing the plant essence. He'd been holding it wrapped in his arms like a pillow as he slept.

"Mr. Wagner, Mr. Armstrong would like to talk to you in

the conference room. Please follow me," said a Secret Service agent.

They left the guest compartment. The conference room was situated farther forward, and in front of that was the staff office which, together with the president's quarters, occupied the front of the plane. In the rear was the press room and the Secret Service section. The agent knocked on the conference room door and opened it for Tom. He stepped inside and the door closed behind him.

"Take a seat, Mr. Wagner," Chief of Staff Armstrong said, gesturing invitingly. Tom picked a seat and sat down, placing the case on the table in front of him. "You know, sooner or later, you're going to have to hand that over," Armstrong went on, with a nod toward the case.

"I'd feel a lot better if I could hand it to the president in person," Tom said. "A lot of good people died for what's inside it."

"I understand. But think about where we are. You're in the most secure airplane in the world, and President Samson is sitting just a short distance ahead of us. You can trust us." Armstrong picked up a small radio and spoke into it. "Rupert, would you come to the conference room, please?" Moments later, there was a knock at the door and Rupert entered.

"Sir?"

"Rupert here will take your case and personally give it to the president."

Rupert nodded. Tom hesitated, but then pushed the case across to the Secret Service agent. Rupert picked it up and left the conference room.

"See? Better already," said Armstrong. "Now tell me everything that's happened in the last forty-eight hours, every detail."

Tom gave the chief of staff a full account of events, starting with the TV report in Nizhny Novgorod. He told him about Noah, Friedrich von Falkenhain, the police at the hospital, Sienna Wilson, and the two CIA agents in London.

"Could you put me in touch with the family of Agent Jack . . . I'm sorry, I never learned his family name? I'd like to pass on my condolences. Jack basically saved my life."

"I understand, of course, but I'm afraid we can't."

Tom nodded. He knew that agents' families were protected. They would probably never find out what really happened. KIA—killed in action, as the military would say. He had given his life in the service of his country; that's all they would be told. Plus an American flag folded into a triangle and, in Agent Jack's case, a star on a marble wall.

"What's going to happen now with the essence, or the biological weapon, or whatever it is that's in there?" Tom asked.

"It will go to one of our high-security labs and be examined by the best scientists we have. But most importantly, it won't fall into the hands of terrorists. Now I want you to go back there, order something good to eat, and enjoy the rest of the flight. We'll sort everything else out as soon as we get to Washington. I'm sure the president will be able to find a minute or two for you then."

Tom stood up. Armstrong shook his hand, thanked him for his service, and called in the agent to take Tom back to his seat. Following instructions, Tom ate dinner, then closed his eyes again and slept soundly.

So soundly, in fact, that he missed the landing, and was rudely awakened by four FBI agents with their guns leveled at him.

"Mr. Wagner, you're under arrest. You have the right to remain silent. Anything you say can and will be used against you in a court of law. You have the right to an attorney. If you cannot afford an attorney, one will be provided for you. Do you understand these rights?" one of the agents intoned while the other three dragged Tom down the steps of the plane. The FBI man reading him his rights, to Tom's amazement, had Sienna's case in his hand.

"Stop! What is this? What the hell? Armstrong, you asshole!" Tom shouted after the chief of staff, just then ducking calmly into a waiting limousine after making sure Tom was safely out of the way and no longer able to harm his president.

51

IN CADILLAC ONE, THE PRESIDENTIAL STATE CAR, EN ROUTE TO WASHINGTON

"Do we have the essence?" President Samson asked his chief of staff.

"Of course, sir."

"Then Tom Wagner was successful. I'd like to congratulate him personally."

"That won't be possible, Mr. President," Armstrong replied.

Samson looked pointedly at Armstrong. "Why not?"

"Sir, as I've said multiple times, in my opinion, your plan to use Tom Wagner is dangerous. The man is not trained to our standards. He operates more like a jackhammer than like a scalpel. His methods only caused more havoc in London."

"I know, but—"

"My God, sir, with all due respect, Wagner's incompetence caused the loss of two agents and our most important CIA base in London." Armstrong leaned toward the president, a motion presumably meant to suggest familiarity. "Sir, we have to think about our reputation. Our priority now is your re-election."

Samson looked out through the armored window of the Cadillac, which tinted the landscape beyond the window a distinctive shade of green. He was silent for several moments, then said, "Very well, Armstrong. What do you suggest?"

"Do nothing, sir. Simply don't give Wagner any more assignments. If he doesn't hear from you again, and if he can no longer call on you, then he'll crawl back to whatever little forest village he came from in Austria."

The president nodded.

"Mr. President, every mistake we let ourselves make by working with amateurs comes back to you. And we're losing points in the polls. The conservative hyenas at Fox News are just waiting for us to screw up, and with Wagner, screw-ups are a certainty."

Samson sighed. "You're right. Put Wagner on ice."

"Consider it done, sir."

Armstrong reached for his cell phone, dialed a number, and pretended to execute the president's order. While he was talking, the president's phone pinged: a message from Yasmine. He stifled a smile—he didn't want his chief of staff to get suspicious and shut down this contact, too. He wanted to hold onto at least a little freedom, intimacy and independence.

Ready to put the plan into action. Should we go ahead?

Yasmine had written, tacking a few heart emojis onto the end of her question.

President Samson looked across at Armstrong, who was also busy with his phone. Samson thought of his chief of staff's words: *Our priority now is your re-election.* Yasmine had reached the top of the biggest food company in the country. He trusted her. She would guarantee his re-election. He quickly wrote his reply: "Yes. Go ahead with the plan."

52

J. EDGAR HOOVER BUILDING, WASHINGTON, D.C.

Things were not going the way Tom had pictured them. *Escape the long arm of the European law with a quick hop across the pond on Air Force One, only to get thrown to the FBI wolves,* he thought angrily. Not only had the leader of the free world dumped him, the man's chief of staff had stabbed him in the back. Now here he was, shackled in the basement of probably the most secure police building in the world, waiting for hours for someone to hear his side of the story.

The interrogation room was exactly as one would imagine it: gray, grim, intimidating and claustrophobic. Tom was sitting on a metal chair bolted to the floor. In front of him stood a table about three feet square, also firmly bolted down. A two-foot length of chain attached his handcuffs to a steel loop in the center of the table.

So that's it, he thought. Things couldn't get any worse. Yes, he had a knack for attracting trouble, but this was just wrong. He could never have dug a hole this deep for himself.

"Hey!" he shouted at the security camera, its little red light blinking incessantly. "What about my phone call?" He had no idea how long he'd been there. The sense of time was the first thing to go when you were inside a room with no windows. It was straight out of interrogation 101: start by leaving the suspect alone with his thoughts. No air conditioning, no water, no contact with the outside world. Everything from the same bag of tricks. But it wouldn't work with Tom. He knew the tricks.

Getting his phone call would be one thing, but who could he actually call in a situation like this? The people he thought might help him were the ones responsible for him being here in the first place. Hellen and Cloutard were somewhere across the Atlantic, out of reach. Hellen's mother was probably happy to be rid of him. And Maierhofer? Not a chance. Tom didn't give his old boss a second thought. But then he had an idea.

"Call Special Agent Jennifer . . . what's her name . . . Baker! FBI Special Agent Jennifer Baker. I'll only talk to her," Tom shouted at the camera.

He wasn't getting his hopes up, though. So far, even his request for a phone call had fallen on deaf ears. But maybe an hour later, the cell door opened and there she was: FBI Special Agent Jennifer Baker, in person.

"Bet you didn't think you'd see me again so soon, right?" Tom said sheepishly.

Jennifer ignored his familiar, friendly tone. Strict and formal, not even looking at him, she began to speak as she flipped through a file.

"Mr. Wagner, from what I see here, you have been taken into custody on an international arrest warrant. You are under investigation for multiple homicides, kidnapping, stealing a biological weapon, and bombing. All in the last forty-eight hours." She glanced up at Tom. "And that doesn't even take into account your role in the Smithsonian affair. I've also heard that you just returned from Russia, and I can't help wondering what damage you caused there—and who ended up dead."

She was looking Tom directly in the eyes, now. Angry, upset, reproachful.

"There's a reasonable explanation for everything," Tom said weakly. "Look, I'm sorry I never got in touch—" But Jennifer's hand shot up, cutting him off in mid-sentence. She stood up, went to the security camera, and switched it off. Tom smiled mischievously, but only for a second. Jennifer returned and slapped him across the face, hard.

"I'll give you this: you've got balls the size of melons. Last time we met, if I recall correctly, you promised me THE arrest of my career, right? The mastermind behind the Smithsonian job. I'm still waiting."

"I—"

"Plus, you still owe me breakfast!"

"I'm not going to say that's why I'm here," Tom said. "But unless I'm seriously mistaken, that same mastermind is the one who got me arrested and sent down here." He lifted his hands. The chain rattled loudly and the handcuffs dug into his flesh. "Listen to me, please, one last time. And I'll make you just one promise: if you listen to me now, you'll never see me again."

Jennifer thought it over, then nodded. "All right. Let's hear it."

"Turn the camera on again. I want everything above board, on the record."

Jennifer went and switched the camera on again. Then she sat and listened to Tom's story, her eyes growing wider the longer he spoke. As for her Smithsonian case, he went a little further and told her what had happened in Ethiopia.

"That's incredible," she said wonderingly when he was finally finished. There's no way you could make it up. Wow. Let me see what I can do."

Jennifer took the file, stood up, and went to the door.

"Thank you," Tom said. "I owe you." She rapped on the door and it was opened from the outside. "One more thing: can you tell my team where I am?"

Jennifer nodded and left the interrogation room. The door closed, and Tom was alone again.

53

PENTHOUSE, 1781 N PIERCE ST., ARLINGTON, VIRGINIA

Yasmine Matthews was descending the spiral staircase that led from the gallery to her living room below. Every time she went down these stairs, she stopped and looked out the window. From her penthouse she could see the skyline of downtown Arlington, the Potomac River and, on the other side of the river, Georgetown University. On a clear day, she could even see the Thomas Jefferson memorial and the Pentagon to the south. *Not bad for a small-town girl from South Carolina*, she had thought when she first moved into the place. Of course, getting to the top had been difficult, and she'd used a few unorthodox methods along the way, but the road to the top was rocky. Nothing for snowflakes. Her claws were as strong as her ambition, and she had broken some eggs making her omelet.

The ringing of her phone jolted her from her daydreams. She looked down at the display, suddenly nervous. She had expected the call, of course, but she felt apprehensive every time they spoke.

"Ms. Matthews, I hope you're well. Where do we stand?"

Noah Pollock's voice sounded friendly, almost warm, but Yasmine knew it was a façade. The man was not friendly, and very far from warm.

"I have the president's go-ahead."

"And the essence?"

"On its way. We're sending it to our Belize plant today."

"And you will supervise the process personally, Ms. Matthews?"

Yasmine faltered. That had not been part of the deal. She had agreed to make her water bottling plant available for the project, and that alone had meant some major logistical adjustments on her part. If NutriAm's board of directors got wind of the changes she'd already made in bottling and distribution, she might as well resign today. She was already taking serious risks. And now they wanted her to be there in person? If anything went wrong, it would mean not only the end of her career—she would also find herself in jail.

"Uh, Mr. Pollock, that was not part of the plan."

"The plan has been changed. Do you have a problem with that?"

Yasmine said nothing. Noah let several seconds pass, and each one felt like an eternity to Yasmine.

"Then that's settled," he finally said. "You should keep in mind who it was who put you in the CEO's chair."

"Yes. But if anything goes wrong, I can kiss my career—"

"If anything goes wrong, your career is the least of our concerns. You know how far this goes. You knew what you were letting yourself in for. So don't start pissing in your designer panties now. Get the job done."

Noah had not raised his voice at all, but his tone had taken on an intensity that terrified Yasmine. "Of course. I'll arrange a flight to Belize right away," she said meekly, her voice trembling.

Noah's tone returned to normal. "Everything will go according to plan. You don't need to worry about your career," he said, and hung up.

54

A DARK SIDE STREET, WASHINGTON, D.C.

He'd parked his car in a dark alley. The overhead lamp cast a pale glow on his injured face. He looked at his watch. He hated lateness with a passion, especially with something so important at stake. Too much had gone wrong already. He had underestimated Tom Wagner once again. Another glance at his watch. His contact was already two minutes late. Friedrich von Falkenhain rubbed his aching chest. Tom had fired seventeen bullets into his bulletproof Kevlar vest. Two had grazed his side, but those had just left scratches. He hardly felt them. But his bruised and broken ribs . . . he certainly felt those. Every breath hurt. But he was still alive. *Thank God Wagner is a good shot*, he thought grimly.

Two firemen had found him in the rubble, and he had murdered them and escaped through the hole blasted in the back wall. AF's global network had quickly patched him up, arranged new papers for him, and put him on a plane to D.C. He had actually arrived in Washington before Tom. But to the Kahle's disgust, Tom was now sitting in the basement of the J. Edgar Hoover Building, FBI central, and had been in interrogation for hours. The Kahle had missed his chance to avenge his brother.

He checked the time again, and then he saw it. In the alley opposite, a car appeared and flashed its headlights at him. The Kahle started his engine and rolled across the quiet, abandoned street into the alley on the other side. He came to a stop directly beside the other car, in the shadows of the high buildings. Both drivers rolled down their windows.

A man in a gray suit, bathed in sweat and looking panicky, sat at the wheel of the limousine with the government license plates. He looked into the Kahle's cold eyes. "And then you'll let her go, right? That was the agreement," he said, his hands shaking as he handed over Sienna Wilson's small case.

The Kahle took the case from him. "I'm afraid that's no longer possible. Your wife is already dead."

The man in the other car had no time even to process the Kahle's words before a bullet from Friedrich's silenced Glock splattered his brain across the car's interior.

The Kahle rolled his window up again and slowly drove away. He lay his Glock on the passenger seat, reached for his phone and tapped out an SMS: *Goods obtained. On my way.*

Fifteen minutes later, Friedrich arrived at Leesburg Executive Airport outside D.C. He turned onto the grounds of the small airport from Sycolin Road and drove directly to one of the executive hangars. Passing through the massive rolling gate, which immediately closed behind him, he parked beside the black stretch limo that had arrived moments before.

The limousine driver opened the rear door and Yasmine Matthews got out. She made her way quickly toward the Bombardier Global 6000 jet. Friedrich took the case and hurried after her.

"Mr. Pollock was not wrong. Right on time." She acknowledged the Kahle with no more than a cursory glance. "It looks as if getting the essence wasn't so easy at all."

"Everything in this world has its price," Friedrich replied. Not only had he been injured, but he had lost his chance to take revenge on Wagner. And the way things looked now, it would take a miracle for him to ever get another one.

"You're right about that," Yasmine said, climbing the steps of her private jet. "But let's toast our success. We're nearly there. The president has given us the green light." She proudly showed him Samson's message.

The Kahle followed her inside. The door closed and the plane rolled out onto the tarmac.

55

INTERVIEW ROOM, SECRET PRISON COMPLEX, NEW MEXICO

"I don't want to put pressure on you in any way. We know that you will meet each and every challenge you face here in our institution. As you know, we operate separately from the rest of the federal prison system, and our employees, accordingly, are not just regular prison guards."

Terrance Zane looked immaculate. His three-piece suit was perfectly tailored, his hair parted as if with a ruler, his voice calm but firm. His eyes scanned the seven new employees starting work that day in his "institution," as he liked to call it. Normally, ADX was the highest designated security level in the U.S. prison system. These "supermax" prisons housed the most dangerous offenders: serial killers, terrorists. The conditions in an ADX prison were exceptionally tough, with extreme isolation the standard. In Zane's "institution," they went a step further. In administrative terms, the prisoners here didn't exist: either they had never officially set foot on U.S. soil or, for other reasons—usually related to national security—they were never supposed to see the light of day again.

"No doubt you were surprised at our exceptionally stringent selection process. We employ only the most professional corrections officers here. The inmates in our custody are among the most dangerous criminals and terrorists in the world. Because they are true professionals in their fields, we have to be as well."

His eyes moved around the conference table where the new guards were seated, taking time to gaze intently at each man in turn, but no one in the room seemed unnerved by the tension.

"Welcome to your new home. My assistant, Shelley, will hand out your assignments and send you to your senior officers."

Zane nodded first to Shelley, then to the new arrivals, and left the room without another word. Shelley had a file prepared for each of them. She went around the room, handing them their paperwork, explaining the next steps of their first day on the job and sending them on their way. Shelley's pulse was hammering when she reached the last man. It took a huge effort even to look him in the eye: the man she'd met first just a few days before at the karaoke bar, with whom she'd spent perhaps the hottest night of lovemaking she'd ever experienced, and who had afterward kidnapped her son. And now here he was, sitting in front of her in the uniform of a corrections officer, expecting her to complete the final steps of their bargain. Shelley waited a few seconds until they were alone in the room.

"Did you organize the ID card for me?" Isaac Hagen asked, as calmly as if he were asking about supermarket coupons. Shelley nodded and pushed the card to him across the table. "Access to IT and all server rooms?" She nodded again. Hagen stood up with a grin and patted her chummily on the shoulder. "Good girl," he said, putting the paperwork and the ID card away. "What does my schedule look like?"

"Every night, between 2 and 3 a.m., there's a small window of time when the IT department is not occupied. There's a shift change, then the staff takes about half an hour to get some fresh air. One of them always has a laptop with him so he can react quickly if there's a security problem. Zane doesn't know anything about it, because it is strictly against regulations. But since nothing's ever happened, the IT guys have made it a regular habit." Hagen continued to look at her placidly. "In that half hour, you can get into the server rooms and . . ." her voice faltered, " . . . and do whatever you have to do."

"Well, if it all happens as you've just described it, then by this time tomorrow your son will be free again. How do I know when the IT guys take their break?"

"They'll pass your post, probably about 2.15. Then you're in the clear."

Hagen was on his feet now and heading for the door.

"For you and your son's sakes, let's hope you're right," he said, without even bothering to turn around.

56

J. EDGAR HOOVER BUILDING, WASHINGTON, D.C.

After Jennifer left, a guard had brought Tom a bottle of water and had left him to stew a little longer. Sometime later, he laid his head on his crossed arms and nodded off. He woke with a start when the door flew open and two men in black SWAT gear stormed into the interrogation room. Everything happened fast. One of them yanked a black hood over his head. The other unlocked his handcuffs and bound his hands with zip ties. Then they dragged him out of the room.

"What the hell? Who are you? Where are you taking me?"

The men ignored his protests. In their iron grip, he was dragged down a corridor and into an elevator, then through several doors and finally into a garage. They bundled him into the back of a large SUV, its windows tinted almost black. He was pinned in the middle, between the two SWAT men.

"Where the hell are we going?" The men stayed silent.

A few minutes later, the car stopped and the two men hauled Tom out of the SUV and up an endless series of steps, but he could tell that he was out in the open.

Suddenly, they jerked the hood from his head, and Tom found himself staring at the immense seated form of Abraham Lincoln. A man approached from the shadows behind the statue and Tom recognized him instantly: Vice President James J. Pitcock.

"We won't be needing those anymore," he said, pointing to Tom's hands, and one of the men stepped forward and cut the nylon restraints. Tom rubbed his wrists. He'd had more than enough of handcuffs.

"A hood? Really? To get from the Hoover building to here? We could have walked."

One of the men pushed a bag into Tom's hands—his personal effects—then followed his colleague back to the SUV.

"Thanks, boys," Pitcock called after them. Without a word, they climbed into the SUV and drove away.

Still confused, Tom looked around. Two Secret Service men were close by, but out of earshot—one there at the top, the other down at the foot of the stairs.

"What is this, sir? Why the theatrics?" Tom asked.

"Mr. Wagner . . . or may I call you Tom? How much do you actually know about the assignment President Samson gave you? Yeah, I know, we soldiers"—he clapped Tom fraternally on the shoulder—"we get it drilled into us not to ask questions, or at least not too many." Tom was about to answer, but Pitcock continued.

"Let me guess. You were told that there was a biological agent that had to be kept out of the hands of terrorists, and that the best scientists would then examine this stuff and keep the world safe from it."

Tom nodded.

"What they didn't tell you is that the research team that originally discovered the plant stumbled onto an ancient Mayan recipe at the same time. The essence derived from the plant makes people obedient. But if the dosage is too high, they go berserk and turn into killers, as the team back then discovered the hard way. Administered in small doses, however, it makes people extremely susceptible to suggestion and manipulation."

Tom could hardly believe his ears. An ancient Mayan recipe turns up just when he and his team are on their way to find the gold of El Dorado? Tom had stopped believing in coincidences after the Kahle showed up at the safe house.

"How do you know all this?"

"When Samson gave you this assignment, his slimy little chief of staff came to me and told me about you and the biological agent. He also told me about the president's affair with the CEO of NutriAm, Yasmine Matthews. His only concern was the president's reputation, of course, but the whole thing got me thinking. I asked a buddy of mine, an ex-Marine who works for the NSA, to poke around a little and he came back with some very interesting information. The NSA had never heard of this weapon. So my buddy dug a little deeper and found out that NutriAm recently built a water bottling plant in the same area where the researchers originally found the plant and the Mayan recipe. Then I put two and two together."

"But how does the water figure into this?" Tom asked.

"The water is the medium. In the past, it would have been done with, say, a smallpox vaccine program, but today, with all the psychos and anti-vaxxers out there, they had to come up with a new method. And if it worked with fluoride, it could work with this stuff, too. What could be better for the job than bottled water? Americans are obsessed with water in little bottles."

Tom's head was spinning. "But what does all this have to do with me?" he asked.

"I want you to help me stop Samson and his girlfriend and their plan."

"But the essence is safe. Armstrong gave it to the FBI."

"True. But . . ."

"But what? Please don't tell me it's disappeared. Do you know what I went through to get that stuff?" Tom sat on the steps in frustration and gazed out over the Reflecting Pool toward the Washington Monument.

"You're right. The essence has vanished. And just a few hours ago, they found the body of the FBI agent who presumably passed it on. Apparently, he was being blackmailed, because when they searched his apartment, they found his wife's body. Both of them had been executed. And the NutriAm company jet took off an hour ago. It's on its way to Belize as we speak."

"Okay. How do you see this working?"

"It's not hard. You fly to Belize and do what you do." Pitcock waved his hands vaguely in the air.

Belize? This was starting to get spooky. Hellen was also on her way to Belize. And the CEO had to be connected to AF somehow, otherwise none of it made any sense. The Kahle, Tom suspected, was working for her, probably through Noah. And only a brain as sick as Noah's could have come up with a plan this insane.

Pitcock saw that he had Tom on his side, and he didn't wait for an answer. "What do you need?" he asked.

Tom was still deep in thought. "A contact in Belize would be good. And guns," he finally replied.

"I can organize a flight for you from Arlington, but I don't think I can find you a contact there at such short notice."

"Thanks, but I already have a flight," Tom said. The vice president looked at Tom in surprise. "We'll work out everything else on site. It won't be the first time." Tom stood up and turned to leave. After descending a few steps, he stopped and said, "I do have one last question."

"Shoot."

"Why do you politicians always want to meet here at the Lincoln Memorial?"

Pitcock laughed and spread his arms wide, taking in the breathtaking view of the sun rising over the Washington Monument and its twin in the Reflecting Pool.

Tom used the time until Hellen and Cloutard arrived in D.C. to freshen up and organize some new clothes. The heavy metal t-shirt had served its purpose. A quick trip to Georgetown and the clothes problem was solved. Apparently, he had not completely fallen out of Theresia's favor, because his Blue Shield credit card still worked. Along the way, he stopped at a small motel to take a shower and turn himself back into a presentable human being. He made it to Leesburg Executive Airport right on time.

"*Bonjour*, Tom. We have missed you. It is about time you joined us. Theresia . . . uh, Madame de Mey is not *enthousiaste* that you went off on your own again," Cloutard greeted Tom as he boarded the Gulfstream. The Frenchman was sitting in one of the leather seats. His injured leg had been through quite a lot in the last two days, and he had it propped in front of him. Tom was unsurprised to see that the hand raised to him in greeting held a cognac glass. "Come and join me for a drink."

Hellen had gotten up from her seat as soon as Tom came on board, and she went to him joyfully. But their embrace and greeting were a little awkward, neither sure whether to kiss on the lips or the cheek. Surprised at Tom's reserve, Hellen returned to her seat.

"Just waiting for fuel and for our flight plan to be approved," said the pilot, emerging from the cockpit. "Hey, welcome back. No Cobra officer knocked out cold this time?" he greeted Tom. "Sorry, the boss ordered me back and I couldn't wait," he added.

"No sweat," Tom said. He turned to Hellen and Cloutard. "It looks like you were able to put this crate to good use."

"A knocked-out Cobra officer?" Cloutard asked.

"It's a long story, I can already tell," Hellen said, a little reproachfully. "Tom, what *were* you doing?"

"Please don't keep us in suspense. What has happened since you left Russia so suddenly?" Cloutard said, and he took a swig from his cognac glass.

"I could really use one of those right now," Tom said, with a nod at Cloutard's cognac, and Cloutard immediately poured a glass and handed it to his friend.

"And how did you end up on Air Force One?" Hellen pressed, looking expectantly at him.

Tom dropped onto one of the comfortable leather seats, raised his glass to Cloutard, took a big mouthful, and began to tell his story.

57

PHILIP S. W. GOLDSON INTERNATIONAL AIRPORT, BELIZE CITY

"I used to think I got around a lot, but I see that I only ever went to the boring airports. Now I can add Ethiopia and Nizhny Novgorod to my list, and today Belize." Cloutard was grinning broadly as he, Tom and Hellen descended the steps of the Gulfstream into a hot, humid breeze. "And the climate here is perfect, *c'est magnifique*," he said, putting on his Panama hat.

"I've looked at Cortés's words very closely now and compared it with his map," Hellen said as they crossed the tarmac to the terminal. "We have to go to where Irish Creek flows into New River. From there, we follow Irish Creek upstream, and at some point we're supposed to somehow stumble across the Golden Path."

"That's not very precise," said Tom, absently looking around the arrivals hall. "Maybe we should fly over the area first and see it from above." At first glance, the spacious hall looked like any other airport terminal, but it had a reputation as one of the least secure airports in the world. Security was lax and the staff were easily bribed.

"I agree," said Cloutard. "Trekking aimlessly through the jungle is not likely to be very expedient. We could wander around for months, and that would be hard for me." He patted his injured thigh. "I know this from my Amazon expeditions, when gold fever broke out in Brazil one time. We need to find someone who knows the region." He looked around and strolled off through the terminal.

Tom was gazing off into the crowd. "I'll be right back," he said to Hellen.

"Where are you going?" she asked, but he was already disappearing into the press of tourists and visitors. *Typical Tom*, she thought, shaking her head. Then she hurried after Cloutard.

"Where did Tom go?" Cloutard asked when she caught up.

"I have no idea," she said with a shrug. "So, what now?"

"Trust me, *Mademoiselle*, this is my specialty. We need to charter a usable aircraft and find an experienced pilot, someone who knows the territory."

Hellen nodded. That sounded like a plan.

"Maya Island Air!" the Frenchman announced, and he strode over to where a young woman was standing behind a counter. "*Buenos días, Señorita*. We are in need of a pilot who can fly us over the Mayan ruins. We would like to see them from above."

Cloutard had removed his hat and was using it to fan his face. He was wearing his most endearing smile, and the girl at the counter seemed to have already fallen for his charm, because she looked back at him with a smile straight out of a toothpaste commercial. Hellen rolled her eyes. What did women see in the man?

"*Señor*, I hate to disappoint you, I am afraid we don't offer sightseeing flights. Maya Air only flies to our most important Mayan attraction at Lamanai."

"Then perhaps you can suggest someone who might be able to help us?"

The young woman's face fell. She had been counting on a commission for booking two flights to Lamanai and now realized that she was out of luck. Seconds later, however, she smiled back at Cloutard, once again the professional consultant for flip-flop-wearing tourists.

"Of course, sir. Orange Town Airways is sure to be of assistance. Their counter is over there." She pointed straight across the hall to a counter that did not look very reputable at all. Cloutard thanked the woman and they crossed over to the other counter. Cloutard seemed to ignore the booth's shabby appearance, but Hellen was not impressed.

"François, this looks as if it hasn't been renovated since the 1930s. Or cleaned, for that matter." She made the mistake of leaning on it and jerked away immediately, wiping her forearm in disgust.

"*C'est rien*," said Cloutard. "We are in Central America. Everything here has a little patina."

"Patina is fine. Filth is not," said Hellen, but Cloutard was already talking to the elderly man behind the counter and telling him what they were looking for.

"Sssi, Sseñor. Of course we'll do a ssssighteeing flight for you. Wherever you wan' go . . ."

Hellen pulled Cloutard back from the counter.

"François, the man is totally drunk! I am not going to climb into any airplane if the airline staff have a drinking problem."

Cloutard reached into his jacket pocket and took out his hip flask. He took a big swig. "Ahhh," he sighed. "*Superbe*."

Just wonderful, Hellen thought, annoyed. It was enough that she had to play the responsible parent for Tom all the time. Now Cloutard was doing his best to compete.

"Hellen, he is merely the salesman, so please relax. Besides, we have no choice."

Cloutard explained to the man where they wanted to go and haggled a little about the price. A few minutes later, the deal was sealed and the Blue Shield credit card was put to official use.

"I hope yous have a pleassshant flight and looots of fun," said the man, pressing the tickets into their hands and pointing the way to the gate.

"I've got a bad feeling about this," Hellen said.

Cloutard glanced at her and shook his head with a laugh. "Tom is going to love it if you start with the movie quotes, too," he said.

Hellen ignored him. They made their way through security, noting how slipshod the entire process was. Still, it was some time before they finally reached their gate.

"I'll message Tom to tell him where we are," Hellen said. Suddenly, she stood rooted to the spot. To her and Cloutard's surprise, the same drunk man was waiting to check their tickets.

"Jusssht go ssshtraight on. You can't missa plane . . ."

Hellen shook her head again, but Cloutard only seemed more amused than before.

"The people here are very efficient, that is all. They call it the profitable use of personnel," he said as they stepped out of the terminal and into the tropical heat.

Hellen stopped in her tracks. Her face turned pale and her jaw dropped. Slowly, she raised her hand and pointed to an ancient, silver Douglas DC3, apparently held together mostly by duct tape and prayer. "What a piece of junk!" she cried in horror.

"Bingo! Tom would be proud of you. If you keep it up, you might even score a Star Wars hat trick today!"

Despite his brave front, the sight of the rickety machine also made Cloutard a little uneasy, although he knew the DC3 was one of the most reliable propeller-driven planes ever built.

"Youssh can board now," they heard a familiar voice say.

The drunk from the counter had donned a pilot's cap, and he dropped into the forward seat with all the elegance of a sandbag. Cloutard looked at Hellen and pointed to the fold-down steps.

"After you, *Chérie*," he said, his hip flask already in his hand.

"No reward in the world is worth this," she muttered, just as Tom came jogging across the tarmac. He was carrying a small sports bag.

"We're going up in that thing? You're braver than I thought!" he said with a laugh as he climbed the steps.

58

PHILIP S. W. GOLDSON INTERNATIONAL AIRPORT, BELIZE CITY

"Very inventive, Monsieur Wagner," Cloutard shouted over the noise of the propellers. The decrepit plane shuddered as it began to roll.

"Where did you get all that?" Hellen asked, a little shocked, staring at the sports bag. Inside it were a pistol, several magazines, two machetes, a knife, and two hand grenades.

"From our AF friends. They definitely know we're here. I spotted two guys in the arrivals terminal who seemed unusually interested in us. One of them was talking on his phone. When they realized that I'd seen them, they decided it was time to go. I followed them out to the parking lot and we had a little . . . discussion. Basically, I was able to convince them that they were on the wrong side, and they declared their willingness to help us out with a little donation." Tom took the pistol out of the bag, pressed a magazine into the grip, and pulled back the slide, chambering a round.

"I have no doubt you made a persuasive argument," Cloutard laughed, and he clapped Tom on the shoulder before fastening his seat belt and pulling it tight. Tom checked the other items in the bag, and Hellen took a machete and put it into her backpack. She was sitting opposite Cloutard in one of the fold-down seats that ran the length of the plane on each side. She also fastened her seat belt, and held on tightly to the net hanging from the side of the fuselage. In the rear of the plane, a few crates were secured in place with a safety net. Tom stood up, handed Cloutard the sports bag, and went forward to the cockpit, while Cloutard put his feet on the bag, pinning it in place. Tom made his way forward through the plane, holding onto the exposed struts on the fuselage ceiling as it rumbled down the runway. He returned a moment later and immediately sat down beside Cloutard and strapped himself in.

"The pilot's got more in his tank than the plane does," Tom joked as the slewed into the air.

"Yes. About now, my mother would say that it's so hard to find good help these days," Hellen said, and Tom grimaced at her little sideswipe.

After a few stomach-turning corrections, the plane finally settled onto a course.

"Show me the map," Tom said.

"What, here?" Hellen said. She had her eyes closed and was breathing deeply, in and out, as if she was preparing to give birth, the noise and roughness of the ride obviously getting to her. Cloutard, by contrast, was enjoying himself immensely. He downed another swig of his expensive cognac.

“Sure, why not?” Tom said. “Hand it over.”

With one hand—she didn’t want to let go with both—Hellen fumbled the map out of her backpack and handed it across to Tom. He unfolded it and began to pore over it.

“You’re right. X really does mark the spot,” he said happily. “Except that it’s right in the middle of the jungle. But it’s impossible to use the scale here in any meaningful way—the proportions are all off.”

“The only clear clue is the junction of the two rivers. Maybe that’s why the Spanish never found anything when they used the map—simply because it is too imprecise,” Cloutard murmured.

They sat and looked at one another in frustration—they were flying over the verdant hell of Belize and had evidently reached a dead end.

59

IN AN OLD DOUGLAS DC3 OVER THE JUNGLES OF BELIZE

"Hoooollly mother o' God, what the hell is that?"

Three heads turned toward the cockpit when the pilot started screaming like a madman. Tom ran to the cockpit and the pilot pointed shakily to the jungle below.

"Tha-sssh different than it used to be. Tha-sssh new," the man slurred.

Tom looked down and saw that parts of the jungle had been razed by fire, apparently quite recently. He recalled seeing a report about Central American wildfires on CNN, back in Russia. Strangely, though, the jungle here had burned in very specific bands, as if someone had deliberately set fire to certain areas and then extinguished them again. But looking closer, he could see what the pilot was so excited about.

"Hellen! François! Come up here, quickly," Tom shouted as the pilot swung the plane back to take a closer look.

They hurried to the cockpit, but had to hold on tightly as the drunken pilot banked sharply.

"Oh my God!" Hellen cried. "That's the top of a Mayan pyramid."

"T-treassssure hunners have been runnin' round here for years, and they ain't never found nothin'." The pilot pointed down. "I'm a ge-genius. Thisssh flight's costin' yous double," he slurred enthusiastically.

"Though I hate to say it, it seems the fire was good for something," Cloutard said, ignoring the pilot.

Hellen was beside herself with excitement. She had a feeling that this discovery would change everything. A rainforest like this was like the proverbial haystack, and its needles—Mayan ruins—had always been discovered by accident in the past. But the fires had taken chance out of the equation. She sensed that they were very close to the Golden Path. She, too, ignored the babbling pilot and studied the map, trying to orient herself.

"Yes, this must be what Cortés meant. We have to get down there!"

"Lady, look arrrroun'. There'ssh nothin' but jungle all around here, and landin' in the middle o' the jungle's really not so easy," the pilot slurred as he struggled to level the plane out.

Hellen looked at the decrepit array of dials and gauges on the instrument panel, and it was suddenly crystal clear to her just how old this rattletrap was. She felt a wave of nausea. By modern standards, the cockpit of the eighty-year-old plane was barely even rudimentary. The most obvious elements were two control columns that looked like someone had cut off the top third of a steering wheel. The seats were upholstered as much with duct tape as they were with the original leather, and there was hardly a gauge or dial with its glass still intact. Every switch, every bolt, every cover—at least, the ones that still existed—rattled.

"You have to get us down there," Tom said.

"No, no, no, señor. That ain't p-possshhible."

"Si, si, si. That's where we have to go." Tom pulled a few banknotes from his pocket and stuffed them into the breast pocket of the man's foul-smelling shirt.

"Ooohh, thank you, sir. Maybe I can put her down in tha' clearing over there . . ."

He pointed to the spot he had in mind and patted the freshly earned dollars in his pocket—his rum supply was safe for a while. He gave Tom a thumbs-up and turned the plane to the west. Satisfied, Tom turned away, and all three of them stumbled back to their seats as quickly as they could. Hellen and Cloutard were already buckled in when there was a loud crash, accompanied by a massive jolt that sent Tom sprawling. Hellen screamed. The plane dipped its nose and fell sharply. With a huge effort, Tom managed to get to his feet. He peered out the window. The cowling around the port engine had been torn away, the propeller was seized, and the engine was spewing flames and black smoke. Bracing against the side wall, he fought his way back to the cockpit.

"What happened?" Hellen cried, clawing her fingers into the cargo net.

The cockpit was chaos, open to hurricane-force winds. The pilot, turning west, had apparently flown straight through a flock of birds. Several had flown into the port engine, shredding it, and at least one had smashed through the windshield and knocked him out. He had slumped forward onto the control column, sending them into a steep descent.

"A flock of birds, I think. We've lost the pilot," Tom shouted back to Hellen and Cloutard as he pulled the unconscious man away from the controls. Then he jumped into the co-pilot's seat and hauled back on the control column, pulling the nose up just in time. The DC3's belly scraped across the treetops as they began to gain altitude again. It took quite a while with only one engine intact, but Tom managed to get the plane above the low-lying blanket of cloud they'd been flying beneath earlier.

"François, see what you can find back there. I don't know how much longer I can keep this thing in the air."

"*Sacré bleu,*" the Frenchman muttered. He lifted up the seat on his left. Nothing. He tried the one on the right. Also nothing. "Check the seats on your side," he said to Hellen, who was still clinging to the net, her eyes closed tightly, praying for her life. "Hellen!" he snapped, and she started and opened her eyes. Then she too, without loosening her seat belt, began rummaging through the compartments beneath the seats.

"Oh, no, no, no. Not on your life," she cried, lifting up an object.

"Perfect," Cloutard said, and he reached for the large parachute Hellen had just found in the compartment.

"Did you find anything?" Tom shouted back. It was taking all his strength just to hold the plane more or less steady. "We're down to one engine and that won't hold much longer."

He glanced back, and Hellen held up the parachute.

"Please tell me there are more of those in there," Cloutard said to Hellen.

Hellen checked, but all she could find was a second harness without a parachute and a small case with a flare gun inside it. She quickly stuffed the flare gun and a few spare cartridges into her backpack. Cloutard stood up and staggered forward to Tom.

"We have one parachute, that is all," Cloutard shouted over the wind. "Let me fly. You and Hellen should try your luck with the chute."

"No. You two go. I'm already at the wheel." The plane was shaking so violently that it almost knocked Cloutard off his feet. Tom was struggling just to hold a course. "Go! The second engine's going to give out any second. We've got enough altitude for the moment, but not for long," he yelled at Cloutard.

Reluctantly, Cloutard went back to Hellen. He pulled on the parachute and got Hellen into the other harness.

"Are you crazy? We can't jump with one parachute. That's it, my life is over."

"No, no, no, *Chérie*. Theresia would kill *me* if anything happened to you. We can do this! Tandem skydiving, the kids call it these days."

Hellen positioned herself in front of Cloutard, He snapped her harness to his and they waddled together to the rear hatch.

"No! I can't do it! Please!" Hellen cried as Cloutard opened the hatch. Her fear of heights was making her panic. She clawed her hands into her backpack, which she was wearing on her chest. Tom looked back over his shoulder and gave Cloutard the okay.

"Jump!" he yelled. "I'll see you down below." Cloutard took a big step forward and dropped into empty space. Hellen's scream resounded for a brief moment as they disappeared into the clouds.

Tom banked the plane left, hoping to bring it down somewhere close to his friends. The starboard engine began to stutter and smoke, then the propeller stopped turning, and the machine instantly began to drop.

Once he was through the clouds, he saw the open parachute and sighed with relief. When they had jumped, his heart had skipped a beat and he'd wondered if he would ever see Hellen and François again. But right now, he had to focus on somehow getting the DC3 back on the ground, or his worst fears would be realized.

60

IN THE JUNGLES OF BELIZE

"*Merde.*"

"Is that all you have to say?" Hellen grumbled, squirming, still attached to Cloutard's chest. The parachute had caught in the dense canopy of the trees and they were stuck. Which, on the other hand, was not entirely a disadvantage: "We're lucky the trees broke our fall, or we'd be pulp right now, jumping together like that," said Hellen. She'd heard all of Tom's stories. When they had still been together, he'd talked her ears off about base jumping and had tried many times to persuade her to go skydiving with him. It seemed he'd finally gotten her to jump out of a plane.

It struck her like an electric shock: she'd been so focused on her own survival that she'd almost forgotten about Tom. Cloutard seemed to read her thoughts and tried to put her mind at ease.

"Tom has more lives than an army of cats. I am sure he managed to land that old bucket and get out in one piece."

Hellen nodded and fought desperately against a rush of tears. She wanted to believe Cloutard, but Tom's situation seemed truly hopeless. She gulped down her fears. Either way, there was nothing she could do for him now.

She managed to open her harness and pull herself up on Cloutard until she could get a foot on his shoulder and reach a branch. She grabbed hold of it in the nick of time, as one of the branches that the chute had caught on gave way and Cloutard dropped several feet lower. Hellen was left dangling in space but she quickly found a foothold on a lower branch.

Cloutard let out a cry when he fell, and another when his fall stopped abruptly when the parachute tangled again. He was hanging quite close to some stronger branches, and he began to swing the parachute to get closer to them.

"François, watch out!" Hellen called as she made her way carefully down the tree.

"I know, I know, or I'll fall on my face," the Frenchman muttered sullenly.

"That wouldn't be the only problem," Hellen said, and she pointed to the jungle floor. A jaguar, a common predator in the rainforests of Belize, had appeared directly beneath Cloutard. He was still dangling a good ten feet over its head, but it was looking up at him with interest, as if it wasn't sure whether this strange creature might be something it could eat.

"Next time, can we stick to breaking into museums? We could steal the Mona Lisa or find the damned Amber Room. Wild horses could not drag me back to the jungle," he grumbled.

Hellen took the flare gun out of her backpack, aimed at the jaguar and pulled the trigger. She missed, but at least she succeeded in scaring it away. And not a second too soon: moments later, Cloutard fell screaming to the ground.

"Thank you," he said, rubbing his tailbone.

"I can't hear the plane anymore," Hellen said with concern.

"Then let us go and look for Tom," said Cloutard, pointing and tramping off in what he thought might be the right direction.

After half an hour, they had not gotten very far at all. The undergrowth was dense and made progress difficult—the machete helped, but not much. Fortunately, no other jungle dwellers had crossed their path, but there was also no sign of Tom. Their spirits were rapidly flagging.

"I feel like we're going in a circle," Hellen said.

"Do you have any idea which way it is to the pyramid? That would be our best chance of finding Tom," said Cloutard.

"Frankly . . . no," Hellen admitted. She looked around and noticed something off to their right. "It looks brighter over that way. Maybe the fire burned a clearing over there? We would at least be able to get our bearings better."

"You are right," Cloutard said, and he scratched his head. "Strange. It looks as if something is shining, like a reflection of the sun. The light seems to be coming not only from above but as if it is being reflected by something on the ground."

Hellen began walking faster and faster toward the source of light. The trees grew thinner, and she began to run. Moments later, Cloutard heard her cry out excitedly. He followed as quickly as he could, and finally found her kneeling on the ground, pushing aside branches, lianas and stones. His eyes widened when he saw the sun reflecting more and more from the ground underfoot.

"Monsieur Cloutard," Hellen said proudly, "may I present to you the Golden Path."

"Well," said Cloutard. "We are certainly better at this than the Spanish were."

"Now all we have to do is follow it. It should lead us directly to El Dorado," Hellen said, her voice trembling.

Cloutard pushed aside his misgivings about all the murderous creatures prowling through the jungle and followed Hellen.

"I hope Tom finds us soon," she whispered as they went.

They soon discovered that they were, in fact, moving toward the burned clearing. Soon, the top of the pyramid appeared ahead. "That's strange," Hellen said, pointing to it. "The pyramid is that way, but the Golden Path turns off to the right here."

"Maybe it's a secret entrance, like the one we found in Ethiopia. There were several ways into the chambers there."

Hellen nodded. "Let's stay on the path," she said.

Minutes later, their suspicion was proven correct. Through the undergrowth, Hellen saw the remains of a wall, and with her machete she cleared away the vines and bushes. The Golden Path continued down a stairway that led into a subterranean vault.

"The passage leads toward the pyramid," said Hellen. "It looks like you were right, François. We're on the path to El Dorado."

"The pyramid seems to be mostly underground," Cloutard noted. "It has been overgrown and buried for centuries."

They descended the stairs and found torches in fixtures on the walls at the entrance to the tunnel, which was roughly eight feet square.

"You don't happen to have any matches, do you?" Hellen asked, holding one of the torches toward Cloutard. To her surprise, he took a gold Dupont lighter from his trouser pocket and lit the torch. "But you don't even smoke!" she said.

"Yes, but one never knows the ladies one will meet," Cloutard replied, taking the torch from the opposite wall.

"You old Romeo."

Cloutard grinned and took a swig from his hip flask. "Shall we?"

They disappeared into the tunnel and followed the Golden Path onward. Despite the anticipation of uncovering more of this archaeological sensation, Hellen felt a brief wave of sadness wash over her. The uncertainty about Tom's fate was too much for her to bear.

61

SOMEWHERE IN THE JUNGLE WEST OF BELIZE CITY, ON THE GUATEMALAN BORDER

A walk in the park, Tom thought. *If I can land a seaplane in the center of Barcelona, I can do this.* The endless ocean of green beneath him looked soft and fuzzy from above, each massive tree merging seamlessly with the next, all the way to the horizon.

The small clearing that had been their original destination and on which their drunken pilot had assured them he could land was out of the question. It lay in a completely different direction, and the spontaneous course change had upset all their plans. Now the pilot was unconscious and Cloutard had jumped to safety with Hellen. Both engines had failed, one of them was actually in flames, and the plane was not designed to glide any distance, so now it was up to Tom to get the old aluminum beast down safely. He would need a generous dose of luck to survive, but there were ways he could increase his chances.

First, he dumped the remaining fuel—with two dead engines, he wouldn't need it, and at least the plane would not turn into a fireball around him during the rough landing ahead.

Second, he kept the landing gear retracted. He had to set the plane down as flat as possible on the treetops. A final attempt to wake the pilot failed. Tom locked the control column, then climbed out of the pilot's seat and made his way into the back of the plane, where he felt he would be safer. When the DC3 finally hit the treetops—and particularly if it flipped over—the cockpit was the last place he wanted to be.

He buckled himself to the bench seat on one side and wove his fingers into the cargo net. He closed his eyes and sent a silent prayer heavenward when he heard the scraping and splintering of branches on the aircraft's belly.

He wanted to see Hellen again. If he got out of this in one piece, he would have to tell her how he really felt about her, once and for all: that she was the woman for him.

And then it happened.

The nose tilted forward and down. There was a deafening roar. Despite the seat belt, Tom was thrown a short way into the air. Shards of glass and other debris flew through the plane. Branches ripped away the engines and the wings. The fuselage flew on through the dense canopy like a bullet, headed for the ground. Then, with a massive jolt, everything stopped moving. The body of the plane was stuck fast, almost vertically, in the fork of a giant tree.

Tom opened his eyes. Everything hurt. Flying glass had cut his face and hands. He was hanging sideways in his seat belt, still gripping the cargo net. All around, he heard the scratching of branches. The plane creaked and groaned unnervingly with every movement he made, and Tom knew only too well that a branch could break or the machine could tip and fall at any second. Slowly and with extreme caution, he wrapped a few loops of the net around his arm and unbuckled his seat belt with his free hand. He immediately slipped downward, but supported his weight on the net, using it as a kind of ladder to climb down toward the cockpit.

He braced his feet against the bulkhead behind the cockpit and looked out a window. It was a long way down; the plane hung more than thirty feet off the ground. Then he saw the small sports bag with the weapons. The force of the crash had sent it flying forward and it was hanging outside the cockpit, caught on the metal frame of the windshield.

I don't believe it, Tom thought, as he climbed carefully down into the cockpit. The fuselage continued to make alarming noises. When he was already halfway into the cockpit, he looked up: the transport crates that had been tied down in the rear of the fuselage were hanging by a thread now. With Tom's every move, they slipped a little further out of the net holding them back. He had no time to waste. A quick glance at the pilot and it was clear that nothing more could be done for him: a large branch had impaled him through the chest. He was dead, and probably hadn't felt a thing.

Balancing like a gymnast, Tom managed to slip the toe of his right shoe through one of the handles of the sports bag and pull it up to him. The crates above him slipped and caught again, making him shudder. He pushed his arms through the handles of the bag, wearing it like a backpack as he climbed cautiously back out of the cockpit. Now he had to figure out how to get out of the plane.

He twisted the handle of the front hatch, just behind the cockpit. It was jammed. He tried again, harder. Nothing. The scraping and tearing sounds over his head were starting to really worry him. If the crates fell, it was all over. There was nowhere to dodge to. He threw himself at the hatch again. And again. And then it happened: with a loud *snap* the cargo net finally gave way and the crates plummeted through the plane. At the last possible second, the hatch swung wide and Tom leapt through. He held on tightly to the door handle and found himself dangling down the side of the fuselage as the crates exploded against the cockpit bulkhead. Splinters flew in all directions. Tom tried to brace his feet on a branch, but with his swinging and the impact of the crates, the plane finally dislodged. It slid sideways and plunged into the depths. The instant it fell, Tom let go of the door handle and fell with it.

He slammed chest-first into a branch ten feet further down, knocking the air out of his lungs, but he held onto it for dear life. Below him, the fuselage of the DC3 slammed into the jungle floor, a twisted wreck.

I never would have walked away from that, Tom thought. He climbed arduously down the tree, then set off in the direction where he'd last seen his friends' parachute—and where he also suspected he would find the pyramid.

62

IN THE JUNGLES OF BELIZE

After following the tunnel for about fifty yards, the light reflecting from their torches began to grow brighter.

"Oh. My. God," Hellen stammered.

Cloutard saw instantly what she meant. In front of them, the path changed. Not only was the path underfoot made of gold, but little by little, the ornamentation moved progressively up the sides of the tunnel. They passed typical Mayan reliefs, at first carved in stone, but then molded from pure gold. The gold seemed to be growing up the walls, like moss. The deeper they went into the tunnel, the higher it climbed, until eventually even the roof of the tunnel gleamed yellow. Gold as far as the eye could see, and the torchlight only magnified the effect. Cloutard turned in a circle, moving his torch from the base of the tunnel up the walls to the roof.

"This section alone must be worth millions," he said.

Hellen nodded, just as much in awe. They were on the Golden Path—a path that no one, presumably, had followed for hundreds of years. Hernán Cortés himself had likely been one of the last Europeans to come this way. Hellen wanted to get to the end of the passage as fast as she could, but at the same time she found it incredibly difficult not to stop after every step and examine the reliefs and figures surrounding them. Everything was in perfect condition, and she let her fingers glide over the breathtaking, ornate patterns as she went. The flickering of the torches made the gold look almost liquid.

"*Aurum metallicum*," Hellen whispered reverently.

"The metal of light," Cloutard translated, and Hellen nodded. They could not stop grinning. Everything around them was simply overwhelming.

A relief of three figures adorned with quetzal feathers and jade caught Hellen's eye. It was a symbol of the highest social rank in the heyday of the Mayan culture. There were gods and godlike kings, and above them stretched a series of celestial symbols known as a "sky-band." She simply had to stop and look.

She was able to identify the central figure by the Mayan glyphs in his crown as a previously unknown king. The figures were enthroned atop the heads of monsters. Other reliefs depicted the king at war against humans, but also battling supernatural hybrids of human and animal. Hellen was mesmerized.

"Come, Hellen. We have to move on. The tunnel seems to get dark again up ahead. Maybe we have reached the end," Cloutard said, tugging at Hellen's sleeve.

They moved on, and after another thirty yards, the reflections from the walls and roof of the tunnel indeed began to dim. Ahead, they saw only here and there a flash of gold from underneath a dark covering. The walls seemed to be moving, and after a few more steps they stopped in their tracks in raw dismay.

"François, tell me that is only my imagination," Hellen whispered, pointing ahead. They stared at the walls in horror as they realized what was covering the gold: the floor, walls and ceiling were crawling with spiders.

"Brown recluses," Cloutard said glumly. "Their bite destroys living tissue. A few hours after you are bitten, the destruction reaches your bones. I know these creatures from the south of the United States. But there they are relatively small and only bite if they feel attacked. These look bigger. Much bigger."

"But look, the fire frightens them," Hellen said. She waved her torch in various directions and the spiders recoiled from the flame. "So let's give them a little more fire," she murmured. She opened her backpack and took out the flare gun she'd used earlier so frighten the jaguar.

"You are not going to fire that thing in—"

Cloutard got no further. Hellen had already pulled the trigger. A huge flame and a flash filled the passage and Cloutard and Hellen turned away. The projectile bounced off the walls like a ping-pong ball until, seconds later, the tunnel was once again dark and silent. Some of the spiders were dead, but most seemed to have just crept away into holes in the walls.

"Quick, François. The tunnel is clear. It's now or never," Hellen cried, and she sprinted ahead.

Cloutard, cursing, followed. They ran about fifty yards to where the walls once again gleamed with pure gold, then stopped and checked one another's clothes. They had to brush off a handful of spiders, but it seemed they had come through unscathed. Neither had been bitten.

"You and Tom are the same kind of crazy," Cloutard said. "You make a good couple."

His words made Hellen flinch. They both knew Tom had gone down with the plane, but not if he had survived the crash. Hellen suddenly found it hard to focus on the here and now. As thrilling as the tunnel was, not knowing what had become of Tom was just as crushing.

Tom will make it, she told herself, turning and moving on down the tunnel. "Look, the tunnel gets wider here," she said. "Maybe we're almost there."

"Shhh! I think I hear something," Cloutard whispered, raising a finger to his lips.

The ducked low and crept on. The tunnel gradually widened until it ended at a gallery overlooking a room about thirty feet below the level of the tunnel. The light from their torches did not carry far. Cautiously, they looked down into the chamber below. Suddenly, Cloutard threw his torch on the ground and frantically stamped out the flames. Hellen did the same.

"I knew it. There's someone here," Cloutard whispered.

Hellen could see it now, too, and together they peeped over the edge of the gallery. Several flashlights wandered through the chamber below, illuminating it vaguely.

Only now did they realize the vastness of the underground cavern.

"Okay, one last check, *vámonos*," they heard a voice shout, and seconds later the space lit up brightly. Floodlights mounted on tripods were set up around the massive chamber, probably powered by a generator outside.

Cloutard and Hellen ducked for cover, but Hellen's curiosity was too strong. Again and again, she risked a peep over the edge of the gallery. She saw two men close one of several open crates before lifting it onto a hand truck. The crates were all filled with gold—the hall had been picked clean.

"We're too late," Hellen hissed.

"Damn it," Cloutard said. "The noise from the flare gun. We need to get out of here. Someone is sure to have heard it."

"You are right about that, Señor." Hellen and Cloutard spun around and raised their hands.

63

SOMEWHERE IN THE JUNGLE WEST OF BELIZE CITY, ON THE GUATEMALAN BORDER

Tom took out his phone. He had no illusions about trying to call or use the Internet, but the compass app should at least work. But when he looked at the display he frowned. The needle was going crazy. There was something here that could make a compass go haywire . . . was that one of the reasons no one had ever found El Dorado? Tom had read just recently that gold had magnetic properties—at the nanometer scale, true, but still. He put his phone away and kept on in the direction he thought would lead him to where Hellen and Cloutard had come down.

He made sure to follow a straight path: hard enough even in a normal forest, and the jungles of Belize were definitely not a "normal" forest. Most people lost their way in a forest because they only *thought* they were traveling in a straight line. Along with their hands, every human being has a dominant and a less dominant leg, which makes it impossible to travel straight ahead without a fixed reference point. Additionally, some might fall victim to false knowledge—that moss always grows on the north side of a tree trunk, for instance, or that trees, attracted to the sun, tend to lean toward the east. Among the most reliable *real* ways to orient oneself was to line up three trees and stick to that line. That way, one could avoid the risk of simply walking in a circle.

Tom pushed on through the undergrowth and soon stumbled onto a narrow dirt track. To call it a road would have been exaggeration, but Tom could see that one or more heavy trucks had come this way recently. The track did not lead in the direction he was heading, but he decided to follow it for now. It had to lead somewhere.

After following it for a while, he could smell it before he actually saw it: in the distance, the trees thinned out and he came to the spot ravaged by fire not long ago. He crept into the forest at the edge of the blackened area. In front of him, a narrow ravine marked where the fire had stopped. On the other side of the divide, a little uphill from where he was crouched, the upper part of a Mayan pyramid rose from the earth. Someone had built a makeshift bridge over the ravine with two steel beams and a row of wooden planks.

Tom couldn't see much from his position, but in front of the pyramid stood an old Russian military truck, a ZIL-131N. The loading area of the truck was hidden under a canvas canopy, and a man with a cap on his head and an Uzi slung over his shoulder was standing nearby, smoking a cigarette.

When the man disappeared behind the truck, Tom saw his chance. He dashed across the bridge and hid behind a burned-out tree stump on the other side. He was about to creep closer when he heard voices and ducked back into hiding. A man emerged from the pyramid, and Tom was shocked to see that he was holding Hellen and Cloutard prisoner.

I can't leave you alone for one minute, he said to himself. He readied himself to switch to combat mode, but paused. Hellen and Cloutard, their hands clasped behind their heads, were marching in front of their captor, who slammed Cloutard repeatedly in the back with the butt of his Uzi: the Frenchman couldn't keep his mouth shut and was clearly starting to get on the thug's nerves. He and the man in the cap forced both of the prisoners into the back of the truck.

In the meantime, two more armed men came out of the pyramid, wheeling a long wooden crate on a hand trolley. With visible difficulty, they heaved the crate with into the rear of the truck and jumped up after it, while the other two climbed into the cab. The driver started the engine, and a black cloud of smoke belched from the exhaust of the six-wheeled behemoth. The truck would have to turn around before it could drive out.

Tom had to hurry. He ducked into the ravine and ran back to the bridge, staying out of sight beneath the thick planks. A man steering a fifty-year-old monster of a truck over a homemade bridge had to be crazy, but a man hiding underneath waiting for the right moment to emerge and board that truck was even crazier. But that was precisely what Tom had in mind. As the truck rumbled slowly over the bridge, Tom pulled himself up and grabbed hold of the undercarriage. Once the truck had crossed the ravine, he climbed up between the cab and the loading area, a space about eighteen inches wide, and made himself as comfortable as possible. Wherever they were going, it would be a bumpy ride. A pistol in his hand, he kept a close watch on the small window at the back of the cab.

64

BURRELL BOOM, A VILLAGE OUTSIDE BELIZE CITY.

Hours later, after a jolting drive through the jungle, they reached the small historic village of Burrell Boom, just outside Belize City. Founded in the 18th century, it was little more than a stop for tourists on the way to the nearby baboon sanctuary.

Tom was exhausted. Every inch of his body ached. During the drive, he had risked a quick glance under the tarpaulin to see how Hellen and Cloutard were faring. They sat on one side of the truck, hands bound, while the two formidable-looking thugs with their Uzis sat opposite. Around them were several long, narrow wooden crates with rough rope handles. Tom was tempted for a moment to free his friends on the spot. He had the element of surprise on his side, after all. But they seemed to be in no danger at the moment, and he decided to wait. He wanted to know where they were going.

In the distance, on the edge of the village and situated directly beside the Belize River, Tom saw a modern factory complex. *The bottling plant Vice President Pitcock was talking about*, he thought. The truck was heading directly toward it. Tom scrambled back underneath the truck to avoid detection, holding on tightly to the undercarriage. He would not be able to hold out for long in that position, but fortunately the truck was waved through the gate quickly and rolled to a stop moments later. Tom slowly lowered himself onto the ground beneath the truck and waited, out of sight between the dual rear wheels. The two thugs in the back jumped down from the loading area while the other two climbed out of the cab.

"*Bájate, bájate!*" one of them shouted.

Cloutard was already helping Hellen down from the truck. "Patience is a virtue, *Messieurs*," he said, earning himself another sharp prod in the back with the butt of an Uzi. Tom shook his head, grinning.

Three of the men led Hellen and Cloutard into the factory complex while one man stayed with the truck, the guy with the cap who'd been smoking earlier. *You should give those things up. They'll kill you sooner or later*, he mentally chided the man. He was about to roll out from under the truck on the other side when there was a sudden flurry of activity. He paused, watching as the factory gate opened and two black SUVs with tinted windows drove onto the grounds and pulled up next to the truck.

From where he lay, Tom could see only the legs of the people who got out of the SUVs. Four of them wore black trousers and sturdy leather shoes. *Definitely security*, he thought. But the next pair of legs wasn't like the others—

even Tom recognized the red soles of Louboutin pumps. It was Yasmine Matthews, the woman in charge of the entire operation. And things became clearer still when she turned to the last man to emerge.

"Come, Mr. von Falkenhain. Let me show you the filling plant," Matthews said.

Tom was thunderstruck. Friedrich von Falkenhain was *still* alive? *That bald-headed bastard's impossible to kill*, he thought angrily.

"You travel with a lot of bodyguards," the Kahle remarked.

"An unfortunate necessity. As I'm sure you can imagine, our company has been the victim of a number of kidnappings. Over the years, we've had to pay several million dollars in ransom to various guerrillas to set our employees free. If it were up to me, I would not pay a cent for anyone stupid enough to get themselves kidnapped, but our PR people seem to think that we can't afford the bad press. That's the price you have to pay, I guess, if you want to exploit the absurdly cheap labor in these regions. It still works out cheaper."

Yasmine Matthews more than lives up to her reputation, Tom thought. As head of the world's biggest food company in the world, her ruthlessness was legend—a British journalist had once described her as a "cold-hearted bitch."

When Matthews and the Kahle disappeared into the factory with two of Matthews' bodyguards, Tom rolled out from beneath the truck. The other two bodyguards had moved away and were standing by an outbuilding about thirty feet from Tom, talking. Cautiously, Tom peeked over the hood of the truck to see what the smoker was up to. With a soft whistle and a "Hey," Tom lured the man to him. A sharp blow, a hard chokehold, and after a brief struggle the man slumped unconscious.

Tom took the man's cap and jacket and slung the Uzi over his shoulder. Then he rolled his body under the truck. He fished the cigarettes out of the jacket pocket, stuck one between his lips, pulled the cap low over his face and casually wandered over to the door the others had used to enter the factory. He knocked and turned his back to the door. It was opened by one of the thugs.

"*Qué pasa?*"

"*Tienes fuego?*" Tom asked.

The man dug around in his pocket for a lighter and held it out to Tom. A moment later, he realized that the man in front of him was not his buddy, but it was already too late. Tom stepped sharply toward the man and forced him back inside, simultaneously bringing his hand up to press the point of his knife under the man's chin.

"Shhh," Tom hissed, and closed the door behind him. He knocked the man out, then tied and gagged him, and deposited him out of sight behind a few pallets. The two bodyguards at the SUV hadn't noticed a thing. With the Uzi at the ready, Tom crept deeper into the factory.

It wasn't long before he caught up with them. He stayed out of sight behind a conveyor and assessed the situation across the endless procession of bottles sliding past in front of him. Hellen and Cloutard were kneeling about thirty feet away in front of the two thugs, who kept their weapons aimed at his friends' heads. Matthews and the

Kahle stood opposite, their backs toward Tom. The bodyguards were standing some distance off to one side. The group was in the center of the bottling plant, surrounded by a maze of conveyors on which thousands of bottles clinked and rattled their way around the various levels of the factory.

To free his friends, Tom was going to need a distraction. He unslung the small sports bag that had almost cost him his life in the jungle. Looking inside, he had an idea.

65

NUTRIAM WATER-BOTTLING PLANT, BURRELL BOOM, OUTSIDE BELIZE CITY

"What have you done with all the gold you found in the pyramid?" Hellen snapped angrily at Yasmine Matthews. "Those are priceless historical objects. They belong in a museum."

Cloutard pinched his eyes closed and shook his head imperceptibly. But Matthews only laughed and went over to a large steel container strapped to a pallet. She lifted the lid and pushed it aside. Then she reached in and picked up a handful of the gold dust it contained, ostentatiously letting it trickle through her fingers.

"Very simple. We've processed it," she said with a nasty smile. Hellen's heart almost stopped and she began to gasp for breath.

"You . . . you . . . you *what*?"

"*Sacré!*" said Cloutard.

Matthews moved a few steps away and rubbed her hands together to brush off the last of the gold. Then she picked a water bottle, its label printed in gold, out of a box and took it over to Hellen.

"Liquid Gold" Hellen read on the stylish label. Matthews crouched in front of her and went on in a saccharine voice.

"Take a look. Two years ago, someone brought a scientist, Dr. Emanuel . . . something," she began, waving her hand vaguely in the air. "I've forgotten his name. Anyway, he was brought to my attention. Apparently, he'd rediscovered an orchid, the *Orchidea espagnola*, which had long been thought to be extinct. And along with it, he also found an ancient Mayan recipe. When an essence from that orchid is mixed with gold dust, a door opens to the human unconscious. It took quite a while, I can tell you. And we did go through a number of guinea pigs. But we finally discovered that we can use this to make people highly suggestible, not just turn them into bestial killers." She paused. "Oh, so much blood." She waved it off, disgusted at the memory, and went on. "It all comes down to the dosage. And at the beginning, we were using the wrong kind of gold. It only works with a special kind of gold: the gold from El Dorado. Don't ask me the details, I'm no chemist, but what makes it special is a certain magnetic impurity, something at the nano scale."

"Do you mean to tell me that you went looking for El Dorado and turned all that gold into dust because of *that*?"

"Of course. But time was of the essence. We couldn't just go looking for it in the usual way—time is money, you know—so we decided to go straight to the source. The negotiations with the natives naturally came to nothing, so we had to—"

Hellen, completely beside herself, cut Matthews off. "What? What did you do to those poor people?" she stammered.

"She murdered them, probably," Tom called from his hiding place.

The Kahle spun around. "Wagner? Where are you hiding now?"

"Here. But if I were you, I'd be careful."

Tom stepped out of his hiding place, his hands raised. In his left hand, he held a grenade with no pin. In the other he carried the Glock. Five guns instantly swung in his direction.

"One false move and we all go up." Tom waved the grenade meaningfully.

"*Enfin!*" Cloutard said, breaking into a smile.

"Tom!" Hellen's spirits also instantly revived.

"I'm sorry I interrupted you. Please go on," Tom said, and the thugs and security men looked at each other, unsure what to do. Matthews kept her composure amazingly well. She straightened up and signaled to her men and the Kahle to keep their cool.

"Later," she hissed to the Kahle, who was obviously itching to pulling the trigger. "Mr. Wagner, I presume?"

"Thank you! Finally, someone who can pronounce my name."

“As you can see, we have the upper hand. Yes, you have a grenade, but you won’t get all of us with it.” She signaled to her men to keep their guns on Hellen and Cloutard. “And before that thing explodes, your two friends here will be dead.” She paused, making sure everyone continued to keep calm. “If I’ve understood you correctly, you’d like to hear what became of the tribe that lived here? I’m afraid Mr. Wagner is right—”

“They’re probably rotting in a hole somewhere in the jungle, right?” Tom said, cutting off her monologue and taking control. “It was you who burned the jungle, too. Effective, I’ll give you that.”

She smiled, taking Tom’s words as a compliment.

“People like you are nothing but money-hungry scum,” Tom snarled. “That includes you, Voldemort. But I’ll get to you soon.”

The Kahle wanted to shoot, but Matthews held him back with a shake of her head.

“I just want to know one thing. How can you be sure that people will actually consume the stuff you’re making?” Tom had to stall a little longer. He strutted back and forth, staring into the barrels of Uzis and pistols and waving the grenade around.

“Gold has a long tradition in the history of medicine. It has played a role for thousands of years. ‘Danziger Goldwasser’ was supposed to help against depression, and at the end of the 19th century, gold was used to fight syphilis and tuberculosis. People today are obsessed with Bach flowers and the laying on of hands. With the right testimonials, social media, and a few influencers behind us, selling it as the new miracle cure will be child's play."

"You talk a steaming pile of shit, lady," Tom said, screwing up his nose.

"Maybe from your perspective. But you are only one tiny cog in our well-oiled machine. I don't know what you hope to gain from this little show, but you have already lost. The first ship—" But she got no further. Her brain sprayed across the floor and she collapsed like a rag doll.

The Kahle had shot Yasmine Matthews in the back of the head. He swung his pistol to the right and cut down her two stunned bodyguards, too.

And just at that moment, a gigantic explosion shook the entire plant.

66

SECRET PRISON COMPLEX, NEW MEXICO

"I'm going to the restroom. Back in a minute," said Isaac Hagen, now wearing the uniform of a prison guard. His partner nodded indifferently, his eyes not leaving the TV screen, one hand on the cup of coffee that got him through the night shift. As an Englishman, Hagen could not comprehend the Americans' enthusiasm for what they called football.

Hagen stepped out of the room, reached into his breast pocket, and took out the ID card for the server room. He glanced at his watch and hoped for Shelley's sake that she hadn't messed things up. He took the fire escape down one floor and turned the corner just in time to see the IT guys going through their nightly handover and heading outside. Seconds later, he was in the server room. He took out a memory stick that Noah had given him and inserted it into a USB port. His phone pinged. A message from Noah: "I'm in."

From now on, everything had to happen with absolute precision. Hagen left the server room and hurried toward the central wing, where Ossana was being held—another useful piece of information that Shelley had supplied. As he moved, he kept a watchful eye on his phone's display, which showed a countdown. A few seconds later, the hallway around him went dark: Noah had cut off the power supply to the entire complex. It would take a minute for the emergency generators to kick in. Until that happened, the electronic security gates and prison doors were running on batteries, and Noah could use that short window of opportunity to unlock the doors to the individual cells.

Hagen reached Ossana's cell just as it unlocked with a soft click. He jerked the door open. Ossana was waiting. Hagen nodded to her, and they left the cell together. "The power will be back on in thirty seconds, but the surveillance cameras will still be out of commission," he said.

The first security station was unmanned and they got past it easily. They would have to come up with something at the next station, though; by then the power would be back on and the entire night shift would be in alarm mode. They were running down the emergency stairway when the lights came on. They had to hurry. They turned into a corridor and saw the next checkpoint ten yards ahead. There was only one guard, standing behind a counter He was confused by the fact that a guard was in the hallway with a prisoner after a power outage. His confusion was doubled when the security gate opened by itself, just as the pair reached his station. Taken by surprise, he reached for his gun, but Ossana was faster. She leaped over the counter and grabbed hold of the man. His neck snapped with a gruesome *crunch* that made even the callous Hagen wince.

"Next," he said.

They ran downstairs, and after the next checkpoint—this time Hagen took out the guard—they arrived in the garage where the employees' cars were parked. Hagen knew perfectly well that he would not simply be able to leave the prison in the middle of the night after a power outage. But here, too, Shelley had been useful. That morning, she had concealed three packets of C4 in the watchtowers and in the guardhouse at the gate.

Ossana jumped into the trunk of Hagen's Dodge Charger and Hagen steered the car out of the underground garage. As he drove up the ramp, he opened an app on his phone and pressed three buttons with his thumb. Seconds later the explosives detonated, demolishing the watchtowers and killing the guards inside. Hagen stepped on the gas and hoped that Noah had taken care of the final hurdle. He raced toward the electronic gate. The guardhouse was no more than a pile of rubble—the C4 had done its job. Seconds before Hagen's car would have crashed into the gate, it opened as if by magic.

Hagen pressed the accelerator to the floor and raced along the dusty road. They weren't in the clear yet, and he knew it. They were in the middle of the godforsaken New Mexico desert. Hagen roared along at a hundred and twenty miles an hour, as fast as he dared go on that road. He raced over a small rise and on the other side he saw them: four identical Sikorsky S-92 helicopters. He smiled and slammed on the brakes, and the Charger came to a stop in a cloud of dust. He climbed out and opened the trunk. Ossana ran to one of the choppers and jumped inside, while Hagen climbed into another. Moments later, all four lifted off and flew in four different directions: one toward Mexico, the second west toward the Navajo Nation reservation, the third north toward the Jicarilla Apache reservation, and the fourth east toward Texas. Noah had jammed the communications at the prison complex—it would be quite a while before the FBI could even mount a pursuit.

67

NUTRIAM BOTTLING PLANT, BURRELL BOOM, OUTSIDE BELIZE CITY

The explosion destroyed part of the bottling system and breached the outer wall. Plastic bottles flew through the air, and water began jetting from countless openings in the gigantic machinery, as if someone had triggered the sprinkler system. Tom had jury-rigged a small time bomb out of a hand grenade, a piece of duct tape and a cigarette, and had placed it close to the CO_2 system on the other side of the hall.

The Kahle and the two thugs ducked for cover when the grenade detonated but were quickly back on their feet. "Run!" Tom yelled, lobbing his second hand grenade toward the Kahle. Almost as one, Hellen, Cloutard and Tom leaped over one of the conveyors just as the grenade exploded, taking out one of the two thugs. Tom, rolling and twisting back, took out the other with three quick shots. He squeezed off three more at the Kahle, but he was fast enough to find cover behind the machinery.

Tom saw a pistol lying on the floor about ten feet away. He fired a cover round, jumped for the gun, rolled to the side, came up on his feet and ran back. Only now did the Kahle dare to break cover and return fire.

"Take this," Tom said, cutting through his friends' bonds and pressing the second pistol into Cloutard's hands, while Hellen took cover behind a large metal cabinet. Water covered the floor, already up to their ankles. Tom instructed Cloutard to stay put while he crept closer to the Kahle.

"Hey, Wagner. We've been here before, remember?"

"Yeah. And we can do it just like last time, but this time I'll aim lower."

Two more bullets whistled past Tom. He crept around to the other side of the machine and climbed up onto it while Cloutard squeezed off an occasional shot to keep their adversary pinned down. Now Tom was directly above the Kahle.

"Well, Wagner? What do you say? You got the guts to fight like a man this time?" von Falkenhain shouted through the hall, then he squeezed off a couple of shots at where he thought Tom was. The slide on his pistol clicked back. His magazine was empty.

"Sure," Tom said. "How about you?" As he spoke, he dropped onto the Kahle, who looked up, stunned. Water splashed high as they crashed together onto the floor. They struggled in the water for a moment, before the Kahle pushed clear of Tom and jumped to his feet. Quick as a snake, he drew a knife and lunged at Tom. Tom was able to grab the knife hand, then he headbutted the Kahle on the bridge of his nose, forcing him back. Blood poured over the German's mouth and chin.

Now it was Tom's turn to seize the initiative. He leaped at the Kahle and they slammed onto the conveyor belt. The knife fell to the floor, and Tom began pounding his fists into the other man's face like a madman. Off to the right, he saw an array of cylindrical steel spikes, each about eighteen inches long. They rose and fell rhythmically with hydraulic precision: the filling nozzles for the bottles. With all his strength, Tom pinned the Kahle to the conveyor and dragged him toward the nozzles. Bottles flew in all directions. Tom was unyielding, filled with a desperate strength. The Kahle had no chance at all.

"If bullets won't kill you, maybe this will."

The Kahle turned his head to the left and began to shriek as he rolled closer to the instruments of his death, but a final convulsion wasn't enough to free himself from Tom's grip.

"This is for Sienna."

Tom released the Kahle as the steel nozzles descended, cracking cruelly through his ribs and plunging into his chest. The Kahle's scream died instantly, transformed into a gurgling groan. Liquid pumped through the pipes and nozzles into the Kahle's lungs, and watery blood gouted from his mouth and nose. The nozzles lifted again, and Friedrich von Falkenhain slipped to the floor, dead. For good this time.

"Enjoy your drink, asshole," Tom said. Exhausted, wet and covered in blood, he sank to the floor.

Hellen came running over. “Are you all right? Are you hurt?” she asked frantically. When she saw that Tom was still in one piece, a note of jealousy crept into her voice as she continued: “And who’s Sienna?”

“Dr. Wilson. I told you about her. That’s the bastard who shot her,” Tom said, taken a little off guard, and he put his hands up for Hellen to help him up. Both were soaked to the skin.

“We should hurry,” Hellen said. “I think I know what Matthews wanted to say before she was shot.”

Tom and Hellen looked at each other. “The first . . .” said Tom.

“ . . . shipment is already on its way,” Hellen added.

“Ah, *l’amour*,” said Cloutard, who had taken care of the other two bodyguards in the meantime. “You two are so sweet together. Now you are even finishing each other’s sentences.”

Quickly, they left the plant. Time was pressing. The ship with the poisoned water was already on its way to the States.

68

BELIZE CITY HARBOR

Outside, chaos reigned. People were running in all directions. Tom's explosion had torn a gaping hole in the bottling plant. Fire engines and ambulances arrived, sirens blaring, only adding to the mayhem. In all the confusion, it was relatively easy for Tom, Hellen and Cloutard to slip unnoticed into one of the SUVs and drive away.

Following first Burrell Boom Cut and then the Northern Highway, they covered the twenty miles to the Port of Belize in less than half an hour.

"What's the plan?" asked Hellen.

"I have no idea," Tom replied.

"Won't you need a small army to take over a huge freighter?"

"You don't need an army for that. The biggest container ships in the world have a crew of no more than thirty, and this ship is probably half that size."

"But then how do you think you can stop it?" Hellen pressed.

"I'll burn that bridge when I come to it. First we need to get there and get on board."

When the entrance gate to the container terminal came into view, Tom abruptly stopped the car. "We can't just charge in, and even here in Central America not everyone will take a bribe. We'll have to think of something else." Tom thought for a moment and looked around in the SUV. He climbed out and opened the back, discovering Yasmine Matthews' hand luggage: a small suitcase and a Louis Vuitton travel bag. He rummaged through the bags, then closed the back and went around to the rear passenger door.

"Here. Put this on," he said to Hellen, handing her a gorgeous summer dress and a pair of pumps.

"Umm . . . why?" Hellen asked, perplexed, but she got out and did as he asked.

"Ah. I think I know what you have in mind," said Cloutard. "It could work."

"Wow!" Tom gasped when Hellen stepped out from behind the car. A little wobbly in the high heels, she stood in front of him and self-consciously rearranged her hair.

"You think this suits me?" she asked. Tom nodded, his eyes almost falling out of his head.

"Here, these too." He handed her a pair of Chanel sunglasses, then stood back and inspected his handiwork. "That should do it."

Tom suddenly caught sight of himself in the tinted window of the SUV and started. The injuries to his face and the sodden, bloody shirt disqualified him. He raked his fingers through his hair, trying to improve his appearance, but quickly gave up.

"No way," he said. "François, you drive. Remember, low key. Let's go." With that, Tom climbed into the cargo area of the SUV. Hellen jumped into the back seat, and Cloutard slid across to the driver's seat.

"Hello," said the security guy who came to the window when they pulled up in front of the boom gate.

"This is Yasmine Matthews, CEO of NutriAm," Cloutard said, turning on his incomparable charm. "The owner of that ship out there. We have an appointment."

Skeptical at first, the security guard tried to peer through the dark-tinted windows. But when Hellen rolled down the window and frowned at the man, he became a lot friendlier.

"Yes, sir, ma'am. Of course." He bowed, almost groveling.

"Open up, open up!" the man said, waving frantically at his colleague to raise the boom. Cloutard drove onto the terminal grounds, heading directly for the water and pulling the SUV to a stop beside the last building. It was not a very busy harbor, with just a few people walking around. No one took any notice of the black vehicle. Tom climbed out of the back and they looked out over the sea. The harbor itself wasn't deep enough for large ships to anchor, so the NutriAm container ship was moored at the end of a half-mile-long pier that led out to deeper water.

It was a one-way pier, with trucks hauling the containers out one by one and cranes at the end loading them aboard the ship.

"What now?" Cloutard asked. He turned to the left to where Tom had been standing a moment earlier, then turned around further and saw Tom, pistol in hand, waving down a truck that was on its way out to the ship. With his hands raised, the driver jumped down from the cab, and Tom led the protesting man over to the SUV.

"I'm terribly sorry about this," an embarrassed Hellen said to the driver as Tom and Cloutard tied him up and pushed him into the back of the SUV.

"You all can go to he—!" the man shouted. Tom cut him off as he slammed the rear hatch closed.

While Hellen changed back to her regular shoes, Tom outlined his reckless plan: "You two hide in the container. I'll sneak onto the ship and let you out on board," he explained, as if he did this every day. Hellen and Cloutard were speechless, but went reluctantly to the back of the truck and climbed inside the container.

"If we are stuck in here all the way to Miami, I will punch you in the mouth personally," said Cloutard.

"Don't worry, it's one of the last containers. It'll be right on top."

Tom closed the container again, then he climbed up into the cab and drove out to the end of the pier, where a handful of trucks were still parked on a small artificial island. Tom reversed the truck beneath one of the freighter's huge cranes.

While the dockworkers hooked Hellen and Cloutard's container to the crane, Tom climbed down from the cab and sneaked forward to the ship's bow, where he quickly shimmied aboard along one of the ropes that moored the ship to the dock. On ships like this, the bridge was at the stern, so no one was paying any attention to the bow.

The last container was lowered into place and the longshoremen left the ship. Tom emerged from his hiding place and crept along the narrow walkway by the railing to the stern. The ship was about three hundred feet long and had several metal stairways that gave access to the containers. Tom climbed one of these stairways, encountering no one. When he found the right container, he swung the handle and pulled open the door. Two very relieved faces peered back at him.

69

U.S. FREIGHTER "SIN LIBERTAD," INTERNATIONAL WATERS

"*Magnifique*," said François happily.

"Okay, I think it's time we heard the rest of your plan," said Hellen. The large freighter was now on its way toward Miami, heading out toward the open sea. Tom, Hellen and François moved cautiously between the containers, making their way toward the stern.

"I figured we'd go up to the bridge, point a gun at the captain's head and call the cavalry," Tom said.

"The cavalry?" Hellen and Cloutard chorused.

"Sure. The Coast Guard, SWAT, the Navy, whoever. The cavalry," Tom said, waving off his friends' misgivings.

"And you're certain there's no more than twenty people on board?" Hellen asked.

"Definitely. They're mostly mechanics and engineers, and they're probably below deck. There shouldn't be more than four on the bridge."

"Then I can add 'pirate' to my résumé," said Cloutard, smiling. He took out his hip flask and offered it to Hellen and Tom.

"Thanks, but I'm on duty," Tom deadpanned. "Just kidding. Here's to luck!" He accepted the flask and took a swig, then took out his pistol and crept on. Hellen shook her head and followed him. Cloutard took a final swallow of the liquor, then joined his friends on their way to the bridge.

When they reached the multi-story tower looming high at the stern of the ship, they had to be more careful. They might cross paths with a crewmember at any time. As quietly as possible, they climbed the steel stairs outside the bridge. Halfway up, Hellen noticed a bright-orange vessel attached to a kind of slide, its nose pointed down at a forty-five degree angle. It looked like a small submarine.

"What the heck is that?" she whispered, pointing to the vessel.

"It's a free-fall lifeboat," Tom said, climbing on.

When they reached the bridge, they paused for a moment. Cloutard also took out the pistol Tom had handed him at the bottling plant. Then they jerked open the door.

"Hands in the—"

Tom's sentence was rudely interrupted by the loud ratcheting sound of several Kalashnikovs being racked. The color drained from Tom's face. Besides the captain and his crew, the bridge contained ten heavily armed men—

they looked to Tom like Guatemalan guerrillas. *Damn. Looks like Matthews found some decent security for her sensitive freight,* he thought.

He and Cloutard dropped their weapons.

"Funny story . . ." he said as he raised his hands, trying to joke his way out of it. But his feeble attempt to break the ice was brought to an end by a rifle butt slamming into his head.

70

U.S. FREIGHTER "SIN LIBERTAD," INTERNATIONAL WATERS

The monotonous rumble of the ship's engines droned in his head. Tom reached up with one hand, delicately touching a deep cut across his temple.

"Hellen. He's awake," Cloutard said.

Tom sat up slowly and looked around.

"Great plan, Mr. Wagner," said Hellen, exasperated.

"What happened?"

"They knocked you out, marched us down here, and locked the door."

"How long have I been out?" Tom asked. His head felt like a bowling ball.

"A few hours," Cloutard said.

"We're in really deep shit this time," Hellen said. "How are you going to get us out of this?"

"Okay, if you're using expressions like that, Ms. de Mey, things must really be serious." Tom looked around the tiny cabin.

"We've searched it from top to bottom. There's nothing."

Just then, they heard somebody unlock the cabin door. It swung open, and three of the guerrillas barged in and dragged Tom, Hellen and Cloutard outside.

"*Vamonos. Adelante!*"

They jammed a gun into Tom's back, driving him along a narrow passage and up a set of stairs. Hellen and Cloutard were pushed brutally along after him.

"Where are you taking us? What's going on?"

"The captain got new orders. We're going to shoot you and throw you overboard."

Their faces turned white as chalk. Even Tom was at a loss for words. His makeshift plan had gone seriously awry. That had happened before, but until now it had only been his own skin at risk. Now it seemed his recklessness would mean not only his own death, but that of Hellen and Cloutard as well. They were surrounded by a gang of mercenaries, armed to the teeth. Tom knew men like this. They would shoot first and ask questions later, if at all. His mind was racing, but a wave of despair washed over him. He had absolutely no idea what to do. Hellen's and Cloutard's terrified faces only made things worse. They were herded up and outside, where the sun beat mercilessly onto the deck and the shipping containers.

The leader of the mercenaries pushed all three of them to the railing. Tom knew he would not hesitate for a second: he'd pull the trigger, and they would fall into the sea. Over and out. For the first time in his life, Tom truly regretted his recklessness. He hated himself. Hellen's and Cloutard's blood was about to be on his hands. Tears stung his eyes as the leader leveled his Kalashnikov at Hellen.

71

U.S. FREIGHTER "SIN LIBERTAD," INTERNATIONAL WATERS

A clattering suddenly tore through the tension. All eyes turned. Even the leader of the mercenaries was distracted, and he lowered his gun. Tom, Hellen and Cloutard turned around almost simultaneously. Tom instantly recognized the sound—swooping in from the horizon were three U.S. Navy helicopters: two Sikorsky SH-60 Seahawks and a big Sikorsky CH-53E Super Stallion.

The troop of mercenaries turned and looked at their leader in confusion. Two of them started shouting something at him, while two others looked like they wanted to cut and run. The leader bellowed back at them and a loud discussion ensued that soon looked as if it might turn into a brawl, or worse.

This was Tom's chance, and he did not hesitate. Fearlessly, he kicked the leader hard in the chest, and the man flew backwards and crashed onto the steel deck. In the same instant, the helicopters came thundering over the bridge and swung around, hovering over the ship.

"This is the U.S. Navy," a voice boomed through an enormous loudspeaker. "Heave to and stop your engines. You are transporting illegal substances into the United States. Stop your engines immediately and prepare to be boarded."

"Go!" Tom yelled. "That way!" Hellen and Cloutard reacted instantly, and all three leaped into a gap between two containers. Bullets slammed into the containers behind them, and ricochets whined across the deck.

The Navy repeated their demand, this time adding "This is your last warning!"

But the mercenaries didn't seem to give a damn what the U.S. Navy had to say. They opened fire on the helicopters.

"Come on, we have to get to the lifeboat," Tom shouted, pointing toward the stern, and they ran for their lives. A pitched battle was developing around them, and they had to deal with dangers on two fronts. The Navy, of course, had no idea that they were the good guys. A lethal hail of bullets poured from the M134 GAU-17 miniguns mounted on the flanks of the Seahawks. Six thousand rounds a minute rained down on the steel deck, shredding everything in sight. The mercenaries had no chance.

"Hey! We're *friendlies!*" Tom cursed. They had just managed to escape the steady stream of fire and finally reached the lifeboat. Tom jerked open the hatch at the rear of the vessel. "All aboard!" he shouted. Hellen slid inside first, followed closely by Cloutard. Tom got in last, pulled the hatch closed behind him, and climbed up over the rows of seats to the cabin above. Inside the lifeboat were four rows of seats, each facing backward. Hellen was already strapped in, and Cloutard was just tightening his seat belt. Tom buckled himself into the pilot's seat and gripped the steering wheel. He glanced momentarily out of the small window and out over the sea—and could not believe his eyes. The third chopper had moved away from the fight and had flown out over open water. When it turned back toward the ship, Tom saw why. The helicopter flew low and dropped a cylindrical object into the sea. A torpedo. Tom decided to keep that to himself for the moment. His friends were unsettled enough as it was.

"Ready?" he shouted.

"Nooooooo!" Hellen cried, and she squeezed her eyes shut. She was sick to death of all the excitement of the last few days.

"Then let's go."

Tom pulled the lever beside his seat and the lifeboat dropped free—not a second too soon. A deafening explosion shook the craft as it shot down the slide. It was followed instantly by a gigantic fireball that engulfed the freighter's entire bridge, including the lifeboat. Flames licked at the windows of the vessel as it dropped thirty feet into the ocean.

Hellen and Cloutard both screamed, but Tom let out a cheer. The lifeboat slammed into the water, shaking its three occupants like a cocktail.

"Touchdown! The crowd goes wild!" Tom whooped. Moments later, the lifeboat bobbed like a cork to the surface. "Who wants to go again?" he said, laughing maniacally. This was his kind of fun, true, but his relief at their survival was boundless. Saved again at the last second.

"Can we all agree not to ever do anything like this ever again?" Hellen gasped, sitting rigid and unmoving in her seat, her eyes still closed. She was just glad it was over.

Tom piloted the boat away from the danger zone as fast as possible and activated the emergency beacon. The torpedo had blasted a huge hole in the hull of the "Sin Libertad," and it wouldn't remain afloat much longer.

"How do we get out of here now?" Cloutard asked.

"I think this is our ride," said Tom, and he pointed upward. They could hear a helicopter hovering over the lifeboat. Tom opened the hatch. A cable with a harness was already being lowered.

Hellen finally opened her eyes. "Oh my God, now this? I just want to go back to my museum!" she whimpered. But all three of them knew she didn't really mean it. One by one, happy and tired, they were winched up to the helicopter.

72

CAMP DAVID, MARYLAND

"Without a doubt, this is the biggest scandal in the history of our country," declared Fox News anchor Sean Hennessy. "I still cannot believe it. We here at Fox News are speechless." Hennessy shook his head in disbelief. His co-host, Megan Collins, nodded in agreement.

President George William Samson sat alone in the living room of the Aspen Lodge at Camp David, staring at the TV, watching the report heralding the end of his career. When the affair had come to light, Samson had decided —for now—to retreat to the lodge to plan his next moves.

"The Goldwater affair is a black day for the Democratic Party and, of course, for the entire country," said Collins. "Sean, let's recap the events as they've come to light one more time for our viewers. They may have heard it many times already, but it's simply impossible to believe."

"We do have to remember that the people involved are innocent until proven guilty, Megan," Hennessy said to the camera. "Especially because the main suspect in the

Goldwater affair is none other than the President of the United States. But the evidence is overwhelming, and it's all the more damning since it was Vice President Pitcock who brought the affair to light."

Hennessy gathered together a handful of papers and looked across at Collins before he continued. Both journalists were visibly shaken.

"President Samson has apparently been engaged in election manipulation on a scale never before seen in this country. Just as unprecedented is the sheer volume of information now being made public, not only by the FBI, but also by the CIA. But one thing is certain: President Samson, together with Yasmine Matthews, the CEO of the multinational NutriAm corporation, the largest food company in the world, were plotting to *poison* the American people using an ancient substance. Ms. Matthews is not available for comment at present, and insiders have claimed that she has escaped to Central America. We have heard that the diabolical plan has its roots in Belize, from where a ship loaded with bottles of poisoned water was already on its way to the United States. We have Vice President Pitcock to thank for averting this catastrophe, too. Pitcock, an ex-Marine himself, sent a team of specialists to Belize to stop the ship, doing it for his country and the well-being of all Americans. Whatever problems he might have faced in going behind President Samson's back were a secondary consideration— he simply wanted to do the right thing. I have to say: it all sounds unbelievable."

Hennessy looked across to his colleague, who responded with, "Yes, Sean, it *is* unbelievable. It all comes down to an ancient drug used in Mayan rituals more than two thousand years ago. Stay tuned, because we'll be hearing more about that later from one of America's leading botanists, Dr. Joseph Dunham. With the help of CEO Matthews, the bottled drinking water was deliberately laced with this substance in order to make the American public more easily persuadable on an immense scale. In other words: this was an attempt at mass brainwashing."

"That's absolutely right, Megan. What we don't know yet is how big a role the president had in planning this evil plot. But we do know that he must have known about it," Hennessy added.

"All in the name of securing his own re-election," Collins said.

"It's understandable, in a way. His liberal views and planned gun control reforms would have meant his defeat otherwise. Of course, we here at Fox News are following the story closely and will keep you up to date as the FBI and CIA release new information," Hennessy said, passing the ball back to Collins.

"Congress has already filed articles of impeachment against President Samson. For the first time in the history of the United States, we are seeing bipartisan support for the move, with both Democrats and Republicans unanimously supporting the filing. If Samson doesn't resign first, Congress will likely vote to remove him, which would make him the first president ever to be punished in this way," Collins said. "And Pitcock seems to be the first vice-president to have ever really made a difference. The president has announced a press conference for early tomorrow morning, saying only that he will deliver a statement at that time. Let's wait and see."

"Thank God I didn't vote for him," Hennessy said with a smile at the camera.

Samson was now on his feet and looking out over the upper terrace at the estate's beautiful grounds. He wasn't particularly concerned that his career was over. He was far more upset, in fact, that he would not be able to keep his promise to his dead wife. He knew now that he should never have put his trust in Yasmine Matthews, never given her a free hand. Because of his mistake, he would now have to break the oath he had made to his wife on her deathbed—and he would go down in history as the president who tried to poison his own people. But at least he would have the chance to tell the world his side of the story tomorrow morning.

He turned around, picked up the remote control, and turned off the TV, where various political figures, from both the U.S. and the rest of the world, were weighing in with their opinions. Just then, there was a knock at the door.

"Sir, the premises have been secured. I just wanted to wish you good night and good luck tomorrow morning," said Rupert, Samson's loyal Secret Service man. The president turned around.

"Thank you, Rupert. Good night."

But Rupert remained where he was for a moment. "Uh, sir, can I ask you a personal question?"

"Of course, Rupert. As a matter of fact, why don't you come in and have a drink with me?"

"Thank you, sir, but I'm still on duty."

"Nonsense. I'm a fallen star. No one gives a damn about me anymore. Come on."

His colleagues couldn't see this, Rupert knew. He looked around. Samson slumped back onto the sofa and rolled up his sleeves.

"Would you mind?" He signaled to Rupert to bring the drinks. Rupert nodded and went across to the silver tray standing on the sideboard. He poured a glass of whiskey from a Baccarat crystal carafe, turned around, and handed it to the president.

"Never trust a beautiful woman. In fact, never trust anyone . . . " With these words, Samson raised his glass to his bodyguard and took a swig of whiskey. "It will be the end of you," he added in a murmur. Samson leaned forward, put the glass down, and loosened his tie. He felt suddenly odd.

"You have no idea how right you are," Rupert said.

"So what did you want to—" Samson broke off and shuddered. Cramping, he grabbed his left arm and fell back on the sofa. "Help me! I'm having a heart atta . . ."

"Sir? Everything all right?" Rupert asked casually. Ignoring Samson's pleas, he returned to the sideboard. He pulled on a pair of disposable gloves, took out a cloth and wiped his fingerprints from the carafe. Then he picked it up and carried it to the sofa, where the president was just gasping his last breath.

George William Samson was dead. Rupert carefully lifted the president's hand and pressed it against the carafe, transferring Samson's fingerprints. Then he set the carafe on the table in front of Samson, wiped the whiskey glass and repeated the process. Finally, he pressed the president's fingers to a small bottle of sleeping pills, set it down beside the glass, and scattered a few tablets on the table. The autopsy would give suicide as the official cause of death. Then he took out a flip phone and pressed a speed-dial number.

"It's done," he said, and hung up. He peeled off his gloves and left the room.

73

THE WHITE HOUSE, WASHINGTON D.C., NEXT MORNING.

"I, James Pitcock, do solemnly swear that I will faithfully execute the office of President of the United States and will, to the best of my ability, preserve, protect and defend the Constitution of the United States. So help me God."

Theodore M. Campbell, Chief Justice of the United States, held the Bible on which Pitcock had placed his hand and taken the oath of office. They stood in the Oval Office, surrounded by a makeshift inauguration committee consisting of the Washington, D.C. attorney general, the late president's chief of staff, the secretary of state, and another federal judge. Two small teams from CNN and Fox News were broadcasting the new president's hastily organized inauguration live.

"Mr. President, we would like to ask a few questions." The ceremony had just come to an end and the CNN reporter immediately tried to get in before Pitcock's chief of staff could veto the attempt. Pitcock sighed, clearly deeply upset by the turn of events.

"You'll have to excuse me, but I won't be making a statement or taking any questions at this time. This situation is unique in the history of the United States. I'm sure you'll understand that I have to sit down with my advisors first; we have a lot to discuss and a lot remains unclear. I will most likely address the nation this evening."

Pitcock seemed composed, but unsettled. Everything had happened so quickly, and a superhuman burden had landed on his shoulders overnight. The reporter nodded, disappointed, and Pitcock's chief of staff herded everyone out of the Oval Office.

"We're going to need a few hours to look at all the facts and put together the president's address," she said as she closed the door behind the last one.

President Pitcock dropped onto an armchair and stroked the armrests with his hands. "I'll need a little time to adjust," he said.

Rita Sorensen looked at her president. Her expression was hard to interpret. Pride mingled with uncertainty, and enthusiasm with sympathy.

"You can do it, Mr. President," she said as she gathered her papers. Then she, too, left the Oval Office.

Pitcock stood up and looked out through the large windows to the Rose Garden. He turned around to make sure he was really alone, and a sudden change came over him. The furrows of concern on his forehead vanished, the tension disappeared from his posture, the lines of his face relaxed. Slowly, the corners of his mouth turned up into a broad smile. It continued to widen, transforming into a malevolent grin. He stood like that for some time, savoring the moment.

The door opened and his secretary was standing in the doorway. “Sir, I’m sorry to disturb you, but your appointment? The one you told me about before the inauguration? He’s here.”

“Thank you. Show him in.”

74

GENERAL SCOTT WAGNER'S HOUSE, WASHINGTON D.C.

Tom locked the porch door and closed the curtains. He wandered through his Uncle Scott's bungalow one last time, just to be certain he hadn't overlooked anything important. He had to make sure everything was squared away before it was sold. After all the excitement of the last few weeks, Tom had decided to stay in the U.S. a little longer, while Hellen and Cloutard flew back to Vienna to report to Theresia. He needed to settle his murdered uncle's estate, but he also wanted to get a little distance from everything. Too many people had died and too much had changed—at least in part because of him. He had almost lost his beloved grandfather in Russia. He had some things to figure out, especially his feelings for Hellen and how things were supposed to continue with her and with Blue Shield. And nothing cleared the mind like a few days of physical labor.

There wasn't much left to do now: his uncle had been a proponent of a minimalist lifestyle, but he had also been a fan of fast cars. When Tom opened the garage door, he was stunned to find a perfectly preserved 1970 Dodge Challenger R/T convertible. The V8 muscle car was one of the first so-called "pony cars", a style that harked back to the first Ford Mustang. Keeping it would not be cheap, Tom knew, but he could not bring himself to get rid of it. The beautiful machine was already on its way to Vienna.

As for clothing, Uncle Scott had worn a uniform most of his life, and for the few private moments of his life, a track suit or jeans and a T-shirt had sufficed. Tom had packed up his uncle's comprehensive book collection and sent it off to Vienna as well. Everything else had gone to the Salvation Army or ended up in the trash.

A horn sounded outside. His taxi was here. He picked up his duffel bag, slung it over his shoulder, and left the bungalow. He locked the door and dropped the key in the small combination-locked box the real estate agent had installed.

Tom climbed into the taxi. "The airport, please," he said, looking back one last time at his uncle's house as the taxi pulled away.

Suddenly, he found himself thinking of Hellen and what he had realized in the plane over the jungles of Belize. Whatever it was they had, it felt right. He fished out his mobile phone and dialed her number, but heard only: "You've reached Hellen de Mey. I'm not available to take your call, but . . ." Tom hung up. He hated voicemail. Then he looked at his watch. She was probably asleep, anyway. He would try again later, maybe from the airport.

He looked out the window, noticing that the driver seemed to be taking the scenic route. "Hey, the airport's the other way!" He knocked on the partition separating the front and rear seats. But the driver did not react. "Hey!" Tom said again, louder.

The door locks clicked as the driver locked them from the front. A moment later he reached back and closed the small hatch in the partition. Tom heard a hissing sound from the footwell and felt panic grip him. *Gas!* he realized. He pounded wildly at the partition and shook the door, but the gas did its job quickly. Tom had no chance: in less than ten seconds, he passed out.

75

OVAL OFFICE, WHITE HOUSE, WASHINGTON D.C.

"Congratulations, Mr. President," said the man that Pitcock's secretary had just shown into the Oval Office. He and Pitcock shook hands.

"Thank you. Frankly, I'm amazed it all came together. I had serious doubts when you first told me the plan. Please, take a seat." Pitcock pointed to the sofa opposite.

"Thank you," said Noah Pollock, and he sat down. "Our plans are audacious, often opaque, and exceptionally ambitious. That is part of the reason why we have so much influence. By the way, the Leader wanted me to convey his congratulations."

Pitcock inclined his head slightly. "Please pass on my thanks for the trust he has placed in me. I will not let him or the organization down," he said. He paused for a moment. Then, with respect and appreciation in his voice, he added: "It was a masterful piece of work, to say the least."

Noah radiated pride, superiority and a touch of arrogance. "Yes," Noah agreed. "We see once again that people today have no interest in the truth. Their only interest is in sensation, scandal, extraordinary events that they can chatter about on Facebook and Twitter. Hardly anyone can separate fake news and alternative facts from the truth these days. Hardly anyone wants to. In today's society, everyone can have their say on social media, and people think that makes them freer than they used to be. They are not. They are trapped. Trapped in sensory overload, caught up in the desire to be part of something big, to help shape it instead of just being swept along. Why do you think humans fall so easily for these absurd conspiracy theories? Because they're tired of being sheep, tired of those at the top taking away all responsibility for their lives. So we give them a grand conspiracy. When they discover that the president is planning to clinch his own re-election by manipulating people with some ancient Mayan drug, they believe it, because it fits into their view of the world. They are outraged, and they jump on the bandwagon without a second thought. This is the essence of our plans: to give people the *impression* of greater freedom and self-determination—when the reality is the opposite."

Pitcock observed Noah as he spoke. The man was not crazy, not some megalomaniac. He had simply realized how modern society worked and was expertly manipulating it.

"I assume none of those involved knew of this? Not even Ms. Matthews?" Pitcock said.

"Of course not. People function best when you tell them only what they need to know, leaving them plenty of room to form their own interpretations. Every dictatorship in history has worked that way."

Noah suddenly grew more serious, his tone forceful. The lines of his face hardened.

"The Leader will contact you directly very soon. There are a few organizational matters to arrange. In particular, we need several of our people in important positions, where our influence is currently too weak. Everything else will follow, step by step. We have big plans."

They shook hands, and Noah left the Oval Office. Pitcock remained, deep in thought—and very glad indeed to be on AF's side. They had the power, and they held all the cards. He felt sorry for the people who had no idea what was going on behind the scenes. But he felt far sorrier for those who knew what was going on, but who were utterly powerless to do anything about it.

76

UNKNOWN LOCATION

A splash of ice-cold water in his face brought Tom back to the world of the living. He jolted awake, twisting his head in all directions.

Where am I? What happened? Handcuffs dug painfully into the skin of his wrists, bound behind his back. His feet were also chained to the chair he sat on, which was bolted firmly to the floor. A dim light bulb dangled overhead. He tore at his bonds with all his strength, but quickly realized that it was both painful and hopeless.

He looked up. Someone was standing in the shadows.

"Who are you? Where am I?" Tom asked, once he had composed himself a little.

"Right now, where you are makes no difference. And you already know who I am."

Ossana Ibori stepped into the light, and Tom's eyes widened.

"Aren't you supposed to be rotting in some hole in the

desert?" Tom sniped, still tugging at the chains holding him. Slowly, almost gracefully, Ossana stepped in front of Tom and leaned down close.

"I was. And when I'm finished with you, you'll wish you were there and not here," she whispered in his ear. She gave him a long kiss on the mouth, then straightened up and continued in a normal voice. "But the Leader still has some use for you. I'm only allowed to play with you a little. So don't worry, I'm not going to kill you just yet—but believe me when I say your stay here will not be pleasant."

With that, she turned away, switched off the light, and left Tom alone in the pitch-black prison.

77

BLUE SHIELD HEADQUARTERS, UNO CITY, VIENNA. ONE WEEK LATER.

"And what is our dear Mr. Wagner's excuse for not taking part in our meeting today?" Theresia de Mey drummed her fingers on the conference table in annoyance.

"I already told you, Mother. And we are really starting to worry," Hellen said. The anxiety in her voice was audible.

Even Cloutard, who normally propped his feet on the table in these meetings and whose cognac-filled hip flask never left his hand, had concern inscribed deeply on his face.

"I know Tom," he said. "He may not always come across as especially reliable or responsible. But I would trust him with my life. I have seldom met a human being with as much integrity and loyalty as Tom. Something must have happened to him. He was planning to fly to Vienna as soon as he had settled his uncle's affairs. But he never boarded the plane, and several days have passed since then. This is entirely out of character."

Cloutard placed his hand on Theresia's, but she pulled away from him.

"Don't give me that, François. Integrity? Really? And to whom is Tom Wagner loyal? No one but himself."

"Mother!"

Hellen had slapped the palm of her hand hard against the table. Everyone turned and looked at her in shocked surprise.

"I don't care what you think of Tom, but something must have happened to him or he would have been in touch. He tried to call me two hours before his flight was supposed to leave, and that was his last contact. You don't like him? Fine. But I will not allow you to talk about him like that. Apart from you, he has saved the life of every person in this room, more than once."

Hellen's eyes turned to Vittoria Arcano, Theresia's assistant, who was nodding vigorously. Theresia ignored her.

"I've also heard some very different stories," Theresia said, and as if on cue the door opened and Captain Maierhofer, head of the Austrian counterterrorism unit Cobra and the joint European Atlas initiative, entered the room. "Perfect timing, Captain. There are already too many Tom Wagner fans in the room for my liking. Your own assessment of Wagner is quite different, I believe."

Hellen was glaring at Maierhofer before he even opened his mouth. "What is Tom's old boss doing here?" she whispered to Cloutard.

Cloutard only shrugged. "*Je ne sais pas*," he said.

Only now did Hellen realize that another man was standing behind Maierhofer. A giant, in fact. Six foot six and at least 260 pounds of solid muscle: a hulking brute with a crew cut, standing ramrod-straight at attention.

"I consulted Captain Maierhofer because I was sick of watching the Tom Wagner circus," Theresia said. Hellen reached out instinctively for Cloutard's arm. She knew what her mother was about to say, and she needed someone she trusted to hold onto. Captain Maierhofer grinned as Theresia went on: "So I asked the captain to look for a replacement."

"Are you serious? You can't do that, Mother!" Hellen snapped.

"Can't I? After that mess with Palffy, I wanted a team to handle Blue Shield's difficult cases, a team that would find and secure new, and more importantly valuable, artifacts for us. Palffy's plan to put together a team consisting of an elite fighter, a historian and a gentleman criminal"—she smiled at Cloutard, whose expression didn't change—"actually seemed like a good idea. I would never have dreamed that the elite fighter would turn out to be such a loser. But here we are and I have been forced to act." Theresia turned and looked at Maierhofer.

"And I've brought you my best man, Ms. de Mey: Maximilian Rupp," Maierhofer said. "Rupp was one of my Cobras; I trained him myself.. He's been a part of numerous international antiterror units, and is a former member of the French Foreign Legion. He's as reliable as they come. He obeys orders and sticks to the rules."

"And he is no doubt as interesting as a block of wood," Cloutard added, earning glares from both Theresia and Maierhofer. Rupp's posture had stiffened even more while Maierhofer was talking about him. Impossibly, he now seemed to have grown even bigger and more massive than before. He grinned proudly and nodded to Maierhofer.

"He even nods when you call him boring," Hellen whispered in Cloutard's ear.

"They probably removed his brain when he was in the Legion. Soldiers are not there to think, *n'est-ce pas*?" Cloutard replied.

"And what if we refuse, Mother?" Hellen's tone had turned venomous.

"Then I'll find replacements for both of you, too. It's that simple." She gestured toward the door and stared back at Hellen.

Cloutard kicked Hellen's shin under the table. She almost squealed, but she understood his message: for the time being, they would have to make the best of it. If they got fired now, it wouldn't do anyone any good.

But Hellen was a poor actress. She jumped up, knocking her chair over. She felt like throwing something at her mother's head, but thought better of it and ran out of the room.

"She will get over it," Cloutard said, trying to de-escalate the situation. It was not like him at all, but in the course of his extremely successful criminal career he had learned that it sometimes paid to take a step back. Theresia could say what she liked, but it was clear to him, too, that the team would not work without Tom. They had to find him.

In the meantime, Hellen had run to the elevator. She rode it down to the ground floor, needing some fresh air. Leaving the building, she followed Leonard-Bernstein-Strasse toward the Donaupark, a large park covering almost 150 acres behind the United Nations complex.

Hellen walked to the pond and found an empty bench to sit on. The fresh air did her good, but she was still beside herself with worry and furious at her mother. She knew that something had happened to Tom—he would never have just disappeared without a word. That wasn't his style. And her mother's audacity in summarily replacing him with some stupid lump of muscle made her angriest of all.

"Hellen."

She heard someone say her name. Her heart stopped. She knew that voice . . . but it was impossible! She turned her head just as an elderly man laid a hand on her shoulder.

Hellen sat as if frozen, unable to get a word out. She struggled to breathe, and even though she was sitting down, the world around her began to spin. An eternity seemed to pass. Then she said a single word, a word she had not uttered in many, many years.

"Papa?"

— The End —
of „THE GOLDEN PATH“

Tom Wagner returns in
THE CHRONICLE OF THE ROUND TABLE

THE CHRONICLE OF THE ROUND TABLE

TURN THE PAGE AND READ THE NEXT TOM WAGNER ADVENTURE!

CHAPTER 1

MOUNTAINS NORTHWEST OF KANDAHAR, AFGHANISTAN

The three Humvees struggled up the barren, stony mountain road toward the remote rendezvous point. The steep track pushed the military behemoths' V8 engines to their limits. The nine-man squads inside the front and rear vehicles were getting severely tossed around. The truck in the middle, however, carried only a single passenger, a civilian. Smartly dressed in a beige three-piece suit, he nevertheless wore a flak jacket and Kevlar helmet with protective goggles. He looked extremely out of place. Who was he? The soldiers didn't know. Their mission was to get him into the mountains and back in one piece, not to ask questions. When the job was done, they were to forget they'd ever seen him.

The men were not regular soldiers; they were private contractors. Mercenaries. Their job was to support US troops in crisis regions. But they didn't play by the same rules, and their style showed it. Instead of close-cropped military haircuts, some of them wore their hair long and had full beards, and beneath their flak jackets most wore nothing but a T-shirt and jeans. Some had even replaced their helmets with the *kufiyah*, the Arab headdress made famous by Palestinian leader Yasir Arafat in his day.

The snappily dressed man glanced at a portable GPS device. "Not far now," he said to his driver. He pointed ahead. "Just over this hill."

And so it was. Cresting the hill, they saw the shoddy buildings of a small village. In a clearing in the middle, a few kids kicked around a ball that looked as if they'd made it themselves. Horses ate from troughs or drank water in a small corral. At the sight of the Humvees, the women and children scattered like nocturnal creatures under a bright light, disappearing into their dilapidated houses. At the same time, the men emerged from those same houses. The Humvees were surrounded in seconds, the barrels of countless AK47s and even a few RPGs trained on them.

The vehicles rolled to a stop in a cloud of dust and the mercenaries leaped out and formed a perimeter. Crouching, they aimed back at the heavily armed locals. Two mercenaries manned the machine guns mounted atop the Hummers. Furious shouts echoed up and down the narrow valley.

Eyes wide and sweat beading on his forehead, the elegant man watched all this through the dusty windows of his vehicle, his fingers clenched around the GPS.

"We're here to talk to Omar Akhtar Akhundzada," the sergeant shouted in Pashto to the men, lifting his assault rifle—a Heckler & Koch G36K with a laser sight—over his head in a signal that they were not there to fight. The nervousness among the mercenaries grew as their sergeant stood facing the enemy. "Keep your heads, boys," the sergeant said to his men as they kept their rifles trained nervously on their adversaries.

One of the locals shouted a few words to his comrades, and the tension eased noticeably. After a short while, an elderly man with a long salt-and-pepper beard emerged from one of the houses. He wore a white turban and a traditional kaftan. The elegant man slowly opened the passenger door of his Hummer and climbed out. He edged cautiously through the ring of mercenaries and walked toward the elderly man, clearly the leader of this local unit. The Afghan's wrinkled skin was tanned dark brown by the sun. His remarkably friendly eyes looked out intensely from beneath bushy eyebrows, staring at his visitor. The elegant man stopped at a respectful distance.

"*As-salamu alaykum*," he said hesitantly.

"*Wa 'alaykumu s-salam*," the old man replied. Then, in perfect, British-accented English, he said, "Did you bring what I asked for?"

Probably studied at Oxford, the elegant man thought. *Nothing unusual about that.* "Yes," he replied, somewhat awed, and he raised his hands slowly into the air. Then, with great caution, he withdrew a small envelope from beneath his flak jacket and held it out to the leader. With a nod, the old man sent one of his men to fetch it. Then he opened the envelope and poured the two dozen small diamonds it contained into the palm of his hand. He nodded with satisfaction, and murmurs and cheers rippled through the ranks of his fighters.

He replaced the diamonds in the envelope and tucked it away inside his kaftan before shouting a few words to his men. Two of them ran some distance away, and the elegant man and the mercenaries watched as they lifted a trapdoor and climbed down. They reappeared a moment later, dragging a body into the daylight. It was a man, dressed in ragged clothes with a sack pulled over his head. He was feeble, hardly able to stand. His captors dragged his naked, filthy feet across the stony ground. When they reached the elegant man, they dropped the half-dead prisoner into the dust at his feet.

The Afghan leader waved contemptuously, ordering the newcomers to leave as he retired to his house. His fighters, however, did not move. They kept their guns on the mercenaries.

"Help me," the well-dressed man said, and he tried to lift the prisoner to his feet. Helped by one of the mercenaries, they carried the man, groaning in pain, to the cargo bed of the Hummer in the middle.

Maintaining their defensive positions to the last moment, the mercenaries retreated to the other vehicles. The convoy pulled out and disappeared behind the hill, heading back to base.

The elegant man turned back and looked at the man as one of the mercenaries pulled the sack off his head. The man nodded his thanks, then collapsed sideways and went limp. One of the mercenaries began treating his numerous injuries. The elegant man reached for his satellite phone and pressed a button.

"We've got him. Get the plane ready. We'll be at the airfield in two hours."

The three Humvees bumped back down the mountain road, trailing a billowing cloud of dust. Relief was inscribed on the faces of the mercenaries and the smartly dressed man. True, this was what they did for a living, but they all knew that this little outing could have had a very different outcome.

CHAPTER 2

PANTELLERIA, AN ITALIAN ISLAND OFF THE COAST OF TUNISIA - FOUR MONTHS AFTER TOM WAGNER'S KIDNAPPING

Thomas Maria Wagner looked down from the top of the small hill and out over the sea. The rising sun glittered golden on the calm waters. His mount snorted, nostrils flaring, and champed at the bit.

"Easy, boy," Tom said gently. He stroked the majestic stallion's neck as it stamped restlessly on the spot. The sun rose slowly from the shimmering Mediterranean, and a cool breeze blew across the small volcanic island. Though it was midwinter, the island was so close to Africa that the temperature could reach the 70s even at this time of year. When the sun had risen fully and hung ablaze just above the horizon, Tom pulled the reins around and spurred the horse forward. He rode at a gallop along the steep, rocky coast until he reached his limit, quite literally: a ten-foot electric fence with surveillance cameras surrounded the estate where he was being held.

But his situation had definitely improved, and not only by comparison to the dark hole where he'd been left him to rot for weeks after being abducted. It was better than his regular home too, a houseboat in Vienna. After weeks of solitary existence in the dark, he'd woken one day in a soft bed on this island. The view was better, but he was clearly still a prisoner. The hermetically sealed estate was secured by high fences and countless gunmen guarded both him and the area.

Why was he here? Why wasn't he dead? What did they want from him? Questions and more questions, day in and day out. But for now, Tom had decided to do nothing and accept his fate, at least outwardly. He wanted to know why AF was going to all this trouble to keep him alive—Absolute Freedom, the global terrorist organization, never did anything without a good reason. Tom had made it his goal to destroy the network. AF was responsible, after all, for the death of his parents.

The only thing that really hurt was that he couldn't tell his friends that he was all right. Hellen would be sick with worry and Cloutard was probably scouring the world for him. But Tom was sure he would see them both again.

The luxurious estate had its own pool, and just before Tom reached the main building, he slowed the horse's gallop to a walk and turned toward the stables at the back. A woman in her mid-20s met Tom with a friendly smile.

"How was he this morning?" Sofia asked. The stable master's daughter had been his riding teacher for several weeks.

"Outstanding," Tom replied as he swung his leg over the horse's rump and dismounted. "I never thought I'd like riding a horse. But with one as magnificent as this, it's easy."

For a moment his mind returned to Hellen and their chance meeting almost a year earlier, months after they had separated. Horses had played a role there, too.

"You see, Signore, it is really not so difficult. You have come a long way."

"Thank you, Sofia." Tom handed her the Lipizzaner's reins and she led it back into the stable. He pulled his riding gloves off with his teeth, removed his helmet, and placed the gloves inside it.

"Sofia?" he called after her.

"Si, Signore?"

"When are you finally going to come with me? I'll go and get ready. Meet back here in ten minutes?"

"Oh, no, no, no, Signore. I am too young to die," she joked, and she gave Tom a radiant smile.

Pity, Tom thought. He turned away and went to the main building to get changed. A few minutes later, he set off along the path to the coast.

Sharp stones dug into the soles of his feet. His eyes were closed and the wind brushed at his face. A hundred feet below, waves crashed rhythmically onto the rocks. He enjoyed the deceptive peace of the moment, but it could not last forever. It was the calm before the storm. Tom opened his eyes and looked out over the endless sea. He simply could not get enough of this view. But the peace he felt came to an abrupt end when he saw something in the distance.

Focus, he said to himself. *You knew this day would come. You've waited for it*. The wind grew stronger and the crashing of the waves louder. He checked the zipper on his wetsuit one last time, then rotated his head until his neck cracked. He closed his eyes and took a deep breath in and out. Every muscle in his body tensed. He was ready. Without opening his eyes, he leaped forward with all his strength. Less than three seconds later, he slammed into the cold sea. It was not Acapulco, but it still gave him a kick. He was an adrenaline junkie, in his element when things were fast and dangerous. When his head broke the surface, he felt a rush of joy.

But it did not last long.

Want to know what happens next?

THE CHRONICLE OF THE ROUND TABLE

(A Tom Wagner Adventure 5)

The first secret society of mankind. Artifacts of inestimable power. A race you cannot win.

The events turn upside down: Tom Wagner is missing. Hellen's father has turned up and a hot lead is waiting for the Blue Shield team: The legendary Chronicle of the Round Table.

What does the Chronicles of the Round Table of King Arthur say? Must the history around Avalon and Camelot be rewritten? Where is Tom and who is pulling the strings?

Click here or open link:
https://robertsmaclay.com/5-tw

THE TOM WAGNER SERIES

THE STONE OF DESTINY

(Tom Wagner Prequel)

A dark secret of the Habsburg Empire. A treasure believed to be lost long time ago. A breathless hunt into the past.

The thriller "The Stone of Destiny" leads Tom Wagner and Hellen de Mey into the dark past of the Habsburgs and to a treasure that seems to have been lost for a long time.

The breathless hunt goes through half of Europe and the surprise at the end is not missing: A conspiracy that began in the last days of the First World War reaches up to the present day!

THE SACRED WEAPON

(A Tom Wagner Adventure 1)

A demonic plan. A mysterious power. An extraordinary team.

The Notre Dame fire, the theft of the Shroud of Turin and a terrorist attack on the legendary Meteora monasteries are just the beginning. Fear has gripped Europe.

Stolen relics, a mysterious power with a demonic plan and allies with questionable allegiances: Tom Wagner is in a race against time, trying to prevent a disaster that could tear Europe down to its foundations. And there's no one he can trust...

Click here or open link:
https://robertsmaclay.com/1-tw

THE LIBRARY OF THE KINGS

(A Tom Wagner Adventure 2)

Hidden wisdom. A relic of unbelievable power. A race against time.

Ancient legends, devilish plans, startling plot twists, breathtaking action and a dash of humor: *Library of the Kings* is gripping entertainment – a Hollywood blockbuster in book form.

When clues to the long-lost Library of Alexandria surface, ex-Cobra officer Tom Wagner and archaeologist Hellen de Mey aren't the only ones on the hunt for its vanished secrets. A sinister power is plotting in the background, and nothing is as it seems. And the dark secret hidden in the Library threatens all of humanity.

Click here or open link:
https://robertsmaclay.com/2-tw

THE INVISIBLE CITY

(A Tom Wagner Adventure 3)

A vanished civilization. A diabolical trap. A mystical treasure.

Tom Wagner, archaeologist Hellen de Mey and gentleman crook Francois Cloutard are about to embark on their first official assignment from Blue Shield – but when Tom receives an urgent call from the Vatican, things start to move quickly:

With the help of the Patriarch of the Russian Orthodox Church, they discover clues to an age-old myth: the Russian Atlantis. And a murderous race to find an ancient, long-lost relic leads them from Cuba to the Russian hinterlands.

What mystical treasure lies buried beneath Nizhny Novgorod? Who laid the evil trap? And what does it all have to do with Tom's grandfather?

Click here or open link:

https://robertsmaclay.com/3-tw

THE GOLDEN PATH

(A Tom Wagner Adventure 4)

The greatest treasure of mankind. An international intrigue. A cruel revelation.

Now a special unit for Blue Shield, Tom and his team are on a search for the legendary El Dorado. But, as usual, things don't go as planned.

The team gets separated and is – literally – forced to fight a battle on multiple fronts: Hellen and Cloutard make discoveries that overturn the familiar story of El Dorado's gold.

Meanwhile, the President of the United States has tasked Tom with keeping a dangerous substance out of the hands of terrorists.

Click here or open link:
https://robertsmaclay.com/4-tw

THE CHRONICLE OF THE ROUND TABLE

(A Tom Wagner Adventure 5)

The first secret society of mankind. Artifacts of inestimable power. A race you cannot win.

The events turn upside down: Tom Wagner is missing. Hellen's father has turned up and a hot lead is waiting for the Blue Shield team: The legendary Chronicle of the Round Table.

What does the Chronicles of the Round Table of King Arthur say? Must the history around Avalon and Camelot be rewritten? Where is Tom and who is pulling the strings?

Click here or open link:
https://robertsmaclay.com/5-tw

THE CHALICE OF ETERNITY

(A Tom Wagner Adventure 6)

The greatest mystery in the world. False friends. All-powerful adversaries.

The Chronicle of the Round Table has been found and Tom Wagner, Hellen de Mey and François Cloutard face their greatest challenge yet: The search for the Holy Grail.

But their adventure does not lead them to the time of the Templars and the Crusades, but much further back into mankind's history. And the hunt into the past is a journey of no return. From Egypt to Vienna, from Abu Dhabi to Valencia, from Monaco to Macao, the hunt is on for the greatest myth of mankind. And in the end, there's a phenomenal surprise for everyone.

Click here or open link:
https://robertsmaclay.com/6-tw

THE SWORD OF REVELATION

(A Tom Wagner Adventure 7)

A false lead. A bitter truth. This time, it's all or nothing.

Hellen's mother is dying and only a miracle can save her...but for that, the team needs to locate mysterious and long-lost artifacts.

At the same time, their struggle with the terrorist organization Absolute Freedom reaches its climax: what is the group's true, diabolical plan? Who is pulling the strings behind this worldwide conspiracy?

The Sword of Revelation completes the circle: all questions are answered, all the loose ends woven into a revelation for our heroes — and for all the fans of the Tom Wagner adventures!

Click here or open link:
https://robertsmaclay.com/tw-7

THRILLED READER REVIEWS

"Suspense and entertainment! I've read a lot of books like this one; some better, some worse. This is one of the best books in this genre I've ever read. I'm really looking forward to a good sequel. "

"I just couldn't put this book down. Full of surprising plot twists, humor, and action! "

"An explosive combination of Robert Langdon, James Bond & Indiana Jones"

"Good build-up of tension; I was always wondering what happens next. Toward the end, where the story gets more and more complex and constantly changes scenes, I was on the edge of my seat"

"Great! I read all three books in one sitting. Dan Brown better watch his back."

"The best thing about it is the basic premise, a story with historical background knowledge scattered throughout the book–never too much at one time and always supporting the plot"

"Entertaining and action-packed! The carefully thought-out story has a clear plotline, but there are a couple of unexpected twists as well. I really enjoyed it. The sections of the book are tailored to maximize the suspense, they don't waste any time with unimportant details. The chapters are short and compact–perfect for a half-hour commute or at night before turning out the lights. Recommended to all lovers of the genre and anyone interested in getting to know it better. I'll definitely read the sequel."

"Anyone who likes reading Dan Brown, James Rollins and Preston & Child needs to get this book."

"An exciting build-up, interesting and historically significant settings, surprising plot twists in the right places."

ABOUT THE AUTHORS

ROBERTS & MACLAY

Roberts & Maclay have known each other for over 25 years, are good friends and have worked together on various projects.

The fact that they are now also writing thrillers together is less coincidence than fate. Talking shop about films, TV series and suspense novels has always been one of their favorite pastimes.

M.C. Roberts is the pen name of an successful entrepreneur and blogger. Adventure stories have always been his passion: after recording a number of superhero audiobooks on his father's old tape recorder as a six-year-old, he postponed his dream of writing novels for almost 40 years, and worked as a marketing director, editor-in-chief, DJ, opera critic, communication coach, blogger, online marketer and author of trade books...but in the end, the call of adventure was too strong to ignore.

R.F. Maclay is the pen name of an outstanding graphic designer and advertising filmmaker. His international career began as an electrician's apprentice, but he quickly realized that he was destined to work creatively. His family and friends were skeptical at first...but now, 20 years later, the passionate, self-taught graphic designer and filmmaker has delighted record labels, brand-name products and tech companies with his work, as well as making a name for himself as a commercial filmmaker and illustrator. He's also a walking encyclopedia of film and television series.

www.RobertsMaclay.com

Printed in Great Britain
by Amazon

24062092R00202